CHASING KILL

BRANDT LEGG

BOOKS

By Brandt Legg

Chase Malone Thriller

Chasing Rain
Chasing Fire
Chasing Wind
Chasing Dirt
Chasing Life
Chasing Kill
Chasing Risk
Chasing Mind
Chasing Time
Chasing Lies
Chasing Fear
Chasing Lost

*As always, this book is dedicated to
Teakki and Ro*

Vinci Books

vinci-books.com

Published by Vinci Books Ltd in 2025

1

Copyright © Brandt Legg 2020

The author has asserted their moral right to be identified as the author of this work in accordance with the Copyright, Designs and Patents Act 1988. This work is a work of fiction. Names, characters, places and incidents are the product of the author's imagination or are used fictitiously. Any resemblance to actual persons, living or dead, places and incidents is entirely coincidental.

All rights reserved. No part of this publication may be copied, reproduced, distributed, stored in any retrieval system, or transmitted in any form or by any means, including photocopying, recording, or other electronic or mechanical methods, nor used as a source for any form of machine learning including AI datasets, without the prior written permission of the publisher.

The publisher and the author have made every effort to obtain permissions for any third party material used in this book and to comply with copyright law. Any queries in this respect should be brought to the attention of the publisher and any omissions will be corrected in future editions.

A CIP catalogue record for this book is available from the British Library.

Paperback ISBN: 9781036705251

Printed and bound in Great Britain by Clays Ltd, Elcograf S.p.A.

Chapter One

Watching a man who would never again know freedom, who'd been in hiding far longer and under greater fear than himself, Chase Malone felt suddenly frightened.

"The world has turned upside down," he said, thinking about his own time on the run, now spanning nearly two years.

Wen, his partner, and a former spy, met his eyes. She, too, had been staring intently as the man walked away, weaving in and out of the pedestrian crowds. "Isn't that what we're trying to fix?"

"I'm not sure we can ever win," he replied, as they stood on a busy street in Moscow on a warm afternoon. "Do you think they'll get him?"

"Sooner or later," Wen said sadly. "I'm surprised he's lived this long."

As so often happened between Chase and Wen, their thoughts mirrored each other's. Wen had become a fugitive before Chase, and was a large part of the reason he was no longer a free man. Yet standing in that constrained city, its breeze scented with arugula and beef, both were grateful for what they had—so much more freedom than the man who'd just left them, a person whom many hailed as a hero, and others deemed a villain.

"He's a man without a country," Chase said, his gaze still following the person they'd just spent forty-five minutes with. "It's ironic that we would ask for his assistance."

"He gave up his freedom for many of the same reasons we did," Wen said.

"Do you think he'll help us?"

"He's a cautious man, but as soon as he verifies that we're not one of his enemies, he will." Wen, trained in psychology, had an uncanny ability to read people. It had saved their lives countless times. Of course, her training in all aspects of espionage, weapons, and martial arts, had also gotten them through many more horrendous situations.

They could still see him, and thought it curious that he'd never once turned back to so much as glance at them. "He must trust us. Five hundred feet away and he hasn't looked over his shoulder." Chase's blue eyes squinted, trying not to miss anything, while he rubbed at an old injury on his arm.

"No, he has somebody watching us." Wen scanned the crowd, as she'd been doing since before the man had arrived. "He has limited resources . . . probably aren't many people on his team . . . certainly one . . . maybe as many as three." She'd identified two suspects already. "We've been under surveillance the whole time. They're still out there."

"Which ones?" Chase asked.

Without looking directly at them, Wen described their appearances and locations. "They're good. I can almost always ID the watch, but these are very, *very* good."

Wen had taught Chase many things since she'd come back into his life two years earlier, yet he still couldn't flush out the pros. Even with all the people constantly after them, it remained difficult for him. Many pursuers they'd identified, others they simply called "the shadow people"—a mysterious group who'd been trailing them relentlessly for unknown reasons.

Chase's life as a billionaire engineer in Silicon Valley seemed far away and long ago. But as he watched the man turn a corner and finally disappear, he couldn't help but wonder about the infamous person with whom they'd just met.

As difficult as it is for me to get some decent sleep, for Edward Snowden, it must be next to impossible.

"There!" Wen whispered urgently.

"One of Snowden's people?" Chase asked, not sure why there was so much alarm in her voice.

"No. Someone else. Someone coming for *us*!" The ex-Chinese agent's lithe body whipped around after giving Chase the 'go now' eye.

Chase instinctively thought of the shadow people, and began to run.

Chapter Two

Chase followed Wen into a narrow alley between two buildings older than his country of birth. He knew she'd already figured out where to run. Wen always had a plan. Immediately upon walking on a new street, entering a building, a room, anywhere, Wen assessed the best escape route, strategic places to fight, every angle of pursuit, and hundreds of other variables mere mortals would never consider.

Her training and experience allowed her to create a strategy out of thin air. However, in this case, she'd had lots of time to plan. Snowden and Wen had chosen the location because of its openness, abundance of exit points, and public crowds that would make an ambush—even in a professional hit—difficult.

They rounded a corner. "Another!" Wen said breathlessly.

Chase saw a second man approaching and realized they were in real trouble. He followed automatically as Wen darted into a building.

The bustling streets and city noises evaporated. They were suddenly in a colorful wonderland of toys and brightly painted wooden Russian Matryoshka nesting dolls of every size—some taller than Chase himself. Their presence caused an immediate disruption as they burst into the store among only a small handful of customers.

"We've lost our young son," Wen called out in perfect Russian. "Have you seen him?" She held out her hand to indicate a child no more than three feet tall.

The shopkeeper, a round, gray lady, gave an immediate look of concern, but shook her head. "*Nyet.*"

"Is there a back door?" Chase blurted out in English.

Wen repeated the question in Russian.

The shopkeeper lit up and pointed to the rear of the store, seemingly happy to be able to give them a positive response. Wen and Chase had never stopped moving, because even if there had not been another exit, they would've had to get as far inside the building as possible before the fight began. Chase pushed through the heavy wooden door, ejecting them out onto a winding side street.

"Listen," Wen said, commotion erupting from the toy shop behind them. "At least one of them is close."

"We're going to have to confront them at some point," Chase yelled, looking for a good place to hide as they sprinted past dumpsters, empty pallets, and discarded barrels.

"We're in *Moscow*. This is not a good place for a fight. We don't need any extra attention."

"I know, but—"

"It will do us no good to defeat the shadow people, only to get taken into custody by the Russian FSB. This is one time where escape is the only way we can win."

"How many are there?"

"I saw two. That means four."

Chase wasn't going to ask *how* she knew that. He'd learned that she always knew. "Then our best way to escape is to cut down their numbers," he said, pointing to a cut out in the curve that held two dumpsters.

Wen nodded reluctantly, knowing what he was thinking.

As the two of them wedged themselves together in the tight space, Chase realized the odds were they would never get off the street alive.

Chapter Three

The nearest man following Chase and Wen moved down the ancient street as if he were a ghost, sliding amongst the shadows. There was competence and purpose in his gate. He was not going to be surprised, and although not from Moscow, or even Russian, he knew the pulse of the place.

Every corner, every doorway, every crate or dumpster, was a potential trap, and yet, in the time it took to inhale, he'd decided how much caution each required.

His targets could've already been down the road, somewhere else, in another building, yet the man seemed to know they were still on that street. Chase watched him through gaps in the scratched, rusty, black steel sides of the dumpsters, both impressed with and scared of the man coming for them.

When the tall stalker was less than fifteen feet away, he began moving faster with each step. Chase wanted to ask Wen if she believed the man was an American, but it was far too late for words.

Eight feet. Chase hardly dared to breathe. Once he was

within two feet, Chase knew they were about to be discovered and made his move—bolting into the street, hoping to make it across to the other side where a disaster of pallets, arrayed like a shipwreck against a loading dock from another century, awaited him.

Chase slid like a player going into home plate. Expecting a ricochet of bullets to spark the painted bricks of the dingy building, he dove into the debris, hoping to find enough cover. Instead, the familiar cadence of Wen issuing commands rose over the hollow crashing of stacks of crates and pallets. She'd come out of the dumpster amidst a cascade of crushed corrugated boxes and unrecyclable styrofoam, slamming down upon the momentarily distracted man, who had been intent on pursuing Chase and failed to account for the more dangerous of the pair.

Anticipating more trouble, Chase looked up and down the street. It only took Wen a few seconds they knew they didn't have to interrogate the man. They'd been running from secret assailants and mysterious people intent on doing them harm so often, that it was almost more important to find out *who* he was than to get away—*almost*.

After tangling with Wen, the man was barely conscious, and even if he'd *wanted* to cooperate, was too groggy to talk. She cursed herself for hitting him so hard.

A quick search unsurprisingly revealed no ID. Wen pocketed his Glock 23 pistol, her favorite brand of gun. Chase helped her lift the man into the dumpster. After exchanging a quick glance, they continued their long unspoken debate: to kill, or not to kill.

"He can't stop us," Chase said as he shoved a metal bar into the locking hasp of the dumpster lid.

Wen felt the pull of her training telling her to put a

bullet in the man's head, but she was not that person anymore, and there was no time to consider it further.

They resumed running, knowing there were at least three more pursuers waiting.

As she came around the corner, Wen spotted the second man, so they turned and ran the opposite direction. "Three and four," Wen shouted as two more appeared. They were surrounded, but it was obvious the men after them did not want to alert the Russian officials any more than Chase and Wen did, because they hadn't shot at them yet.

"Stop!" one of them yelled in English. Wen swung the Glock 23 toward three and four, her mind looking for angles, estimating the number of shots. She'd already checked and knew the man in the dumpster had equipped the Glock with a high-capacity magazine. Knowing he hadn't fired one of the .40 caliber bullets meant she had all twenty-two rounds in which to waste the three men who were inching toward them. The gun felt light in her hand, less than thirty-two ounces. She aimed.

"Stop!" the one behind her repeated. "Tess sent us!"

Chase, who, unlike Wen, wasn't an expert in weapons, didn't know he was holding a Glock 19, with an optional thirty-three round mag of 9mm bullets. He only knew he had a pistol, and was about to start firing. Yet when he heard an American voice claiming Tess had sent them, he instinctively hesitated. All along, he'd believed "they" were the shadow people. Tess Federgreen, head of the ultra-secret Corporate Intelligence Security Section, which had been formed as a joint operation of the CIA, NSA, and FBI, with a mandate to prevent war between corporations, seemingly showed up at quintessential times. Chase and Wen had a love-hate relationship with her—mostly hate.

At the same moment, Wen, who had already been reluctant to engage in a firefight on a Moscow street, twisted, dropped, rolled, and sprang back against the stunned man behind them. She had her Glock against his head before any of them could effectively respond. "Start talking," she growled.

Chase kept his gun pointed towards three and four, one of whom held his gun tensely aimed at Wen. The other covered Chase.

"Not here," her hostage said.

"It's here or in the afterlife," Wen said, jamming the gun hard into his temple. "You choose."

Chapter Four

Three and four exchanged a frustrated glance. One of them sighed, held up his gun hand, and slowly reached inside his suit jacket. "Getting my phone," he said slowly.

Chase clenched his jaw, ready to fire.

The man carefully withdrew the device and tapped the screen. A moment later, he flipped it around, and Chase was staring at the face of the woman who had caused so much distress in his life, while also saving it several times.

He wanted to laugh.

He wanted to shoot the phone.

He wanted to run.

Instead, he lowered his gun and cleared his throat. "Was this necessary, Tess?"

Wen shoved the man she'd been holding, slid the Glock into her pack, and jogged to the man holding the phone. Before Chase could stop her, she'd snatched it, yelling at Tess.

"I could have killed your agents! Do you realize how lucky you are?"

"Or how lucky *you* are, Wen. It seems it could have gone either way. And yet here we are, talking like old friends," Tess said. Although she'd changed her silky, shoulder length hair to different shades of blonde, to brown, to auburn, this time it was pinned tightly back, revealing the delicate, chiseled jaw, and determined, unwavering green eyes.

One of the agents ran over to free the man from the dumpster. Since they knew right where he was, Wen assumed all the agents must have had standard CIA tracking tags on them.

"I'm not your friend!" Wen yelled.

"I know," Tess replied calmly. "But I'm yours."

"What's going on?" Chase asked as he took the phone and moved toward a doorway to avoid drawing attention. All the agents had put their weapons away and turned their backs to lend them the illusion of privacy.

Before Tess could answer, Wen resumed her verbal attack. "I came *this* close to shooting them, and probably dislocated the tall one's jaw before depositing him in the dumpster!"

"But. You. Did. *Not*," Tess said, sounding like a therapist dealing with a hysterical patient.

Chase put his hand on Wen's shoulder, trying to calm her. Instead, she huffed off.

"We don't like killing people for no reason," Chase said to Tess.

"Says the man who's left a trail of bodies around the globe."

Wen, now leaning against a wall a few feet away, groaned angrily.

"What do you want?" Chase asked Tess impatiently.

"I've been hunting the two of you for weeks."

"How'd you find us?" Chase looked at the four agents

who had now taken up casual, yet defensive positions around the street. To protect them? A noble thought.

"I'm not sure I would've found you, except you happened to meet with the one person in the world who's more wanted than you are."

Snowden, of course, Chase thought, and wondered about the amount of surveillance *he* must be under by the US, Russians, and probably Chinese. He hoped he hadn't blown his cover or caused him any trouble.

"Why were you meeting with Snowden?"

"It's none of your business," Wen snapped from the wall.

"Silly girl, *everything* is my business. That is why I exist." Tess gave Chase a look as if to say, *Keep your little China doll under control.*

"Arguing on a back street in the middle of Moscow probably isn't a good idea for any of us," Chase said, leaning against a wall, folding his buffed arms and actually relaxing momentarily among *sort of* friends—or, at least, not outright enemies.

"I went to all this trouble to find you because we're up against a very smart and very dangerous enemy."

"Who is *we*?" Wen asked.

Tess ignored her question. "There is a person, or persons, hacking the unhackable."

"Is there such a thing as unhackable?" Chase mused.

"Apparently not." She paused for a moment. "Anyway, this person is taking down power grids, infrastructure, financial systems . . . targeting everything that runs on computers."

"*Everything?*"

Tess nodded. "So far it's been teasers, but this person, going by the screen name of "Killcore," has made it abundantly clear that he can get into anything. Corporate networks, power plants, nuclear facilities, mass transit, hospitals, pipelines, aviation, defense—deployed, remote, and pentagon—even our intelligence networks."

"*He?*" Wen sneered. "How do you know it's one person? And maybe it's a *woman!*"

"Can't you have people at the NSA figure this out?" Chase asked after glancing to Wen with an exasperated look. Wen blew him a kiss. "Why do you need *us?*"

"I haven't been looking for you because I need your help. I've been trying to find you because, Chase, you're the number one suspect."

Chapter Five

Typed characters danced across one of the thirty-six monitors in an immaculate, windowless room located three floors below a newly constructed low-rise office building, lost in a sea of dozens of identical structures.

The letters raced into words, which quickly formed the following sentences: "*The federal Rivers and Harbors Act of 1938 authorized more than fifty water projects, including the construction of two massive dams west of Houston, Texas . . .*"

Graphics and satellite images were inserted into the text. A man, sitting next to the screen, looked up from the book he was reading to admire the pictures. *They have no idea.* His mind unraveled a sequence of events as he turned back to his Kindle. Although halfway through the thriller novel, he recalled its opening line. First sentences were usually his favorite because of the way they captured the entire meaning of a novel, thereby catapulting the reader into the story. He often memorized them.

The end of the world, prophesied and feared for millennia, conjures images of fireballs plummeting toward earth, mushroom clouds obliter-

ating cities, and pandemics sweeping the globe. But no one ever imagined it would begin on a cloudy day, as a line of code on a typical computer, in an average building . . .

He smiled at the memory of the words. *Very apropos*, he sniggered to himself. Characters continued to fill the big screen as he resumed his reading.

"The Army Corps of Engineers completed the Barker Dam and Addicks Dam in the 1940s, resulting in the Barker and Addicks Reservoirs. Combined, the dams hold back nearly half a million acre-feet of water . . . "

Distracted from his thriller, the man couldn't help but watch the words streaming onto the monitor, as if secret messages were arriving from a team of code breakers at some exotic and remote location. And the part he'd been waiting for had finally come; the boring press release was about to get exciting.

"Today the dams will fail. And all the water, enough to fill two million average size swimming pools, bolstered by the recent heavy rains, will roar into Houston, submerging large sections of the nation's fourth most populous city under several feet of water . . . "

The man smiled, and went back to his book.

The press release continued. At that very moment, news organizations around the country were receiving the same document. *"Hundreds of thousands of gallons of contaminated wastewater will be released into the floodwaters, creating a health emergency . . . "*

Even as people in the media were reading the description of the disaster, it was occurring. The notification was both a warning and an announcement. The disaster was no accident. The floodgates had been lifted mere minutes before the release was sent.

The man was tempted to go online to watch the scrambling live coverage of the event, but he'd rather read his thriller. He had been held in government custody for a long time without access to the books he loved. Now that he was a free man again, his intent was to catch up on the reading he'd missed. All those titles loaded on his Kindle were his only goal.

That, he thought, *and to assist Killcore in wreaking havoc.*

Oh, and, of course, to make sure Chase McLone and his lovely girlfriend die a slow and painful death.

"Patience," he said aloud. "Patience."

Chapter Six

Chase looked at Wen, knowing she would be thinking that Tess was weaving them into yet another plot, another trap.

"You know I didn't do this," Chase said, turning back to Tess on the video-call.

"Yeah, I know." She looked down. Her worn cowboy boots grounded her while navigating the unjust and political world she juggled. Strangely, they also lent her levity. Tess smiled, yet she was not happy. "But no one else knows. And everything points to you."

"What?"

"All the strikes come through Balance Engineering."

Once a mighty and rising star among Silicon Valley elites, Chase and his partner, Desmond "Dez" Jefferson, had created RAI, a startlingly advanced artificial intelligence system, and SEER, an acronym for Search Entire Existence Result, which employed advanced photonic quantum information processors and utilized deep learning, AI, quantum algorithms, and virtually every data point in digital existence, to predict the future with stunning accuracy. There were other inventions, too. Some complete, some still in development.

Ever since he'd gone on the run, Balance Engineering had been run by Dez, a widely respected and well-liked African American engineer whose brilliant mind was the perfect complement to Chase.

Balance now conducted its operations in total secret. To the outside world, it hardly existed. Yet now, someone had cracked the shell, and whomever had gotten inside was trying to destroy Chase.

"Tess, it's *not* me. Tell your bosses—Do you actually *have* any?"

"Don't you know the Dylan song? 'Everyone's gotta serve somebody, It may be the Devil or it may be the Lord, But you're gonna have to serve somebody . . .'"

"Oh-kay," Chase said, a little unnerved at hearing her sing. "Just tell them I'm not this killer dude."

"It's *Killcore*."

"Whatever, just tell them!" Chase snapped.

"I wish it were that easy." She sighed. "You're not exactly an *upstanding* citizen."

Standing on a Moscow back street, his confused and wounded look made Tess laugh.

"You've broken more US and international laws than I can even count," she continued, absently spinning the turquoise bracelet she always wore. "You're in the company of a foreign agent."

"Ex-agent!" Wen snapped. "And what crimes?" A rat scurried from beneath a dumpster and caught Wen's eye.

"Murder, espionage, extortion, trafficking in contraband, destruction of property, and about a million weapons charges . . . those are just the ones that come to mind. It's an awfully long list. I could pull it up if you want."

"Most of those were done at *your* behest."

"Try proving that. I'm the head of an agency that doesn't officially exist, inside of the most powerful intelligence apparatus the world has ever known."

"I'm happy *you* said that and not me. I can still subpoena you."

Tess laughed. "It would be amusing to see you try."

"We're wasting time," Wen said. "What do you *want?*"

"Always cutting to the bottom line, aren't you, Wen?" Tess said. "I like that about you."

"Are these men here to arrest us?" Chase asked.

"No. They're going to escort you out of Russia."

"Sounds like the same thing."

"It's quite different, I assure you."

"Why do we need to leave Russia?"

"Because if you're going to prove your innocence, you need to return to the United States."

"Are there currently any arrest warrants for us in the States?" Wen asked.

"Yes, I'm afraid. Quite a few."

"Then why would we go there?"

"Because Killcore is here."

"If you know that, then that proves I'm not him," Chase said. "And I think it would be a lot smarter for me to be as far away from the man impersonating me as possible."

"The 'man' could also be a woman," Wen said.

"Quite right." Tess smiled. "But you should be here, where the action is. He's pretending to be you for a reason."

"Which is?"

"That's what you need to find out. And anyway, dear, innocent Chase, the arrest warrants are international. There's nowhere for you to hide."

"We'll see about that," Wen said with the confidence of a woman who had been in hiding for nearly two years.

"This is the worst cyber threat we've ever faced," Tess said, looking away from the camera, scanning something on a screen that appeared to disturb her. "There has never been someone who could do this much damage. Killcore's skills are frightening. He appears to be brilliant in his grasp of manipulative abilities with technology. If I didn't know better myself, I'd *swear* that Killcore is you."

"You told me once that I couldn't trust you."

"Did I? I meant you *shouldn't*, but sometimes you have to, even *if* you shouldn't."

Three armed men appeared at the end of the street.

"Go!" shouted one of the CISS agents.

Chase and Wen took off.

"She set us up!" Wen yelled as they ran.

"No I didn't," Tess, still on the phone, yelled back. "It's my people back there fighting off the Russians so you can get away!"

"We're in the middle of Moscow, with Russian agents after us," Chase yelled at Tess. "How far are we going to get?"

"Head to Novoslobodskaya Station," Tess said. "I have a team there."

Chase looked at Wen questioningly.

Wen nodded.

"Okay," Chase said, believing the last thing Tess wanted was to see them wind up in the hands of the Russians. He also knew Wen couldn't stand trusting their fates to Tess.

"I can get you out, but you must do exactly what I say," Tess said, her voice partially garbled. "And for God's sake, don't kill anyone."

Chapter Seven

Chase wasn't prepared for what they found inside the Novoslobodskaya metro station. It reminded him of a strange, elongated church. They walked briskly along the hard, checkerboard floor past a blur of massive, ornate, stained glass windows in bright primary colors in between grand arched openings leading to stairs, platforms, and corridors.

Wen used her practiced, yet still remarkable skill to somehow continuously check behind them while also scanning the area in front of them and still appear casual. Although Chase had seen her do it on hundreds of occasions, it amazed him each time. He did his best to spot potential trouble, like security guards, but knew the real threat was likely about to burst into the station through the same entrance they'd used.

"This place looks a bit like Alice in Wonderland," Chase said, wondering if at any minute Tess might decree, *"Off with their heads!"*

Chase and Wen tried to blend in with the locals while

pretending the authorities—people with guns and orders to kill—weren't after them. Endless brass moldings magnified the marble arches and separated them from a white, misty ceiling, punctuated only by a long line of conical chandeliers—probably alert spies as well.

A quick memory flash reminded Chase of a friend at MIT expounding about Moscow's world famous subway stations, each very different, all like museums, containing art and incredible design.

Tess had been silent since they'd entered the station. "Where do we go?" he asked as quietly as possible, fearing the comment would echo throughout the transportation cathedral's hard walls.

"Is she still there?" Wen asked after ten seconds with no response.

"I'm still here," Tess finally replied. "Having trouble picking you up underground."

"Can you get us out of here?"

"We still have a chance," she replied, sounding preoccupied.

"Then do something quick," Wen said. "They just found us."

Shots broke through the murmur of commuters, instantly replacing the routine din with screams of terrified passengers. The trampling of running feet created panic and provided momentary cover for Chase and Wen. The acoustics made the sound of each shot reverberate perhaps five times louder than it should have been.

A massive stained-glass panel exploded inches from Chase as bullets meant for them destroyed the seventy-year-old masterpiece. Shards of colored glass and metal tore into the crowd. The noise ratcheted up again as the gunfire, shouts, and sounds of terror amplified.

"Don't kill anyone!" Tess's voice commanded from the phone.

"They're shooting at us!" Chase yelled back.

"I understand that, but I can't get you out of there if you kill a Russian agent."

"I'd prefer *not* to be carried out in a body bag," Chase barked.

Wen returned fire, wishing for some other form of cover. Ironically, all the trash cans had been removed from Moscow's subways to help prevent terror attacks.

"Can you get to a train?" Tess asked. "One should be coming in less than a minute."

Chase didn't answer, but followed Wen, who was already heading through one of the arched openings. They emerged onto the now mostly abandoned platform. They ducked behind another column as a new gun battle broke out behind them.

"My team has arrived," Tess said. "Get on that train."

"There isn't a train yet," Chase said.

"Is *your* team allowed to kill Russian agents?" Wen asked as she fired back, careful not to hit anyone.

"That's a complicated question."

"Explain it," Chase said. "We've got time. Just waiting for a train."

The gunfire from the terminal magnified, but so far no one else had made it to the platform.

"It should be there now."

"It's *not* here!"

They heard another stained glass window shatter.

"It *has* to be." Tess sounded uncharacteristically frazzled.

"Why?" Chase asked as more gunshots echoed. "Aren't trains ever late in Moscow?"

"Not today."

"There's too many," Wen said, peering back through the terminal, which now looked more like a disaster area.

"Could they have stopped it?" he asked. "Wait . . . here it comes."

The CIA agent from the dumpster stumbled into the archway, and fell dead.

"One of your agents just—"

"I know."

"How do we know they won't get us on the train?" Wen asked as they moved toward it.

"We don't!" Tess snapped.

"Then why—?" Chase began to protest.

"Just get on the damned train *now*!"

Chapter Eight

The director of the FBI got up from his desk and walked slowly to the window, trying to catch his breath. *Something isn't right,* he thought, then staggered back and caught himself. *I'm in trouble.* He made his way back to his desk, where there were two phones—his secure cellular device, and a landline. One button on either phone would get him instant help.

The last thing he saw were the pictures of his wife, children, and grandchildren, as he crashed to the floor, taking a stack of classified folders and a desk lamp with him.

It would be ten minutes before an assistant found his unresponsive body. Seventeen minutes after that, an EMT would pronounce the FBI director dead.

During those same twenty-seven minutes, other high-ranking US government officials also collapsed. It wouldn't take long for investigators to realize these weren't coincidental, natural deaths. That the common denominator was that each victim had a pacemaker, or in the case of an under cabinet secretary and an army colonel, insulin pumps.

Even before all that information was known, the CIA had received a message from Killcore claiming responsibility. The message was quickly analyzed, deciphered, and dissected for intelligence.

Inside "Mission Control," a secure basement room of the undisclosed CISS headquarters building in Vienna, Virginia, Tess watched the crisis deepen. The expansive space, filled with wall-sized monitors and computer terminals, looked like a futuristic version of NASA's Mission Control—thus the name. Three select groups of nine technicians and eight analysts worked the data twenty-four-seven, as if searching for treasure.

"The current digital footprints all—not surprisingly—lead back to Balance Engineering and Chase Malone," an analyst told Tess.

She nodded, knowing as soon as it happened that Chase would be fingered again, never mind that he was running for his life in the Moscow underground. He could have set the events into motion earlier, or he could have a team, a network, involved with his schemes. Chase Malone was more than a brilliant man—he was driven.

What drives him? He's on a quest. A man who has everything, yet risks it all, and his life, every day . . .

An assistant interrupted her thoughts. "Tess, the president is on the line."

As she listened to the only person in the world who could overrule her, Tess watched one of the big screens.

Large sections of Houston were underwater, thousands of homes flooded. An estimated seventy thousand residents were seeking shelter. Hundreds were yet to be rescued. At least eighty-four people were reported to have been killed, including a family of five, whose car was swept away by the raging waters.

An unknown number of persons are still stranded in their homes, a FEMA report stated. *Dozens of volunteers in boats are struggling to reach the trapped people.*

Tess watched as the National Guard poured into the ravaged area. The president had already declared the city a Federal Disaster Area, and all of it had been done intentionally.

"Why don't you believe this was Chase Malone?" the president asked at the end of his rant.

"I know him. I worked with him. This *isn't* him. This is a set-up."

"So, in your scenario, some madman used a sophisticated artificial intelligence program to predict the weather and take over these dams at *precisely* their most vulnerable point, to create the perfect storm? And then laid a trail of digital breadcrumbs leading back to your billionaire friend?"

"Exactly."

"*Why?*" the president asked. "Why not just do the crime? Why bother to frame someone? What does that get him?"

"Revenge."

"Really? Doesn't that seem a little too Game of Thrones? Does Malone even *have* someone who hates him that much?"

"Chase has more enemies than you." The highly powerful Tess Federgreen smoothed her silk pant suit and sat tall in the ergo-simulated chair, narrowing her sharp green eyes, knowing on so many levels who this man was, how little the president knew about everything, how much she had to play into his game, and how well she played it.

He scoffed. "That seems unlikely. However, let's pretend you're right. If someone's going to all this trouble to destroy Malone's life, why not just kill him?"

"Because Malone is harder to get to than you." She bit into a green apple.

The president grunted. He knew Tess didn't exaggerate, yet this seemed ridiculous.

"Killcore does seem intent on ruining Chase, but that's only a distraction. He's going after world stability." Tess had to hide a chuckle, even though her job was to assure everything stayed in working order. *How ironic,* she thought.

"Where is he?"

"Malone, or Killcore?"

"Right now, the entire National Security team, and every single one of my intelligence advisors, is telling me they're one in the same. Everyone but you."

"Chase is in Moscow." Her voice was deadpan.

"Of course he is. Probably meeting with Vladimir Putin and Edward Snowden."

Tess decided that would be too much information. "We're pulling him out."

"Do you *have* him?"

"We will in a minute. I'll have to get back to you."

"What?" the president asked. "Tess? What the hell?"

The line was dead.

Chapter Nine

Chase pushed through a group of passengers trying to get off the subway car. Wen lagged a few seconds behind in case agents came through the arches. As she turned to join Chase, the throngs of commuters abruptly reversed direction, having heard the gun battle. The mob's ensuing fear created a stampede back into the subway car. Wen fought against the crushing swell, immobilized by the press of bodies against her. She could neither see Chase, nor hear her own shouts to him, but she was inside the train, and believed he was also still onboard. The train jerked ahead, pulling out of the Novoslobodskaya metro station.

Chase had become jammed into a corner before they departed and had not been able to see Wen enter. While still trying to hear Tess, he fought his way through the packed car. With the phone on speaker, pressed to his ear, he was grateful that the Astronaut had enhanced their phones, one of the abilities addressed being subterranean reception. He wasn't sure how it worked, but remembered something about more devices in the area meaning a stronger signal—some kind of quantum relay system—and there were hundreds of devices around him.

When Tess's voice came through, Chase silently thanked the Astronaut. Tess was their life-line.

"Can you still hear me?"

"Yes," he said, checking the screen. "But I can't see you."

"You'll . . . have. . . make do . . . my voice then . . . already know . . . beautiful I am." The signal crackled in and out.

"Aren't the authorities going to be waiting for us at the next stop?" Chase asked, still working his way back through the car.

"Yes . . . alrea. . . there."

"Then how?"

"You're gett. . . off before the next. . ."

Before Chase could push for more details, he spotted Wen. The two of them forced a seam through the ranting and shouting riders. Even though their words were in Russian, Chase knew the commotion was centered around the terror at Novoslobodskaya metro station.

Finally, Chase and Wen reached through the last knot of people, clasped hands, and pulled themselves together. Before either one could speak, Tess continued, "In . . . two minutes the . . . will stop. You . . . get off imme. . . ."

"What?" Chase asked.

"The train wi. . . stopped. . . a matter . . . seconds. . . be a pulse set."

"What's that mean?" Wen asked, struggling to hear Tess above the continuing commotion of scared riders.

"It doesn't matter," Tess replied.

"It does if it involves something I need to defend us

against." Their heads were pressed tightly together, listening to Tess, as they inched toward the exit doors.

"It's . . . electronic," Tess continued. "We. . . through the system. It . . . appear to be . . . maintenance glitch. You . . . long . . . have . . . force the doors."

"When you say seconds?" Chase asked.

"Three . . . then it starts . . . again."

"We need more information!" Wen snapped.

"I can't tell you details while . . . crowded train . . . Russians, many of whom . . . English better than I do."

"How about a different language?" Wen asked.

Tess, very aware that Wen was fluent in more than half a dozen languages, was not, and there was no time for her to stutter through her high school French. "I'll tell . . . need to know."

Wen checked the time, knowing they only had sixty seconds left before the stop. "We need to know *now*! We're about to get off in the middle of a dark tunnel under Moscow, and could lose contact with you at any moment. Tell us where we have to go."

Tess could not argue with the logic, and shivered at the thought of the two of them standing stranded in the middle of a subway tunnel waiting for Russian agents to close in from either direction. "Do you . . . Bunker-42?"

Chase had never heard of it.

Wen immediately realized there might be a way to escape. "Yes, of course. But we're nowhere near it. It's on another line." Wen reviewed the Moscow subway map in her head. She knew, from MSS training, that the Soviets had maintained Bunker-42 during the Cold War. The top-secret facility, located more than two hundred feet underground, operated as an emergency command post, part of the Moscow anti-aircraft district, and a communication center. Two secure tunnels connected it to the Moscow subway.

"What is it?" Chase asked, trying to picture a Cold War nuke site.

Wen quickly recalled the details—in the event of a nuclear attack, the complex could support six hundred people with enough food and water for thirty days. However, Bunker-42 had been declassified in 2000, and long since decommissioned. "But that's at the Taganskyaya station," Wen continued. "That's the opposite side of the circle."

". . . another Bunker," Tess said. ". . . hasn't been decommissioned. And . . . far more sophisticated."

Chapter Ten

Mission Control was filled to capacity. High level personnel from other agencies were jammed in with technicians and analysts as Tess directed the effort to find Killcore.

"He's hit Bank of America," the head of the FBI's financial crimes division said with more than a little panic in his voice as rows of numbers rolled across one of the big screens.

"Killcore just took sixteen million from Wells Fargo!" another man yelled from somewhere in the room.

Tess whirled around to check on the team monitoring Citibank, which had just finished updating their security measures based on the earlier Killcore attacks. "Citi has to hold," she muttered to herself, knowing that if Killcore could penetrate these newest defenses, which had been done in collaboration with the NSA's lead encryption group, there might be no way to stop him. "If we can't prevent this, then figuring out *who* Killcore is will be the least of our problems," she said to an assistant CIA director, who was also watching the Citibank accounts.

"He just got into Equifax," an analyst called out. The credit agency had long been a target of hackers. However, for twenty-one months, no one had successfully breached their data.

"Damn," Tess said. What made it even more brazen was the speed at which the break-ins were occurring.

"How is he getting into all these places simultaneously?" an NSA employee asked while Tess spoke into her phone again.

"There has to be a team helping him," another tech speculated.

Tess thought of Wen, who kept reminding her that Killcore could be a woman instead of a man, as most in the room assumed. Tess had tentatively convinced most of those gathered in Mission Control that Chase Malone was not Killcore, however, some were still not sure. Her upcoming face-to-face with Chase and Wen would be critical. The intelligence community had to stop being distracted by the possibility that Killcore was Chase. Tess knew it was technically possible, but at the same time believed it wasn't.

"He's in Citibank!" someone yelled, as they all turned their attention back to that screen.

Tess allowed herself only a moment of fear before she fought it off. "Are we on him?"

"I've never seen anybody as brazen as this guy," the FBI financial crimes man said. "He's picked off all the major banks right in front of us while we were *watching*!"

"God help us if he starts going after the stock exchanges," an analyst added.

Tess had the very same thought. However, her mind had immediately moved way beyond that. *Where is Killcore going next? What is he after? How can we stop him?* Then, looking back at the screen, she whispered, "Who is Killcore?"

"Did you say something?" the FBI man asked.

Tess shook her head, concentrating on the only real clue they had as to his identity, the lead they had been wrestling with for days: Killcore's connection to Chase Malone.

"We've just traced the Wells Fargo hack," an analyst said, interrupting her thoughts.

"Balance Engineering?" she asked, already knowing the answer.

The analyst nodded, not surprised.

Tess spoke more instructions into her phone.

Another technician moved additional streams onto the "big board." Bank of America, Citi, and Equifax breaches were all locked in and traced. "They're all coming from Balance."

"Chase Malone is going to have a lot of explaining to do," a woman from the NSA said.

"Malone is a brilliant engineer," an FBI financial crimes agent muttered. "It's unlikely he would be so careless as to leave a trail *this* obvious. One can only assume that Tess is right on this." He raised his eyebrows and shrugged. "Chase is being set up."

"But why?" the woman asked. "Killcore must know that we'll figure that out, and then use Malone to find him."

"So far, that hasn't been working for us," Tess said.

"Killcore's inside Morgan Stanley," a man and woman shouted simultaneously from the middle of the room. That bank's data switched onto the big screen, and they all watched in amazement as Killcore unmasked encrypted names and addresses of the account holders.

"He's transferring eight million to . . . Balance Engineering's bank account," a technician reported.

Tess suppressed a laugh, knowing it would not have been appreciated given the gravity of the situation. However, she couldn't help being amused by Killcore's audacity. "He's toying with us. *Actually* ridiculing us," she said.

"It's outrageous," the FBI man said. "And unnerving."

A moment later, the laughter Tess had swallowed turned to bile when Killcore swiftly hacked into Mission Control and changed all their screens to NSA data streams.

Chapter Eleven

Reception in the Moscow subway tunnel fell apart. Chase and Wen had to keep moving blindly until he heard Tess again. "You're having us walk into a high-security Russian military installation?"

"No, you won't get that far."

"I'm sure we won't," Wen continued, watching the other passengers, looking for any signs of recognition, but was confident they couldn't hear Tess since *she* could barely hear the CISS director, and the phone was touching her ear.

More static, then Tess was back mid-sentence. ". . . –ember you'll have . . . –ee seconds . . . stops." Garbled syllables. "Once you're off, you'll . . . looking for yellow paint marks . . . wall. They'll be something . . . ones painted . . . di– . . . ded highways. There'll be hundreds of marks, but . . . twice as thick as the others, about . . . inches." Tess's voice broke up into a garble of static.

"I didn't hear. How many inches thick?" Chase asked as Wen checked the time.

"We're down to fifteen seconds before it stops," Wen said.

"*Six* inches," Tess came through again.

"Got it, then what?"

The whole next sentence from Tess was incoherent.

"Say again?"

"Eight seconds," Wen said.

"Tess? *Tess?*"

"Past the yellow . . . box . . . look for why . . . then."

When they finally reached the door, the signal came back just long enough for them to hear the word "box" again. The car suddenly lurched and slowed. Chase, unsure if it was actually going to stop, began clawing at the doors. Only after the train's movement paused did the safety mechanism release and the doors open. To the surprise of the already traumatized passengers, Chase pushed Wen out, then squeezed through into the darkness.

However, before he got his foot down onto the rough concrete ledge, the doors closed, trapping his right ankle. The train started away, dragging him, hopping, along beside it. Two large men pulled on the doors, which still hadn't latched. Wen yelled. Chase looked up and saw in a few feet the train would crush him into a massive concrete column. The men inside saw it, too, and although the riders around them looked panicked, the two men displayed nothing but stoic determination. Wen ran after the car as it picked up speed. Chase lost his balance and went down, the train pulling him along on the rough concrete until, at the last instant, the men prevailed and forced the doors apart only inches, but enough to release the door's hold, to cheers from those inside. Chase sprang free and rolled into the column, but with far less impact. Instead of being smashed and broken, he was scraped and bruised.

"Close! Are you all right?" Wen asked, helping him to his feet.

"Ask me tomorrow. Let's find the yellow line."

After almost two minutes of searching the now oppressively dark tunnel with only the light of their phones, they found it.

"Now what?" Wen asked.

"I don't know. I never heard the rest, but there was something about a box."

Wen raised her phone near the wall. "There."

"That's it?" Chase asked, looking at what appeared to be an electrical relay enclosure about ten feet from the yellow mark.

Wen walked back and forth. "No other box."

"Okay," Chase said, pulling out his multi-tool, an item he tried never to be without. A few seconds later, the cover was off. "Any ideas?"

She peered inside at the mess of wires and switches. "Does anything seem like it doesn't belong?"

Chase studied the wiring while Wen nervously looked in both directions down the dark tunnel, anticipating trouble.

"Here," he said, seeing a worn wooden peg buried below a tangle of colored wires. The box dislodged, and Chase barely caught it before it would have crashed onto the tracks. Behind it was a latch. "The box is just a dummy."

He tugged on the latch. A section of concrete opened at a seam, providing a tight space for them to crawl into. Chase was somehow able to hang the electrical box back up before pulling the vault shut behind them.

The dank, stale air closed in quickly. Wen led the way, hoping her light would last.

"We spend entirely too much time in tunnels," Chase said, trying to get a signal, knowing it was useless.

"There," Wen said, pointing to a rusted metal hatch. "Look, there's a panel."

It was faded, but a neatly printed diagram, that looked as if it had been written with a magic marker a hundred years ago, explained—amazingly, in English—that the hatch would lead through a back ventilation shaft to the Command Center. Following the tunnel to the left, one would soon reach a steel ladder to the street.

"I vote we take the street," Chase said. "I'm not in the mood to be shot or taken prisoner, at least not while we're in a Communist country."

After a long crawl through a narrow, curving tunnel, they came to rusted steel foot holds built into the concrete. Wen wasted no time, relieved to finally be able to stand, grabbing the first rung and climbing up the dark shaft. Without using his light, Chase could not see Wen above him, and it took much longer to reach the top than he'd expected.

"We don't know what's on the other side," Wen said, her head bumping against what she assumed was a manhole cover. "Get your gun ready."

Chapter Twelve

Franco Madden walked outside and lit a cigarette. He didn't used to smoke, but it came with his new identity, and he liked the habit: the nicotine, the ceremony of packing a cigarette, lighting it—always and *only* with matches—and flicking ashes.

But, most of all, he loved the slow suicide of it.

He checked the phone. Still no call. It irritated him that one of his partners was not as timely as he and Killcore were. However, they needed Costa—at least for now.

While he continued to wait and smoke, Franco thought back to when he'd first met the short, muscled, Chilean native.

Aaron Costa had been an MIT graduate, and could have worked at any number of startups or the biggest tech companies. But the chairman of GlobeTec, where Franco was head of Security at the time, had made it a priority to get the best brains on his payroll. TruNueral, one of GlobeTec's subsidiaries, had a big secret project underway, and needed talent.

The Chairman had personally put together starting packages that were twice as rich as those Apple, Google, or Microsoft were offering. Still, Costa had been reluctant until Irvin Sliske, then the CEO of TruNueral, made an unannounced visit to Costa, and somehow closed the deal. Franco found out later that he'd given Costa an envelope containing twenty thousand dollars in cash—a signing bonus to what was already, by far, the highest offer he'd received.

It wasn't the money, Costa said, that had swayed him. "It was the determination with which they were soliciting me," he later said. Costa wanted to be with a company that was going to change the world, while surrounded by the brightest minds in the field. TruNueral was all of that—or, at least it *had* been before Chase Malone betrayed them.

A few months later, Costa and Franco met when Franco was providing security at a TruNueral company retreat. Costa had been reading his favorite science fiction novels during the mandatory downtime. Franco had walked by and, as he often did, showed off by quoting: "'The children were playing while Holston climbed to his death; he could hear them squealing as only happy children do.'"

Costa flipped back in the book and smiled, impressed that Franco knew the first line of *Wool* by Hugh Howey. The two conversed animatedly about the book, as well as others they had read. Inevitably, they sparked up a friendship, one that would change the world.

Braced against the wall in the dark shaft above the Moscow subway, Chase reached for his phone. "We might be able to get reception," he said, touching the screen.

"I see you made it," Tess's tense voice came from the speaker a moment later. "Open it."

"I've tried," Wen replied. "It won't budge."

"I'm talking to someone else," Tess said.

"*Who?*" Wen snapped back, positioning her gun.

"Your rescuers."

Chase was about to say they didn't *need* to be rescued, but then remembered they were trapped in a narrow underground shaft with half the Russian Army and a large contingent from the Federal Security Service closing in below them.

The manhole cover turned out to be a concealed and secure hatch that could only be opened from above with a six-digit combination.

"Those are *our* people," Tess said as the hatch opened, knowing Wen might shoot them. "I have a situation here. I'll get back to you when I can."

"Wait," Chase said, but she was gone.

Three women dressed in black helped them out, then quickly closed and secured the tunnel again. Chase looked back, and could not tell where it had been. They had emerged in a lightly wooded section of what appeared to be a small park.

"Hurry," one of the women said in accented English.

"Where?" Wen asked.

"We have a car."

Chase saw they were actually in what wasn't more than a few rows of trees separating some small apartment buildings, someone's feeble attempt at community beautification in a drab, post-Stalinesque Soviet residential complex.

In the fading light of the day, as the sun dipped behind a thousand-unit structure, Wen scanned the area. Her instincts told her they were still not safe. "How much farther?"

"Through here. Not far."

They reached a late-model white sedan, which Wen immediately approved of, knowing it would blend in.

"You will need to ride in trunk," one of the women said in broken English.

"No, we don't," Wen said.

"Sorry, it is necessary."

Wen was ready to take the vehicle by force and leave the women behind. One of them seemed to sense this and let out an exasperated sigh. "We take chance risking this to help you. To get you out of Moscow."

"I know, but—" Wen started.

"We appreciate it," Chase interrupted. He pointed at the trunk. "*That's* just not going to happen."

"Then you stay here," the third woman said.

"Look," the first woman said, opening the trunk. "It has safety. It can open from inside." She crawled into the large trunk and pulled it shut. A second later, it sprang open. "Presto," she said, crawling out. "Simple."

Wen inspected the interior handle which released the lock.

"We must hurry," one of them said. "You come, you ride in trunk."

"Let me test it," Chase said. He got in and Wen closed the trunk. A second later, he sprung himself.

"Good. Okay," one of the women said. "Satisfied we are not killing you?"

Wen climbed in with Chase and pulled the trunk closed. The car started immediately, and bounced along the rough grassy trail until it dropped off a curb onto the pavement and sped away.

Chapter Thirteen

For nearly an hour, Chase and Wen endured starting and stopping, swerving, hills, and curves, until, finally, the car found some consistent speed. Wen seethed, not at having to ride in the trunk, she understood that logic, but at being dependent on people she didn't know, didn't trust, and who were somehow loosely connected to Tess, another woman she certainly didn't trust.

Yet, on the other hand, Chase held her comfortably, and whispered in her ear, "Its dark, we're alone—"

"Not funny," she shot back. "This might be the end of us."

"What will be, will be." He winked, yet she couldn't see him. His hot lips found hers for one long, sensuous kiss.

Wen sighed deeply before saying, "That's enough."

"Okay," one of the women yelled loudly as the car rolled to a stop. "Get out now."

Wen had her gun pointed to the trunk's opening as Chase tripped the knob.

"Whoa," a stocky man, silhouetted against the dim backlight, said, holding up his hands.

"Who are you?" Wen asked.

"Sorry about her, Victor," one of the women said. "She is a paranoid wench. Does not appreciate us saving her life."

"I am one of the good guys," the man said, his hands still in the air.

Wen kept her gun aimed as she pulled herself from the deep trunk. Chase quickly got out behind her.

"Unless you can fly an X3," Victor said, "you might want to stop pointing that thing at me."

"I can fly it," Wen said, still ready to shoot them all.

"Your phone is ringing," one of the women told Wen.

"No," she said suspiciously, but then it vibrated. Expertly, Wen extracted her phone, never taking her gun or eyes off Victor.

"Wen, please," Tess's voice came through the speaker. "I don't have the time or the patience to babysit you. I've gone to a lot of trouble to get you out of Moscow, and now out of Russia. Get on the damned helicopter, and stop pointing your gun at our friends, or I'll tell them to leave you to the FSS, who, if they don't *kill* you, will quickly trade you to the Chinese."

"We don't need—" Wen began before Chase raised his hand in a calming gesture.

"We'll go along," Chase said.

"Play nice, Wen," Tess added.

"Until I see *you*," Wen said bitterly.

"I'll look forward to our meeting," Tess said, ending the call.

"Okay?" Victor said to Wen, lowering his hands.

She nodded.

In his worn leather jacket, Victor looked like a tough

World War II ace. "I am Victor," he introduced himself, patting his chest a bit too hard. His smile seemingly flashed a sparkle, and he offered his hand out to Wen. "I guess you have had a lousy day, or maybe very bad week or something. I do not know."

Wen eyed him carefully, then shook his hand without saying anything.

"I'm Chase. It's good to meet you. We appreciate your help, and yeah, it's been kind of a rough *year*, really."

"Sorry. We will get you home, then maybe it gets better." Victor rubbed his hands quickly together, faster and faster, until it seemed he would take off. He was a hyper guy, which normally made people uneasy. For some reason, Chase liked him.

They walked over to an old barn the size of a small warehouse, its weathered boards barely seeming to hold the structure upright. Inside, on an oversized flatbed, waited one of the most impressive helicopters Chase had ever seen.

"Modified Eurocopter X3," Victor said, beaming like a proud schoolboy. "Top speed of regular version." He spanked the side of the sophisticated machine with a flat palm. "Is a tiny bit under five hundred kilometers per hour, but this one, I think, does more more than Five-fifty." There was that smile again, with the sparkle on his teeth.

"What kind of engines?" Wen asked, impressed.

"It powered by two Rolls-Royce Turbomeca RTM322X turboshaft engines," he said, whistling. "They generate more than twenty-three hundred horsepower. *Each*."

Wen smiled for the first time all day. "You'd better fly. Where are we going?"

"Latvia," one of the women said. She handed Chase a paper bag.

"How far to the border?"

"Not too far," Victor said. "Maybe six hundred kilometers." He nodded and raised his bushy eyebrows. It was hard for Chase to take this stocky man seriously, with his protruding belly used to vodka and Doktorskaya Bologna.

"We ought to be there in ten minutes in this thing," Chase said waving a *no, but thank you* to the paper bag.

"Almost, my friend," Victor said, "But really more close to ninety minutes." He turned to Chase. "Take the bag. The best peroshkas you'll ever taste." He kissed his fingers.

"Might attract attention at that speed," Wen said.

"We fly low," Victor said as the helicopter was pulled out of the barn. "Low and fast."

Victor lived up to his promise, and delivered them to an airfield where a CIA chartered jet was waiting to whisk Chase and Wen to the United States. Once airborne, another call came in from Tess.

"He killed Hank Stram," Tess began, audibly fatigued.

"The director of the FBI?" Chase asked.

"Yes. I'd been working with him personally on the case."

"How?" Wen asked.

"He hacked the director's pacemaker."

Wen looked questioningly at Chase, as if to ask if that were even possible.

"There should have been security protocols," Chase said. "All life-dependent medical devices have them."

"Apparently Killcore is not bothered by security protocols." She bit into a fresh green apple. Tess was known to leave partially eaten apples around her office. Assistants continually found and discarded them.

"How do we know it was him?" Chase asked, while Wen was still processing the fact that it was even possible to do.

"Because he wanted us to know it was him," Tess said gruffly. "Two senior CIA officials, and three more at the Pentagon, all had heart attacks within minutes of each other. All had pacemakers. And just to make sure we didn't miss him, he killed at least thirty-eight people at the UVA Medical Center."

"More pacemakers?"

"This time he hacked into insulin pumps, dialysis machines, blood monitoring . . . I'm not a doctor, but apparently there are a lot of computers keeping people alive. He knocked the power out for the entire hospital, then disabled the switches that would turn on the emergency back-up generators."

"Who would do something like that? Going after sick people. Why?" Chase instinctively reached for his multi-tool, and like a worry stone, squeezed its handles, his fingers following the edges to all the parts.

"He's sending a message," Tess said.

"That he's a psychopath?"

"Yes. He doesn't care. He'll cross any line." She tossed the apple, with three bites gone, into a trash can.

"But what does he *want*?" Wen asked. "Why is he doing this? What is his ultimate objective?"

"We don't know yet."

"He's going to too much trouble just to be framing me," Chase said.

"I agree," Tess said. "But you're the best link we have to him, our best chance to stop him. And there's something else."

"What?" Chase and Wen's eyes met, deeply, openly, knowingly.

"I have to tell you in person."

Chapter Fourteen

Dean Johnson looked around suspiciously, and, seeing no one, pulled a phone out of the glove compartment of his brand new, midnight-blue, Ford Mustang convertible. Working as a "cyber-spy" had made him careful, but not *this* careful.

Breaking the law had made him this careful.

His ridiculously long title—Deputy Director of Cyber Security, National Cyber Security Division, Office of Cybersecurity and Communications, Cybersecurity and Infrastructure Security Agency, United States Department of Homeland Security—didn't begin to cover the layers of bureaucracy he had to wade through on a daily basis, all of it meant to keep the United States ahead in an ongoing cyber war. "World War III," he'd once quipped to a colleague, amused by his foretelling. "Only the public is expecting nukes and smart-bombs. They don't get that *this* world war is all being fought in cyberspace, and it's even *more* dangerous, because it's invisible." He leaned in conspiratorially, grinned, and snapped his on-going piece of sugar-free gum.

Dean was part of the team that coordinated with the National Security Agency, Central Security Services, US Cyber Command and the Cyber Division of the FBI, National Cyber Investigative Joint Task Force, CyWatch, Domestic Security Alliance Council, InfraGard, the National Cyber Forensics and Training Alliance, DHS's National Cybersecurity and Communications Integration Center, the Critical Infrastructure Assurance Office, the National Infrastructure Protection Center, the Federal Computer Incident Response Center, and the National Communications System, a tangled mess of alphabet agencies and sub departments—egos, careers, and power trips—that was constantly clashing.

A light breeze came in through the open window, suddenly making him sneeze several times, so he closed it. He got lost for a moment, seeing only the lofty trees. His eyes followed their trunks down to a sidewalk, and then the expansive, dusty parking lot where he sat and waited.

He punched in thirty-seven digits that would, after a convoluted process of connections and reroutings, put him in touch with Franco Madden, the insanely vengeful and highly intelligent former head of security for the massive conglomerate GlobeTec. These days, he preferred to call himself simply a *facilitator*.

Dean's job was to collaborate with the private sector, government, military, and intelligence stakeholders. The collective mission meant a constant stream of historic and real-time data, with projections being integrated between agencies. Ultimately, Dean's slender fingers and keen mind got him to be one of the top officials tasked with conducting risk assessments to mitigate vulnerabilities and threats to the nation's information technology assets. This meant overseeing problematic exchanges and/or attacks, along with other activities affecting the operations of civilian, military, government, and private sector critical cyber infrastructures. His department also provided cyber threat and vulnerability analysis, early warning, and incident response assistance for public and private sector constituents.

He'd never been a very brave man. His mother had wanted him to be a classical pianist, which he actually still played, but only for stress relief.

The call failed to connect. That sometimes happened. He tried again.

Combatting national security cyber threats might have sounded interesting, but to Dean it had become tedious, frustrating work, and something he thought could never be won. "Every day there's a different threat, every day it's harder to tell who the enemy is and who it is not." He believed that the United States was doing as much, or more, than any other nation in the arena. "It is an endless, unwinnable war," he told himself regularly, and so he justified his actions. He could see the entire playing field, and he knew—better than others—that this was the new normal. It didn't make him crazy or angry, just tired. So he'd decided to change it. He also knew all those same bureaucratic mazes shielded him from getting caught.

Another call failure. Dean tried not to get nervous. A lot was going on now, meaning encrypted call traffic was tighter, but they could also be onto him. He looked around the parking lot and saw nothing suspicious.

But it wouldn't be suspicious, he thought. *It would look normal.*

Looking into a computer screen, he could quickly spot anything that was not right. It was his talent. But in the actual world, things were harder for him.

He tried the call one last time. Thirty-seven digits.

Dean liked his vacations. He was smart about it, keeping them modest in appearance, but on vacation, he spent lavishly and freely—alcohol, prostitutes, gambling, whatever and whenever he could. It was just play money to him. And he didn't believe any of the secrets mattered that much because everyone was ahead of everyone else at some point. Cyber advancement was a fast-moving field—hackers, viruses, spyware, and, most important of all, tracking. They could look inside any computer, co-opt any phone, using their cameras to spy. Tracking, eavesdropping, and watching —*everyone*—through their devices, and they did it using completely complex set-ups that boxed in whoever they were after. It didn't matter how many innocent devices or people were caught up in the web. The perpetrators would never be found out, either, because they were the United States government, and they acted with impunity. It was, after all, for the better good.

"Screw them!" Dean suddenly blurted, angry at what the US Government had become. "Empire builders!"

His eyes started to itch. He suffered from extreme allergies from everything—animal dander, dust, pollen . . .

He looked nervously at the phone. "Why isn't it connecting?" He envisioned friends of his inside an NSA secure dry-room intercepting his call and recording every word. "They can't know," he whispered, testing himself to see if he believed his own words. "They *can't*," he said firmly. And he knew they didn't, because he was too good.

Chapter Fifteen

The plane carrying Chase and Wen taxied into a spacious hanger. Even before the jet engines shut down, the large doors sealed the cavernous space behind them. Chase and Wen, anxious to leave CIA custody, were relieved when stairs rolled into place and they were allowed to exit freely. However, as they descended the steps, Chase spotted Tess with a team of armed men.

"So we are not allowed to leave?" Wen asked, as they reached the bottom of the stairs, upset that their weapons were in a carry-on bag sealed by their handlers.

"I'm afraid not immediately," Tess said, with her trademark smile that simultaneously conveyed friendliness and femme fatale.

"I knew we couldn't trust you," Wen said.

"What is this?" Chase asked.

Tess walked up to Chase, until their faces were only a foot apart. "Who is Killcore?"

"I already told you, I'd never heard of Killcore until you told me about him."

"I believe you."

"Then let us go!" Wen said, glancing around at the elite operatives surrounding them, calculating how many she could kill before they stopped her, looking for every angle of advantage, a way to escape.

"I've been directed and authorized to administer sodium pentothal, to waterboard you, cut off a pinkie, do whatever to get the answers we need—to *kill* you if necessary. So don't bother me with your whining about how inconvenient this is for *you*." She glared at Chase like an angry parent.

"We can help you more if we're out there," Chase said.

"I know." She nodded to one of the IT-Squad members, the elite CISS operatives proficient in both special ops combat and computer technology. Immediately, Chase and Wen were seized and cuffed. Wen knew it was coming, and had already reluctantly concluded that this was not the place to fight.

A few minutes later, they were in the back of a large SUV, racing through dark streets outside of Boston.

Inside a warehouse on the edge of an office park, Squad members led Chase and Wen into a secret CIA facility. "I need you to take a polygraph," Tess said to Chase.

"You're kidding, right? Lie detector tests aren't reliable."

"No, they're not, and with practice, a smart guy like you can fake your way through, but this isn't for me. If I let you go, I need to show that we had reason to believe you."

"Is it that simple?" Chase asked.

"No," Wen said. "This isn't for her superiors. It's so *we'll* believe she is letting us go, but they'll be trailing us, monitoring our every move. This is just to give us a false sense of security."

"You're a smart woman," Tess said. "But humor me."

If the test was just for show, it was the full double-feature. After an exhaustive ninety minutes, it ended with the big question from the man administering.

"Are you Killcore?"

"*No*," Chase said emphatically.

After another half hour of waiting in a small room, while Wen invented a hundred ways to escape, Tess told them they were free to go.

"I know you'll want to dump it as soon as possible," Tess said, handing Wen the keys to a government car, "but please, just park it somewhere. We'll know where to find it."

Wen resisted the urge to say something sarcastic or mean. They all knew at least the first part of their journey would be tracked. Wen intended CISS wouldn't know where they were by the end of the day.

"Thanks for taking the test, Chase. I really do believe you."

"Then I passed?"

Tess nodded and smiled. "But you're not out of trouble. We need to know *who* Killcore is, and obviously he has a problem with you, so . . ."

"We'll find her," Wen said. "If Killcore wants us, she's going to get us. But not in the way she plans."

Tess raised her eyebrows. "She?"

Chapter Sixteen

Dean's long, encrypted call to Franco finally clicked through. He sighed, relieved. A few more seconds, and Franco would be on the line.

He appreciated Franco's role in his life, but didn't care too much for him. It wasn't as if he hated the guy, he just didn't really like him, and found him to be a little weaselly. Yet he also thought him fascinating. It seemed as if Franco had read every book ever written, and could quote their first lines from memory. Initially, Dean thought Franco had just read the first few pages of all those books. However, several times during the five years that the two had known each other, Dean tested his knowledge by having in-depth conversations about books Dean knew well. On every occasion, Franco always knew the intricacies of their plots. In fact, Dean, who read a lot himself, had never managed to come up with a book that Franco hadn't also read. It was a remarkable trait, especially for a man Dean would otherwise consider shallow. He couldn't quite reconcile the strange ability to read and memorize so many books with Franco's other passion: killing.

Maybe it's not a passion, Dean thought, while waiting for this "killer" to pick up. *But he's very good at it, and seems to enjoy it a little too much.* Maybe not the actual act itself, but the chess match leading up to "ending a quarry," as Franco referred to killing.

As soon as he heard a sharp, clipped voice, Dean could almost taste the salt air of his next vacation.

"Do you have them?" Franco asked.

"Yes," Dean replied. The two of them were always careful, even though they were on untraceable burner phones, to never speak in specifics. They knew better than most that the NSA was always listening to every call. The specific data in this case were classified security codes for Air Force clearance across all military intelligence networks, including a link into "Heaven," the ultra-classified intelligence computer/satellite network of US spy agencies.

"Footage of my parents' place?" Franco asked, using their code.

"Yeah, it's good."

The data would be sent into a secure digital dropbox encrypted with limited access. Dean had devised a rotating, crossover, two-siphon, hack-proof, random "coin slot," which would transform the data every few seconds. The sources and destinations also changed constantly to avoid detection and be virtually untraceable should any of it be discovered during the process or at some later time.

They needed these Air Force codes in order to access FAA data. It was a long way around. Franco had wanted to just get the FAA information directly, since the DHS also handled cyber threats for that agency. However, Dean had cautioned that as soon as the CIA began searching for the source of the hacks, it would be too obvious.

"Believe me, we don't want to give Tess Federgreen one more clue to find us," Dean said.

Franco couldn't argue with that. He hated the woman.

Nearly two years earlier, after a TruNueral operation went wrong, CISS agents had grabbed Franco, locked him in shackles, and flown him on a CIA plane back to Washington, DC, where Tess Federgreen had been waiting, and would have a million questions for him.

However, in spite of all the power Tess assumed she had —and, he had to admit, she was a great force—The Chairman, the man in charge of GlobeTec, a massive international conglomerate that owned TruNueral, held power Tess couldn't begin to imagine.

Before the CIA flight even landed at Joint Base Andrews, outside Washington, the president of the United States had ordered Franco's immediate release. The Chairman had made a call, and his will would be done. Tess, furious, could not refuse the order, but issued her own that Franco be tailed and surveilled to the fullest extent of US intelligence capabilities.

The Chairman had told Franco to come to his New York offices immediately. Franco, happy to be out of custody, knew three things—Tess Federgreen would have him followed, and, because he knew too much, the Chairman was going to have him killed.

The third thing was that neither of the first two things were going to happen.

Franco contacted a friend who had left the company to form his own start-up fourteen months earlier. Aaron Costa's new firm, Code-or-Col-or LLC, concentrated on the two areas Franco most needed—protecting one's identity in the modern cyber-connected, facial recognition world, and making one's life, and corporations, hack-proof. The pair used Code-or-Col-or technology, that had previously belonged to TruNueral, to assist Franco in vanishing.

Costa's scrappy and cunning attributes were partly due from his upbringing in a poor family deep in the rainforests of Chile, where long hours of physical labor were his only future until escaping the lifelong treachery of cultivating maca for the rich. He'd hoboed his way to America, learned English, became a computer tech, married, got citizenship, then divorced. He hadn't spoken to his parents since he'd left at age fourteen. He'd brought Franco in on his side project after he'd found a way to reverse engineer—meaning that actually doing hacking and changing identities could be far more lucrative in seeking to protect clients: Code-or-Col-or. It also gave Franco a platform to destroy the three people he most despised: Tess, the Chairman, and Chase.

"Are you still there?" Dean asked after some silence.

"I'll talk to Costa later," Franco replied, snapping back to the present. "We're almost there."

"The plan is working quite well," Dean said. "Which means I can soon leave the government."

"Twenty-four more hours and . . . "

"No one will even notice I'm gone," Dean finished with that nervous laugh which always unnerved Franco. It reminded him of Bella Lugosi.

Franco smiled. "Yes. In twenty-four hours, the world will be unrecognizable."

Chapter Seventeen

Inside a downtown Boston loft, Chase and Wen gave a brief account of their escape from Russia to two of the three people they trusted most. The first, Nash Graham, a math savant known as "The Astronaut," had worked with almost every intelligence agency in the world before joining forces with Chase and Wen.

"If he is accessing the most restricted and secure networks on earth, I can find him," the Astronaut said.

"How can you be so sure?" Chase asked, leaning against one of the exposed, century-old brick walls.

"Patterns," he replied, as if it should have been obvious. "I'll find him in the patterns."

The second person at the hastily arranged meeting was a young woman called "Bull," a brilliant hacker who'd earned her screen name as a nod to the energy drink, Red Bull, her favorite beverage.

"Nobody can run around the dark web without leaving a digital trail," she said. "Bet I find him before the Astronaut does." Her slight frame, tattooed chest, and short, bleached hair left nothing to the imagination. She was tough, sweet, smart, and hyper.

Chase smiled at her youthful confidence—or arrogance, maybe both. "I wish it were that easy," he said. "But the government's best have not been able to find him—"

"Or *her*," Wen corrected.

"Right." He looked out one of the panoramic windows at the Charles River, meditating for a moment.

"The government might know the moves of every citizen, but that's tracking. *Hacking* is a different thing, and the best is our freelance." Bull pointed to herself. "The second best are working for startups and big tech, and the rest are losers. I'm not even a little surprised the feds can't find this chick." Bull smiled at Wen.

"Tess claims that Killcore is after me," Chase said, repeating the point he'd started with. "Which means we're going to have to be extremely careful. If he finds us, *any* of us, it's going to be easier for him to make it look like I'm to blame."

"I keep telling you," Wen said. "Killcore could be a *woman*."

"Yeah," Bull agreed. "There are at least a hundred beauties like me who can get in and out of your system while we're blowing you a kiss, and you'll never know we just took your last dollar."

"No offense, Bull, but I believe you're one-of-a-kind," Chase said, bowing grandly in her direction. "Regardless, I don't doubt your skills. That's why you're in this room."

"I've been going over the information on Killcore that Tess gave you," the Astronaut began, looking up from his custom-built laptop, dubbed an "AntiMatter Machine" since it couldn't be traced. "It seems that every time they have gotten close to him—or her," he paused and nodded to Wen, whom he adored, "Killcore just vanishes. As if they were tipped off."

"Then you think that it's someone on the inside?" Wen asked. "Someone from the US intelligence community?"

"It would make sense," the Astronaut reasoned. "This level of sophistication, combined with the apparent inside knowledge required to find and exploit these weaknesses, would certainly suggest that if Killcore is not a current or former intelligence operative, then he is definitely getting consistent help from one."

"But why try to frame *me*?" Chase asked, pacing around the airy room, wondering how long they had until someone kicked in the door. "That isn't random. Whoever Killcore is, *she* must have a good reason, a very specific one, for pinning this on me."

"An ex-girlfriend, perhaps," Wen said, winking.

"I hope not," Chase said. "Because I don't remember any women I knew before you."

"Maybe you two want to be left alone?" Bull asked, sipping an espresso. "We really aren't doing anything important, just trying to save the world."

"What else is new?" Chase said.

"Have you run this past Dez?" the Astronaut asked.

The question surprised Chase. "I thought you didn't think SEER could do anything that *you* couldn't," Chase replied, referring to Balance Engineering's secret Search Entire Existence Result advanced photonic quantum information processing, deep learning, AI, quantum algorithm system that Dez operated.

"I have come to appreciate the capabilities of SEER, and don't mind letting you and Dez do all the tedious work while I concentrate on the more important analysis," the Astronaut said. He rarely missed a joke, and he never laughed. "The data we have on Killcore, his attacks, and specific approach, can be used by SEER to predict his future moves. To catch someone like this, we need to be there before he is."

"We haven't had a second since we've gotten back in the country. Dez will be my next call," Chase said, nervously looking at the door again. "But first, we need a plan. Tess sent the data here, which means this location is no longer safe."

"I beg to differ," the Astronaut said. "I have developed protocols . . . " He checked his screen. "Right now, Tess believes we are eight miles from here."

"How do you do that?" Wen asked.

"I made everything look as if she sent the data to Norway, and that created a back-channel track to Ireland, back through Texas, and—"

Wen, sorry she asked, held up both hands.

"If they can't find Killcore, they are never going to find us," the Astronaut finished.

"That may be true," Chase said. "But I'm not as worried about her locating us as I am about Killcore finding us. If there's a connection between Killcore and the US intelligence agencies, then he—*or she*—can track us using that information, and Killcore definitely seems a lot more competent than the CIA or NSA."

"Where do you want us?" Bull asked.

"I have a cabin, completely outfitted. It's never been used, and it's secluded and remote, but not isolated," Chase said to Bull. "It's full of the latest technology. You'll love it there."

"Sounds awesome."

"Nash, I trust you'll find your own undisclosed location?"

He nodded.

"When should we leave?" Bull asked.

Chase looked at the door again, and then to Wen. "Now isn't soon enough."

Chapter Eighteen

Franco checked to make sure the door was locked and that the curtains had no gaps. He'd swept the hotel room for listening devices three times. Finally satisfied, at least for the moment before his obsessive compulsive disorder kicked in again, he sat down next to his phone and looked at the time. One minute until Killcore would call. He was never late.

"Are you watching the news?" Killcore asked, after Franco accepted the call.

"Yes," Franco replied, staring at the fifty-two inch flat screen hanging on the wall of his suite. The television had been tuned into cable news for hours. "I've been enjoying the spectacle. It's quite amusing that no one can figure out what's causing this big mess."

"Amusing?" Killcore echoed. "That's an interesting way to describe it. They don't know how it's happening because I'm not letting them see any trails yet."

"But you will?"

"Of course. I want to be certain that I get credit."

Franco watched "The Traffapocalypse," as the media

was already calling it. "The worst traffic jam ever," one commentator said, citing statistics over scenes of past mega-traffic events flashing on the screen.

"An eleven day, sixty-two-mile back-up along the Beijing-Tibet Expressway," the commentator continued, declaring dramatically, "caused by poor construction planning." Franco thought the one he and Killcore had created was much more thrilling.

"Sao Paulo, Brazil, generally considered the home of the world's biggest and most frequent traffic jams, broke its own record with this one-hundred-ninety-two mile long headache," the commentator groaned, as if he'd been there, then added, "I wonder if the folks at Guinness would consider this the world's biggest parking lot?"

Franco was about to switch channels, but was drawn to the next image of Chicago in a blizzard. "They called Lake Shore Drive a car graveyard during a February blizzard back in 2011, when thousands abandoned their cars in this wintery traffic jam."

"They had a snowstorm," Franco said to the TV. "That shouldn't count."

"What?" Killcore asked. "Who had snow?"

For a moment, Franco forgot he'd been on the phone.

"The media is comparing our traffic jam to others that came before."

"Nonsense."

"Then perhaps the king of them all," the commentator announced, as if awarding an Oscar. "During the first Easter holiday after the fall of the Berlin Wall, a reported eighteen million cars were caught in a bottleneck at the border of East and West Germany, resulting in an unprecedented stand-still."

"Ours is bigger!" Franco shouted.

The commentator seemed to agree. "Officials estimate that four million vehicles are involved in The Traffapocalypse, and that number is expected to double in the next hour as the transportation meltdown expands to Long Beach, Anaheim, Santa Ana, and Riverside."

"Don't forget San Bernardino," Franco added.

"If you'd like to break the German record, we may have to involve San Diego." Killcore said.

"Can we do that?"

After a few moments of silence, Killcore responded, "Just did."

"The freeways are in virtual gridlock," an analyst inside Mission Control told Tess over the phone as her plane carried her back to Washington. "Downtown LA looks like a gigantic used car dealership."

"Killcore?" she asked, as several screens on her plane switched to the west coast.

"He hasn't claimed responsibility yet, but can you see the chaos on your monitors?"

"Yes, I'm seeing it." She watched as a massive brawl involving at least thirty people erupted on the roofs and hoods of cars along Wilshire Boulevard.

"The traffic is impenetrable," the analyst said. "Even police, fire, and ambulances can't get through. Helicopters are the only way emergency services are able to respond, and there aren't enough to keep up with demand."

"*Who is Killcore?*" Tess shouted in exasperation.

"Why is she doing this?" Linda, Tess's deputy, responded from Mission Control. "What could she possibly gain from this?"

"The city is blaming The Traffapocalypse for eighteen fatalities, and scores of injuries. But both tolls are expected to rise dramatically, particularly if the situation isn't resolved by nightfall."

"The *Traffapocalypse*?" Tess asked.

"That's what the media is calling it."

She shook her head. "The media is just helping Killcore."

"She's doing all this just to show she can," Linda said, answering her own question as she pulled her long brown hair into a ponytail, realizing she might have to work through the night.

"No," Tess said. "Killcore has a much bigger plan . . . He's trying to destroy our modern world."

Chapter Nineteen

Chase put the phone on speaker and called his oldest friend as he and Wen headed back to the train station, their first stop in an effort to shake Tess.

Mars, a forty-three-year-old convict at Lompoc Federal Prison, had been expecting the call. A prison guard, on Mars's payroll, walked past his cell and gave him a list of what sounded like a cake recipe, but actually alerted Mars to the time Chase would call. The guard had no idea what the message meant, and had no interest in asking questions.

Mars, an ex-lawyer, was like an older brother to Chase, and was considered an honorary member of the family. Chase's parents and brother, Boone, had all been devastated when Mars had been sent to prison. However, he'd made the best of it by crafting a mini-empire from inside, actually earning more money than he'd been making while free.

Within an empty paint can on a high shelf in the prison's large, paint shop warehouse, Mars kept one of his many illegal cellphones. He had become a powerful and connected person throughout the "underworld," and his business dealings reached far outside prison walls—including operations in six countries. Although balding and handsome, he wore his remaining hair Marine Corps short, and his good looks said tough, confident, and *don't mess with me*, rather than being pretty-boy.

After Chase explained their dilemma, Mars asked the same question that had been tormenting Chase and Wen since Moscow. "Who *is* Killcore?"

"I've tried to think of every possible suspect, but I keep ending up back with the shadow people."

The shadow people had been after Chase and Wen almost as long as they'd been together; a mysterious, unidentifiable organization. More importantly, even with all their resources, it was unclear *why* the shadow people wanted them, or if they were just after Chase, or Wen, or both.

"If it's the shadow people, then why would they create this? That doesn't make sense," Mars said. "And certainly points back to the Chinese, or another state-sponsored group."

They had been working on the theory for several months that the shadow people must be originating from either the Chinese, or another government. Chase had been planning to ask Tess for help in identifying which government or agency.

"This might be a chance to test our theory," Chase said.

"The resources needed do seem to exceed an individual or small player's capabilities," Wen said.

"Do you really believe they're going to all this trouble, killing and threatening so many people, just to flush me out?" Chase asked.

"They haven't been able to get you any other way," Mars said. He'd been helping them avoid the shadow people, and others pursuing them, by developing and utilizing a system called "decoying." Reports and sightings of Chase or Wen would occur at random intervals across the globe. Whoever was looking for them would get a constant stream of bad information. Through credit card use, surveillance cameras linked to facial recognition data bases, and a number of other related methods, the sightings would flood in and overwhelm those seeking the pair.

"Good, then we'll finally discover who they are, and what they want," Chase said. "But in the meantime, we need to make sure that we locate them on *our* terms and on *our* timeline. So I need you to step up the decoying efforts."

"If they find us first, then we'll never be able to stop them," Wen said. "That will not only be disastrous for us, but also for the rest of the world."

"We've made some improvements to vIDs, which should help."

The virtual Image Deviation system—"vIDs"—was an incredible collaborative invention created by the Astronaut and Chase. Its purpose was to fool the algorithms that powered facial recognition cameras. The ingenious spray-on application covered a subject's face with hundreds of nano micro-processors, each with a diameter about the size of the head of a pin, and thinner than a human hair. Because the gold specks appeared translucent, they were virtually undetectable to the naked eye on any skin tone.

"We're wearing vIDs now. It's the only way we can vanish from Tess."

"Good," Mars said, checking out the narrow window at the end of the warehouse. He might have had a lot of guards in his pocket, but not all of them. "We've increased the size of our split network. Is that new program you wrote ready?"

Chase had developed new algorithms that could systematically place Wen and him throughout the world in a logical manner, instead of haphazardly, as they used to do it. In the past, they might be "spotted" in India, Belgium, and Columbia all at the same time. Now, the computers would put them in places closer to the last sightings, and within precise flight times, interfacing with airline and train schedules, even bus schedules. Not only were the sightings currently more authentic, they were much more effective in consuming the resources of those pursuing them.

"It's done."

"Great." Mars checked the time. Inmates were counted often, and another count was less than ten minutes away.

"How are you otherwise?" Chase asked.

Mars looked out into the yard where prison guards were roughing up an inmate after breaking up a fight, and to the guard towers and razor wire beyond—part of the attached Penitentiary. "Other than being in prison, I feel pretty good," he said. "Looking forward to the day I can hang out with you and actually meet Wen face-to-face. Maybe even sneak a kiss while you aren't looking."

"You can kiss Chase anytime you want, even if I'm looking," Wen said.

"I meant sneak a kiss from *you*," Mars said, laughing.

"I hope you can do that, too," Wen said. "I won't tell Chase."

"I'll hold you to it," Mars said with a grin. "Meantime, you two stay alive."

Chapter Twenty

Franco burst out laughing as the mayor of Los Angeles tried to explain The Traffapocalypse.

"They are so incompetent," Killcore said. "They are so easily controlled. Shutting down the traffic signals was easy. Their safeguards are weak. I created a program that forced the systems offline in an order that would optimize the problems. A series of events occurred, leading to the most efficient and rapid deterioration of the engineered flow, resulting in systematic gridlock."

Franco smiled. "'Hail! I have become helpless! But I go forward . . . I have come from the uttermost parts of the earth and received my apparel . . .'"

"Excuse me?"

"The Book of the Dead," Franco raucously sneered. "Very apropos."

"Odd."

"City officials are estimating that it will take up to forty-eight hours to untangle the mess."

"Now I would agree with your previous word, 'amusement.' By my calculations, it will be five full days before they get back to normal. And that's only *if* I stop corrupting their systems immediately—which I will not."

"We have other issues to discuss," Franco said.

"Chase Malone?" Killcore asked.

"Yes. Apparently Tess Federgreen believes he is not responsible for our attacks."

"I anticipated this."

"I know. And you mentioned another way to increase his culpability."

"Yes. Obviously, one way would be to attack the Chairman of GlobeTec, or any of his vast holdings, since that is a clear motive for Malone. However, that would also make *you* a suspect, since you used to work for him, and because the Chairman wants you dead. I assume you would neither like to be a suspect, or allow the Chairman to have you murdered."

"Obviously not."

"Right. Then, since others in the intelligence community are not as convinced of Malone's innocence as Ms. Federgreen is, our next move is clear. We will attack her directly."

"She's not easy to get to," Franco said, momentarily distracted by a fiery image on the TV of a burning tanker on the highway. "Especially since she's never leaving the CISS headquarters building."

"Yes. I explored cutting power to the building, which would have forced them to leave. However, CISS employs an off-network, off-grid, generator system. Thus far, I have found no routes to circumvent."

"Did you somehow start that fire on the LA Expressway?" Franco asked, watching the fire spread to multiple other vehicles.

"What fire?"

"It's on the cable news out of Los Angeles."

"No, that is just a convenient byproduct of slamming millions of vehicles together in a Rubik's cube configuration. You see, if you jam up so many vehicles and people with no way out, all kinds of awful and unexpected things are bound to happen."

"Now, how do you propose reaching Tess?"

"She has employees," Killcore said. "The *employees* leave that building. Get it?"

Franco almost blurted out, "I love you," to Killcore, but stopped himself, knowing it would be highly inappropriate. Still, he felt fortunate to be working with somebody so brilliant and so very diabolical. And yet, there were definitely things he didn't trust about Killcore, and much he didn't understand. He'd had problems in the past with similar working arrangements that had not ended well. However, he believed neither Chase Malone, Tess Federgreen, the Chairman, nor anyone else could stop what he, Costa, and Killcore had put together. Costa had predicted this kind of success early on, while Franco had doubted it. Although, now, he knew he'd been wrong. Everything was coming to fruition; the plans were falling into place. The world was going to change, and Franco would be remembered.

"Linda Moore," Killcore suddenly said. "Deputy to the director of CISS has full CIA NSA credentials, and Top Secret security clearances." Killcore continued rattling off details about Moore, including age, height, weight, current address, list of known associates, and so on.

Franco ceased to be impressed by Killcore's ability to reach these ultra-classified places, even though he was still excited by the convenience. As he continued to listen to the facts about Tess's deputy, he began to laugh, knowing Linda

Moore was about to suffer a pawn's fate. Sometimes Franco worried he might be turning too sadistic in his revenge and lust for power. He felt like an overly vengeful character in a thriller novel.

I enjoy being an antagonist, he mused.

Franco usually consumed several books a day. He'd been a speed reader since elementary school, fascinated with the idea that just twenty-six letters in the alphabet could create millions and millions of different narratives. Twenty-six letters rearranged an infinite number of ways to convey stories, ideas, schemes, plots, twists and turns, all of it from such a limited palette of so few symbols. And yet he recognized that the endless reading had somehow made him a little crazy. He wasn't quite *normal*. Each aspect of the thousands of books he'd read had imprinted themselves on him so that he was just a bit schizophrenic—in a literary kind of way. This realization had come long ago, and unnerved him, but he'd grown used to it, so that now it didn't scare him as it once had.

Franco embraced the recall of lines from books. It wasn't only the first ones he recited from memory, but whole passages, even complete chapters. The most important to him, though, were indeed the first lines. He cherished them because they set the tone for the entire story. They were the enticement to wander into the cave, to venture down the dark forest paths, to board the spaceship knowing he would likely never return, and if he did, he'd be forever changed. Those first lines lured him in, beckoning like a drug to an addict, and he'd long given up trying to escape.

"We will see what Linda Moore has to say," Killcore said, concluding his ranting profile.

"I don't think we should kill her," Franco said, offering different advice than he normally gave.

"Yes," Killcore agreed. "Our message is better heard if sent in terror rather than mourning."

Franco looked back at the screen, the Traffapocalypse death toll was approaching one hundred. *Those silly people have no idea of what awaits.*

Chapter Twenty-One

Ten minutes after Bull and the Astronaut left, Wen finished wiping a laptop after transferring its important data to a flash drive. She looked up, suddenly in horror at seeing a red laser dot appear on Chase's forehead. "Get down!" she screamed, throwing the computer at the window. Shattering glass, blowing the laptop apart, the high caliber bullet continued through, passing only millimeters above Chase's head before blasting a chunk out of the hundred year-old brick wall.

As he dove to the floor, more rounds tore up the room. Chase scrambled for cover, and in the confusion, didn't see Wen get to the door and dash out. A second later, the shooting stopped. It took him at least fifteen seconds to follow her out of the loft. By the time he reached the ground floor, Wen was heading into the building across the street.

He knew she couldn't miss a chance to catch the shadow people, but as he ran after her, looking in all directions for would-be assassins, it crossed his mind that maybe it was Tess's CISS IT-Squad bullets he had just dodged.

As if on cue, his phone rang. Immediately, he recognized the number as Tess's direct cell phone. He touched speaker, as a car swerved to avoid hitting him, and continued running toward the entrance of the building where Wen had gone.

"What?" he barked.

"You need to get out of the street and take cover."

"Why?" He looked around, trying to see how she was watching him. Obviously she now knew where they were. "Are you shooting at us?"

"Of course not. My agents just saved your life . . . *again*."

"Then who is it?" Chase asked, still unsure if he believed her. He found the door to the stairs, taking them up two at a time.

"I was hoping *you* could answer that question."

"Yeah, well, that's actually an ongoing problem for us."

"I bet it is."

"They seem to find us everywhere," he said breathlessly.

"Who?"

"I don't know."

"Go back down and cover the lobby!" Wen yelled from above.

Chase changed directions, retracing his steps. "We don't know who it is," he repeated.

"Could Killcore have sent them?"

"I guess, but this has been going on a long time—long before Killcore." Chase found a corner where he could see the front and back entrances, as well as the door to the stairs. He crouched down, caught his breath, and kept his gun ready.

"What was before Killcore?" Tess asked. "How long has Killcore been planning all of this?"

"I'm not Killcore, how would I know?"

"I'm just saying, if these people have been after you . . . I need to know everything you know about them. Killcore could have been trying to kill you for years. It may lead us to him."

"You know all I know. We've got nothing on them."

"When do you encounter them?"

"Whenever they try to kill us."

"I want to know where you've seen them. Dates. Was it before or after your reunion with Wen?"

"Do we have to do this *now*?" Chase asked, looking apprehensively at all the entrances.

"What else are you doing?"

"The mountains of California, Paris, Moscow . . . " He named several other places.

"And they haven't killed you yet?"

"I'm talking to you, aren't I?"

Tess was impressed. She had long been amazed at their resourcefulness and staying power. "Who else would be after you if it's not Killcore?"

"I don't even know why *Killcore* is after me," Chase said, exasperated. "I don't know who *it* is."

"'The man doth protest too much, methinks.'"

"Hamlet," Chase said, annoyed. "Are you doubting me again?"

"To doubt you again, I would've had to stop doubting you before, and I haven't."

"Then why did you let us go? And don't tell me it has to do with Flint Jones," Chase said, recalling his former head of security and friend, who'd had some kind of personal relationship with Tess. "His deathbed promise still holding sway over you? I told you, you were released from that."

An attractive woman hurried through the lobby, rushing past him.

"You don't get to release a promise made by another," she said, more bitterly than was typical for the western, boot-stomping, heart sick, wannabe prairie girl. Chase had always known her to keep her emotions even.

He was getting antsy waiting for Wen, and stood up, aiming his gun at the stairs door.

"Careful who you shoot at," Tess said. "I've got agents in that building."

"How convenient. You've got agents in the building where the bullets came from. Who should be doubting whom?"

"For a brilliant man, you're a fool sometimes, Chase. A simple *thank you* for saving your life would be the gracious way normal people would respond."

The door from the stairs suddenly flew open. Chase pointed his gun and almost pulled the trigger before seeing it was his soul mate.

"Two assassins, dead before I got there," she said angrily.

"My agents saved you," Tess said across the speaker, as if Wen might appreciate her efforts.

"Your agents killed our only hope of finding out who those men were!" Wen growled.

"No ID?" Chase asked.

Wen looked at him as if he should know better. "There never is."

"We'll run them through facial ID," Tess said, as if she'd just volunteered to pick up their dry-cleaning.

"You won't find anything," Wen said flatly.

Chapter Twenty-Two

Chase parked the car that they would never see again. "We didn't wreck it," Chase said, as he and Wen hustled into the train station. "Didn't even get in a good chase with it and leave it scuffed up a bit."

"You know Tess is going to be expecting this," Wen replied, as they passed through the heavy, brass-framed glass doors.

"It's a busy terminal," Chase said. They quickly melted into the crowd.

"How many agents do you think she has following us?"

"Twenty, maybe thirty."

"With Killcore occupying them, I don't think she can spare that many." Wen pulled the SIM card out of her phone, then held out her hand. Chase gave her his phone. She did the same thing to his, then tossed both cards in a passing trash can.

"Now the fun part," Wen said, motioning to a restroom sign. They ducked into the men's room and went together into a handicap stall. Two men already occupying the restroom exchanged sly smiles, but they weren't going to tell.

The Astronaut had scanned Chase and Wen back at the loft and discovered tracking chips in their shoes.

"I still don't know how they got those chips into our *shoes*," Chase said, standing on one foot and slipping off his leather sneaker.

"One of those agents did it on the flight from Russia, or maybe during the polygraph. But they were good. I didn't catch it . . . and I was watching."

"So we didn't take them out back at the loft because . . . ?"

"We want Tess to know we're at the train station, and that we have no idea she has trackers on our person. If we'd already taken them out, we never would've gotten this far."

Chase nodded. He'd been too busy thinking about Killcore and the shadow people to give it any thought.

Wen carefully took the trackers out of their shoes and handed one of the chips to Chase while he re-tied his shoe.

"We need to get these on two different trains heading in different directions," she said.

"That should be fun," Chase said, encountering an amused teenager as they left the stall.

"Right on," the kid said. "Any more girls in there?"

"Uh . . . " Chase stuttered.

"Don't Bogart the joint." The kid cracked up. "No worries, dude, lips are sealed."

A few minutes later, down by the tracks, Chase saw a crew member about to board and was able to slip his chip into a pocket on the man's pack.

"We don't have much time now," Wen said. "They'll get suspicious when they see us split up on their monitors, so we need to split up for real, in case they've got eyes on us."

She told Chase where to meet her. Wen spotted a woman with a shopping bag and dropped her chip in. Almost simultaneously, the woman picked up her bag, making the chip bounce off the side and onto the ground.

Wen got down on her knees and searched for it under a row of chairs.

"What you looking for lady?" a little boy, who must have been around eight, asked.

"Oh, I lost my keys."

The boy looked around. "Is this your key?" he asked, holding up the silver chip.

Wen pulled out a five dollar bill and handed it to him.

"Thanks!" the kid said with wide eyes.

For a moment, she considered letting the kid keep the chip, before fearing it could get him killed.

She smiled at the boy and waved goodbye, noticing a soldier squaring away his duffel. She caught his eye and winked at him while just managing to toss the chip in before the serviceman pulled the strings tight and tied it off. "Mission accomplished," she said to herself.

Chase walked briskly back to his meeting place with Wen, continually checking for tails. As he approached her, it was evident by her stance that she'd finally caught sight of their surveillance. Their eyes met across the distance. She looked off, steering him in another direction. Following her eyes, he saw the south entrance and veered off before getting too close to her. He headed to the entrance without looking back, as if never intending to meet her.

A couple minutes later, Wen was next to him on the

curb in front of the entrance. She took his arm and said, "We're going to get in the cab."

"Are they watching us?" he asked nonchalantly.

"It's possible I lost them, possible I didn't. Either way, it's possible there are more out here, so we just have to hope they're still following the chips."

"Okay," Chase replied as they entered a cab. "But those chips are on trains that are probably pulling away right now, and we're not on those trains. If they saw us . . . "

"I don't know," Wen said. "It depends on *when* they saw us. The chips aren't big enough to be that accurate. They might pinpoint location within five hundred to one thousand feet, so if we were still close enough, we might have just pulled it off." Wen compulsively watched out the side and back windows of the cab, but found no evidence they were being followed.

Chase snatched her chin and kissed her quickly, deeply. "Just so you remember, okay?"

"Okay." She smiled, a beautiful, innocent, very Wen smile. The one that melted the billionaire like nothing else.

She'd asked the driver to take them to Norwood Airport, but ten minutes into the ride, she asked to be dropped on the next corner in Ashcroft. Chase paid, and they jumped out, alert to anything unusual. They jogged another block, walked into a restaurant, and continued all the way through, going out the back door. Keeping up a fast pace, they completed another block, crossed through an alley, and emerged at a busy intersection, where they could see a white sedan idling in a loading zone on the other side. Nervously, they waited for the light to change, watching everyone. Finally, they got across, and jumped in the back of the sedan. The driver was a man they knew and trusted—a member of The Cause, an underground movement also known as "WOLF" by its members. The group had originally been started by a few radicals, intellectuals, and activists intent on bringing about income equality throughout the world, but had quickly evolved into a full-fledged revolutionary movement seeking to bring down the current world order and the elites.

"How'd it go in Moscow?" the man asked as he pulled the car out of the loading zone and merged into traffic.

"I think he's going to cooperate," Chase said.

"And Wen? Do you agree?" the man asked, looking at her in the rearview mirror.

"Changing the world is a complicated profession," she said. "Edward Snowden is not an easy man to predict. I believe we have a very good chance, but without stopping Killcore, it won't matter."

"Perhaps your mission in Moscow and the situation with Killcore is connected," the man said, having been briefed on the Killcore details by the leader of The Cause.

Chase and Wen looked at each other. Things had suddenly become incredibly more complex.

Chapter Twenty-Three

Killcore sent out thousands of malicious files, malware, and spyware, as if launching a flurry of digital missiles. They began extracting precious information almost instantly as large amounts of data were exfiltrated. The reports were automatically compiled. An incredibly sophisticated algorithm would decide the best way to utilize the bounty. Plans were drawn, and attack scenarios were created without any input from Killcore, Franco, or Costa. Although Killcore would have the final say on what attacks were launched, the speed and efficiency of the operation made tracking and finding the mastermind nearly impossible. The world was changing.

Corporations, government agencies, and the military began flooding the NSA with reports of major breaches and hacks. Tess used her authority and diverted hundreds of personnel from other intelligence agencies and CIA divisions to work on trying to contain the data hemorrhaging and locate the source of the hack.

Later in the ride, with Chase asleep, the driver caught Wen's eyes in the mirror and brought up the conversation again. "If Snowden and Killcore are—"

"Everything is connected," Wen said, echoing her thoughts, which had overheated during the silence.

"Could Snowden actually be Killcore?"

She shook her head no, but answered, "Anything is possible."

"Then he would have to be working with Russian hackers."

"It would be difficult without official help," she said, deciding that made it less likely. She had looked into Snowden's eyes, and believed the former intelligence community officer and whistleblower was different. She relied on her highly developed intuition and years of training to read people, and she believed him. "If Snowden helps us, maybe more than our initial objectives can be met. We may be able to find Killcore from the inside."

"Then you don't think Snowden is Killcore?"

"No."

"Are you willing to bet civil stability on that?"

They had crossed from Massachusetts into Connecticut, and Wen stared out the window at the passing rural backroads without replying. Her thoughts had wandered back to Tess Federgreen. The CISS director had located them in Moscow, as it seemed she found them often—too often.

"The CIA and NSA could easily already have everything they need to find Killcore, but they aren't looking at it the right way," Wen began. "Their tools are being used incorrectly, on the wrong problems, at the wrong places. It's happened repeatedly over the last five or six decades . . . America sought supremacy, first from the Soviets, and then from Russia and China. As the three great powers struggle for dominance, the constant churn produces a steady stream of mistakes."

Their conversation continued while the man drove farther away from Boston. He compulsively checked the rearview mirror, while Wen also turned around constantly, looking at the road behind, inspecting every car they passed, scanning the landscape, buildings, and billboards, especially near bridges.

"We lost the CIA," the driver said, trying to put her at ease.

"At this point, I'm less concerned with Tess than with the shadow people and Killcore."

"There are a lot of people trying to get you," the driver said.

"More than ever."

"Do you ever get tired of all the running?"

"I wish we had that luxury," Wen said. She looked over and watched Chase sleeping. She smiled, because she knew he could rarely sleep in cars or on planes.

"He trusts you," Wen said to the driver.

The driver glanced into the mirror and saw Chase asleep. "I don't know about that. But he trusts *you*."

Tess marched into Mission Control at the CISS Headquarters building. "Where the hell are they!?"

Everyone knew she was asking about Chase and Wen,

but no one wanted to respond, because they didn't have the answer she wanted.

Linda Moore stepped forward. "We're back-checking satellites and drone surveillance now, but we don't know."

"How is that possible?" Tess snapped as she went to her console and began flipping screens herself.

"They had a plan."

"Of course they had a plan! Wen *always* has a damn plan."

"The best guess is, they are already out of Boston."

"Heading in which direction?"

"We don't know."

"Find them, people! How hard could this be? They were *just* in our custody!"

"Incoming!" a technician yelled. "Killcore is carpet bombing the internet."

"Where's it coming from?" Tess asked, less worried about the damage Killcore was inflicting this time, and more anxious to get a location.

"Isolating it now."

"Where?" Tess asked again after fifteen seconds of silence.

"Closing . . . Western United States."

"Scramble IT-Squads," she barked to Linda.

Linda wanted to ask, "From where?" but started pulling up ready-teams in the western US.

"Colorado . . . Denver."

Tess watched breathlessly as the satellite map zoomed in on Denver.

Linda was already getting the Albuquerque, Wichita, and Salt Lake units moving. "We have a Squad in Denver!" Linda yelled, as if they'd won the lottery.

"Get SWAT and FBI mobilized now!" Tess ordered.

"Here," the tech said, as a building came into full view. "Killcore is in there."

"We're coming for you," Tess said coldly, in a tone an ancient warrior might have used against a distant and merciless king. "We're coming."

Chapter Twenty-Four

Chase stirred as the car hit some rough pavement. "Where are we? Was I asleep?"

"Yes, you were," Wen replied softly, kissing his cheek. "Connecticut. We should be there soon."

"Any sign of . . . anyone?"

Wen turned around again and looked at everything behind them. "No. I think we got rid of Tess, at least for now. And since Tess got rid of the shadow people, it always seems to take them a little while to regroup."

"How are they finding us?" Chase asked rhetorically. "I'm starving." The two of them had spent days with the Astronaut and Bull trying to figure out who the shadow people were, what they wanted, and how they were possibly tracking them when almost no one else in the world could. "Tess thinks it's possible that Killcore is sending the shadow people, or he *is* the shadow people, or whatever."

"This is all I got," the driver said, throwing a bag of dried apricots into the back.

Wen looked as if the idea was an interesting one, and

played with it in her mind for a couple of minutes. Finally, tired of the silence, Chase added, "But if that's true, it still means we don't know why they're after us, since we don't know why *Killcore* is after us, and that brings up—"

"Something even more disturbing," Wen said, finishing his statement. "If Killcore is part of the shadow people, that means he's been planning whatever he's doing now for years."

"Yeah," Chase said, uncomfortable with that idea. They discussed the ramifications a little longer, and then Wen sent a message to the Astronaut, suggesting he explore any connections Killcore might have to the shadow people.

Soon they arrived at a small private airfield and bid farewell to their driver. The pilot waiting for them in the small Learjet 60 XR was also with The Cause. Although he had never met them, he knew of their reputations. He was very friendly and conversational. Wen, never one for small talk, let Chase handle the casual chatter as they boarded and readied for takeoff.

After landing in St. Louis, Chase called Tess from an untraceable phone the pilot had given him.

"Where *are* you?" Tess asked in a tired voice from Secure, the room at the end of Mission Control that utilized virtually every conceivable anti-eavesdropping technology. She watched the drama taking place in Mission Control through the glass walls separating the areas.

"If I wanted you to know that, I wouldn't have gone to so much trouble to make sure you would have to ask."

There was silence for a beat, and then she responded in the most rigid, angry voice he had ever heard from her. "Do you think this is a game? That you're somehow safer running around solo out there? You don't seem to understand what Killcore is *doing*. You don't seem to *get* it."

"I do get it, Tess. But the government is also after me. And, as you said, Killcore is causing a lot of trouble, and I don't want a lot of trouble."

"Is that what you think? Killcore is causing a *lot of trouble*? I guess you aren't that smart, Chase, because if you were, you'd realize just how *fragile* the system is."

"The system?"

"The world order, the economy, the United States government, civilization, *all of it*. It feels permanent because it's all you've ever known. It seems like we've got a nice, long, consistent history, a rock solid foundation that the modern world is built on, but we're all just hanging on by threads."

"Listen, Tess—"

"No, *you* listen. As technology grows exponentially, and power is more accessible to the oppressed, their ability to connect and organize, and the government's likewise ability to track and watch all these things converging right now, expands as well." She started pacing manically back and forth. A couple of assistants left the room to give her privacy. "And Killcore comes out of nowhere, seemingly knowing *just* what buttons to push to take advantage of the precarious plight of the world. We're perched on a damned precipice. We're holding on, and keeping it together, but it's slipping. Everything was close to falling into destruction and anarchy, even before Killcore." She swept her hair aside before clenching her fist in targetless frustration.

Chase held a moment of silence as Wen met his eyes. They both seemed baffled by the dire worldview that pragmatic Tess had just painted. *Could it be that desperate?* They knew The Cause was working to take advantage of some of those same conditions she'd outlined, yet even with their superior knowledge of the players and events shaping the present dramas in the world, they didn't believe the fragility was as great as Tess was declaring it to be.

But they also knew Tess abhorred exaggeration.

An instant flash between their eyes confirmed they'd both had the same realization.

What if Killcore was a member of The Cause? What if he'd grown impatient with the pace at which the rebellious group was proceeding, and had taken matters into his own hands?

The Cause had some of the smartest people in the world as members, people who knew that the system was broken, that change *had* to come, and were trying to get ahead of it before it was too late—either because a bloody revolution might precede their efforts, or the elite's, holding the top two percent of the world's wealth, could forever lock their iron grip on any potential change.

The shadow people, someone from The Cause, Snowden...
Who the hell is Killcore?

Chapter Twenty-Five

Tess, leaving Secure, still stewing from the call with Chase, found Mission Control much quieter than it had been during Killcore's bank attacks. However, the tension was far greater as all eyes watched three IT-Squads. The elite group of highly trained "secret agents" were almost always in the field. On a typical day, they were conducting operations in dozens of countries around the globe. The IT-Squads, consisting of highly trained men and women, belonged to the NSA, but were under the command of CISS. And while they were armed with HK MP5N 9mm submachine guns and HK Mk 23 SOCOM .45 ACP pistols, they rarely used them. Their preferred tools were the highest technology the US intelligence community had in its arsenal. These IT-Squads had one purpose: obtaining and disseminating the most powerful and dangerous weapon of all—information. With Killcore's increasing threat, almost all IT-Squads had been reassigned to one mission: find Killcore.

Tess's second in command, Linda Moore, a thirty-nine

year old woman whose long brown hair and doe-like brown eyes gave her impression of a sweet kindergarten teacher, was instead a seasoned intelligence analyst, with Georgetown law and political-sci degrees, fluency in three languages, and years behind the scenes of highly classified missions. Linda had come in late from the Pentagon briefing concerning the Killcore crisis. Normally, she would have immediately updated Tess on the status from the Pentagon. However, being that they were in the midst of an ongoing operation, Tess brought Linda up to speed instead.

"We found and broke down a section of Killcore's routings," Tess began. "And with some help from Jack's team over at the NSA, we were able to isolate his location."

"How long did it take to strip it down?"

"Four hours," Tess replied.

"The NSA team said they were venturing into new territory. Even Jack has never seen a cloak and evade set-up like this."

"The servers moved?" Linda asked, watching one of the tracking routes on monitor three.

"Somehow, Killcore is co-opting satellite time and refocusing real estate all over the place—twenty-nine countries."

The deputy's expression of concern and surprise mirrored Tess's. "This has to be more than one man."

"Or woman," Tess corrected, remembering Wen's words and wondering if Chase and Wen were going to be surprised at who they found in this building—or could they themselves be inside?

"Or woman," Linda agreed, looking at the building. "Where are we? What do we know?"

"Denver, obviously," Tess said, motioning at the Rocky

Mountains in the background of the wide, skyline view. "This building's ownership changed hands most recently fourteen months ago. We're trying to run down the current landlord, but it's a Nevada Corporation. There seems to be one tenant, Scales Up Inc. Four stories perimeter—"

"Wait, Scales Up?"

"Yes, do you know something about them?" Tess asked, not taking her eyes off the screen.

"Scales as in balance? Balance Engineering? Their logo is an abstract scale."

A sick feeling surged through Tess's stomach. "I hadn't made the connection," Tess admitted. "Too coincidental not to be something."

Tess relayed the latest information, and the increased likelihood that this could be a trap, to the commander on the ground. Dozens of SWAT and FBI agents covered the perimeter. However, CISS had the lead since it involved cybercrimes and Killcore. IT-Squads were in charge.

"Team leader, team leader, building is locked, we're forcing."

The IT-Squads breached the building by quickly laser-cutting through the locks.

"We are inside the lobby."

Tess and Linda watched as IT-Squads took the stairs. FBI agents came in behind them, securing the elevator and all exterior exits. Tess still held out hope that Killcore was inside. They were continuing to receive pings from his ongoing operations.

"What is Killcore doing?" Tess asked a technician.

"Right now we're still triangulating the original signal. It's originating from inside that building," he replied. "All native IP addresses match our coordinated tracings, and are locked. Any transient signals tracing strays are still linked to Denver. Right now he's inside Lockheed Martin's internal network."

"Tess, I think we've got him," Linda said. "He's active and operating from that building." She pointed to the screen, showing agents spreading throughout it.

"Doesn't this seem a little too easy?" Tess said, knowing they had to get him now. Killcore had already swept through Boeing, and now Lockheed Martin. Apparently his evening plans were to strip major defense contractors of salable data.

"*Easy?*" a technician, who'd only had four hours of sleep in the last day and a half, questioned. It had taken the coordinated efforts of the entire US intelligence apparatus and countless specialists within the top agencies, and outside consulting with many of the major US tech firms, in cooperation with several other nations, to get to the point where they were now, in Denver.

"A relative term," Tess admitted, crunching on an apple. Maybe they *did* have Killcore. It really hadn't been easy, after all, but in terms of Killcore, it still nagged at her. With all he had done, how had he made such a mistake that allowed them to get there?

Her thoughts were interrupted by another report from Denver.

"Team leader, this is Squad leader, first floor clear. There is a lower level, proceeding now."

Another Squad member reported from the lower level. "Lower level, we got a server room. Fully active."

Everyone in Mission Control watched as the IT-Squad entered the server room.

"Servers are shutting down," the man reported.

"Are they still in Lockheed Martin?" Tess asked loudly.

"Yes, Killcore is still inside Lockheed."

She looked again at the darkened servers. "There must still be more servers. Keep going!"

Linda looked at Tess, unsure now what Killcore was doing. "He knows we're in the building."

Chapter Twenty-Six

Franco glanced at the phone's display. *RESTRICTED*. Although in the middle of multiple illegal operations, the former head of GlobeTec's security wasn't worried about the identity of the caller. Only Killcore had this number. Franco accepted the call immediately.

"We lost Denver," Killcore said. "I made exit prior to their raid. CISS, FBI, CIA, SWAT . . . an overtly magnified production."

"Weren't you cutting that a little close?"

"I expected them. It was amusing. They think they have time."

"'Psychics have seen the color of time, and it's blue,'" Franco said, quoting the first line of *Blown Away* by Ronald Sukenick.

"Does it make you feel intelligent to quote books like that?"

"No. It's just something I do," Franco said, annoyed at the question. "It relaxes me somehow. I really can't help it."

"The CIA is going to identify you as a suspect soon."

"I'm surprised they haven't already."

"They have something."

"It'll be fine. I wish I could see the look on Chase Malone's arrogant face when he figures out that I might be Killcore."

"He'll only think that for a moment," Killcore said. "It won't take him long to realize that you're not smart enough to be me."

Franco wasn't insulted. He was well aware of his limitations, and the vastly superior intelligence his partner possessed. However, he believed it would take Chase longer to decide he wasn't Killcore, and even once he did, it would still drive him crazy.

Franco smiled at the thought.

"I have just sent the communication," Killcore said.

Franco took a moment to savor the enormity of those words. He could imagine it being the first line of a techno thriller novel.

I have just sent the communication, telling them they have thirty-six hours before the world digresses into total anarchy.

"How do you think they'll respond?"

"They will be worried. Having now glimpsed what we are capable of, and because we are making no demands, they will believe we plan to do it."

"And we do," Franco added. "The only thing that can stop us is if they find all the servers first."

"They haven't even figured out yet that they need to find the servers. They'll be too busy trying to save lives to worry about servers."

Dean Johnson followed CISS's progress on his encrypted laptop. A series of special codes gave him access to the US intelligence's most highly classified network—nicknamed "Heaven" because it "may or may not actually exist," and it was said, "you can only get into it by dying."

"Tess Federgreen, you think you have found me?" he said out loud, as if she could hear his words, and if she could, she would no doubt pick up on the dripping condescension in the tone with which he delivered them. He switched to another screen. "So obsessed with Killcore, you are blind to the reality of your predicament."

He continued to type until a new screen came up, displaying reports on surveillance of Chase Malone. "Hmmm . . Chase, you seem to be everywhere," Dean said to a photo of Chase caught by a cctv camera in Barcelona, Spain. "How can you be in twenty-two different cities around the globe at the exact same moment in time?" He made a face. "Are you a time traveler? I think not. Then this data must be corrupt. It is clever. However, I think there is a way to see through your game."

Dean clicked a few buttons to first filter out worldwide sightings.

"There we are. Only seventeen now. You would not be outside of America while looking for Killcore, since Killcore is, of course, located in this country. Now, I'll simply remove any sightings that would be so simple for a smart man like yourself to avoid, and . . . voila, we suddenly have no credible sightings outside of CISS tracking from Boston. Soon . . . we will have you, my friend. Soon you will be in custody."

Mars, utilizing the most advanced decoying programs ever devised, updated the Chase sightings around the world. They'd set up a network of computers, tablets, and phones that Chase no longer used, or ones that were bogus to begin with, and fed the IP addresses into an AI loop so that anyone tracking his devices would be led to an endless series of dead ends. His favorite, though, was fooling surveillance algorithms to think they had seen someone they had not. Those and other methods made Chase and Wen effectively invisible. He'd managed to keep them alive this long using these methods, but it was getting much more difficult.

The team he had assisting the efforts had grown in recent months, as the shadow people threat increased. However, the past few days had been their most challenging.

"It's as if we've got some kind of virus," one of his tech people reported. "Everywhere I put Chase, there seems to be a tag already waiting there for us."

"What do you mean?" Mars asked as the two convicts slowly made their way around a jogging track.

"Like, I think it, decide where to put him . . . and they *know*."

"Are you giving any kind of leading indicator?"

"No way."

"A pattern?"

He shook his head. "No."

"*Anything* they could anticipate? A trail? A clue? Some thread of—"

"*Nothing*."

"Well, they're getting it somehow."

"I know, but *how?*"

Mars glanced up at the guard tower. "Better computers than ours."

"We've been doing this a long time, and there's never been anything like this. They're so close to cracking us."

The razor wire depressed him, but at least he was minimum security. The towers and wire were for the medium security prison that was also part of their complex. He looked the other direction, past the trees. There was freedom out there, and a better way to save Chase.

Chapter Twenty-Seven

As the server room filled with smoke, the IT-Squads used the small, portable extinguishers they had in attempt to stop the servers from frying.

"It's a full self-destruct sequence underway," the Squad leader reported.

"Leave it!" Tess ordered. "Killcore is still live. He's operating from that building. There must be another server room."

Up on the second floor, they encountered a locked, reinforced steel door. "We're going to cut through."

"Killcore could be behind that door," Linda said.

"He has to be," one of the technicians said. Tess knew that tech had been working for almost three days straight, and could hear the strain in his voice.

Tess paced in the back of the room. She'd been in enough situations like this to already be doubting what they were doing. "It reeks of a set up," she said quietly to no one.

The IT-Squad audio broke through her tense thoughts.

"We are through the door in five . . . four . . . three . . . two . . . one—"

The big monitor lit up with a bright flash and roll of smoke as the doors blew open.

"We have another door."

Tess watched the footage in disbelief. Less than four feet into the opening, there was *another* heavy steel door. She looked back at the technician monitoring Lockheed Martin.

"Bring Lockheed onto one of the big screens," she ordered, checking her watch while the IT-Squad cut through the second steel door. Now on the adjoining large screen, the data feeds from Lockheed Martin played. It amazed Tess, and her NSA counterparts in attendance, how easily Killcore could pilfer the defense contractor's network.

"He's moving through their firewalls, digital defenses, and AI blockades," one of the NSA reps blurted out. "And we're seemingly helpless to stop him."

Another smaller monitor showed the tracing routes, sectioning, and hops Killcore was making to get there. Purple lines merged from connecting red and blue lines, and white dotted blips bounced all over the globe, jumping around like some kind of crazy, futuristic video game.

"Everything is still leading back to Denver," Linda said, while the Squad continued working the door. "It's originating from there. A coordinated, verified target . . . the building we're in." The deputy reviewed all the screens, and then added, "He's *got* to be in there."

"*Someone* is in that building making all this happen," another woman, from the NSA, agreed.

Tess was doing her best to believe there was a chance, maybe even a good one, that Killcore was in that building. The odds all pointed to the fact that they were about to identify the dreaded suspect, capture him, and end his reign of terror. But she had a bad feeling.

"Do we still have nothing bouncing into that building?" Tess asked, a question she had repeated ever since they'd first located the Denver hub.

"All data and signals emanating," an analyst replied.

"It's all going out, and nothing coming in," a tech concurred. "Lockheed and everything else originating in Denver."

"Since all of Killcore's operations are starting from the building," Linda began, "and no data is coming in, then that's where the routing had to—"

"Nothing, we are still clean," another tech announced.

"And are we *positive* there is no way he can get a signal into that building without us knowing about it?" Tess had also asked that question before, but as it was taking so long to get through the second steel door, she had to ask it again. Another team was systematically searching the third floor. She watched as their cameras continued showing empty rooms.

"We're about to find out who Killcore is," the deputy said as the second blast countdown began.

Another technician answered Tess's question. "Absolutely no way the signal could originate anywhere else. It had to be starting from there."

"Damn it!" one of the IT-Squad yelled as they cleared the second door and encountered a third one.

Tess wanted to scream.

While the Squad began cutting *again*, another team moved back into the lower server rooms. The camera left by the first Squad had continued running, and showed the smoke thinning.

"It's still melting," a woman reported.

Tess had been watching the red and black smoke, wondering what evidence had been destroyed.

"Everything is melting, but vents must be taking the smoke out of the building," the woman on the scene's voice came over the speakers. "It's been designed to destroy the servers, but not damage the space."

"They've gone to too much trouble to destroy those servers. What's on them?" Tess whispered to herself, and then, in an authoritative voice, she ordered, "Get into those servers." She feared as they were cutting through the third steel door that the second-floor server room was melting in a similar fashion, or that the doors were only a decoy to give the lower server room time to self-destruct. She verified that Killcore was still inside the Lockheed network, as well as the ongoing breaches into all the other targets.

"Third floor clear," the IT-Squad on three announced. They had checked every office, every space, and found no one up there.

"Killcore has to be on the second floor," Tess said. "Still nothing coming in?"

"Nothing. Still clear."

"Oh my God—there's a *fourth* door!"

"Look, Tess," the FBI man said, pointing to interior and exterior shots being collected on another monitor. "There are no windows on the second floor. Those black, smoky, silver-tinted windows on the first and third floors match the ones on two, but it's really just a band of glass going around the second floor."

"They only *look* like windows . . . They're just reflective glass against concrete," Linda said.

"It's a bunker," Tess breathed in realization.

"Because Killcore *is* in there!" Linda shouted. "We've

got him!" She was almost giddy. "We're about to find out who this SOB is."

However, by the time they got through the fourth, and then the fifth steel door, the celebration was over. The entire second floor turned out to be a massive room of servers, which had all melted.

With guns drawn, they swept the dark, stale room, expecting to apprehend the most dangerous cyber-criminal the world had ever known, but the room was empty.

Chapter Twenty-Eight

Tess, still monitoring the failed raid in Denver, received a message from Killcore, and immediately called Chase.

"Killcore is claiming that in seventy-two hours, he'll have the world on the edge of anarchy."

"At least he's not aiming too high," Chase said. "How can he even *make* a claim like that?"

"We believe him."

"You do?" Chase asked, stunned.

"His abilities are *astounding*," she said, as if the word *astounding* were a new and novel sound which could only be applied to Killcore.

Chase and Wen shared a concerned look. "Who is Killcore?" Chase asked. "How can you not have found him yet?"

"We thought we had him in Denver, but he either escaped as we came in, or was never there to begin with. I suspect it was the latter. Our next best lead is Nevada."

In the middle of his conversation with Tess, Chase read a message from Bull that Killcore could be in Des Moines, and silently signaled Wen to tell the pilot to change course and head for Iowa. At the same time, Wen typed the information to the Astronaut.

"His screen name, Killcore, is obviously a false identity," Tess continued as she pulled up a file on the screen, although she didn't need to. All the facts in the file had already been committed to memory. "But we're using it to track him, and are piecing together a profile. He appears to be male, thirty years old, wealthy, a brilliant engineer—starting to sound familiar?"

"Starting to sound like I'm being framed. All of that stuff can be manufactured on the Internet. You know how it goes."

"I do, but ask your Astronaut to look into it. I think you'll find that this isn't just a quick anonymous online identity. There are footprints going back years."

"It's *not* me."

"I know," Tess said. "You don't even look like him."

"Wait, you've got a photograph of this guy?" Chase asked.

"We have lots of them. We just don't know if they're really him."

"But it *is* a him?" Chase looked at Wen and smiled.

"That's just more evidence she's a woman," Wen said. "She's smart enough to do all of this, then she's smart enough to use a man's picture."

"The front profile paints him as you, but as we've gone deeper, more has been revealed about his true identity."

Pictures came across the screen as Tess read through data and vital statistics. "Forty-one year old white male, screen name Killcore, real name Colin Willis. Former government employee, Dallas Cowboys fan, no military service, likes to read science fiction and fantasy. He's purchased every single Michael Anderle book and Craig Martelle's novels, a lot of space military sci-fi. He's a heavy metal music lover, but is also active in Pink Floyd fan groups. Drives only German vehicles—VW, Audi, Porsche, Mercedes, BMW. Watches mostly British made television series and Bollywood films, in addition to ultraviolent action adventure movies, especially the Terminator and John Wick series. He seems to have supported both Democrat and Republican candidates in the past, and has—"

"Wait, if we know this much about him, why can't you *find* him? Former government employee . . . I mean, don't you have a database?"

"We've been searching. There's no match. He's found a way. He's also antigovernment."

"I thought you said he was a former government employee?"

"Former government employees are often the *most* antigovernment," Tess said in a *you-should-know-that* tone. "For a period of time, he resided in Indiana, and the Maryland suburbs of Washington DC. He is now believed to be in the Chicago area, but that doesn't mean that's where he's operating from."

"What in his profile explains his brilliance?"

"What in *your* profile explains *your* brilliance?" Tess shot back.

"MIT and Stanford's SAIL are at least good indications. Number of patents would be another, net worth . . ."

"We aren't sure. His educational background is incomplete. Appears to be a high school dropout. As I said, he reads a lot. We're tracing him through chat rooms, Facebook groups, and other social media activity, in addition to less concrete methods."

"Meaning you don't have a phone number you can listen in on."

"No, but we do have various email addresses. We're getting into those now. None of them have so far ended in their administrative set-up, or led to any true identities or physical addresses. However, the contents of the messages themselves may yield additional leads. We should know something more in the next hour."

"You would think with this many photos of the guy," Chase said, looking at candid shots of Killcore at an antigovernment rally, others with a group of "friends" at a bowling alley, another where he was showing off a plate of food at a fancy restaurant, "you'd be able to find him. I mean, this has gotta be ten or twelve years' worth of photos."

"Fourteen," Tess said. "That's why we need facial recognition cameras everywhere."

"Always justifying the surveillance state," he snapped.

Tess knew it was a sore point with him, but wanted to make *her* point that if they'd had all that data, Killcore would already be in jail, and this, the worst threat she'd ever faced in her time in the intelligence community, would be over. No bites yet had been taken out of the now bruised apple she'd been holding.

Chapter Twenty-Nine

Bull studied her main computer monitor while keeping an eye on the four others surrounding it.

"I think I've found you, Killcore," she said cautiously, taking a swig from her third can of Red Bull. "You think you're so clever, and yet I tracked you down. Now I own you!"

Bull looked around the empty cabin as if waiting for applause, but there was no one there, and she quickly focused back on the screen, afraid Killcore might slip away again.

"Most mortals would never have seen you in those numbers. The Astronaut would have, of course, but he's more like a superhero, so that doesn't count. I am your worst nightmare, Killcore, because *I* can see you." She flipped him off via the monitor, taunting him in her empty room, secure in the fact that he could not see or hear her. She smiled, happy to have tracked him.

It was time for a celebratory cigarette. Bull had promised Chase she wouldn't smoke inside the cabin, but she had a window open a few inches, a small usb-powered fan, and a can of air freshener in her luggage, so no harm, no foul. She lit up a cigarette and used one of the empty Red Bull cans as an ashtray.

Between drags, Bull kept watching the screen. She could see Killcore weaving through the dark web. "You're into all sorts of mischief aren't you?" she asked him, exhaling a long stream of blue-gray smoke. "But what are you after? And how are you leaving Chase's footprints everywhere?"

She keyed in long, complex commands, coding on the fly. The cigarette dangling from her mouth sent hot smoke seeping into her nostrils. She liked the sensation. *I don't understand why the kids these days are so into vaping, instead of the authentic smoke and heat of actual burning tobacco and paper.*

"Must be careful not to let him see me," she said, talking to the room. "I mean *her*," Bull corrected herself, remembering Wen's claim that Killcore could easily be a woman. Wen knew about such things, had a way of dissecting an adversary, deducing and seducing information. However, in the cyber-world, Bull had her own advantages—understood impressions and movements of male/female hackers in the androgynous digital coding rhythms, and she would soon decide if Killcore was man or woman.

She followed Killcore's every digital move. Wanting to have more answers before she contacted the Astronaut or Chase, Bull kept up the tedious race. "Finding Killcore is impressive, but by itself, it won't solve our problems, or avert the crisis. We need to find out his physical location," she said out loud, inhaling deeply, letting the smoke fill her lungs.

"Where are you right now?" she asked Killcore. "I've got you on the screen, but be a good boy and lead me back to your lair—wherever it is that you are *right now*, where you're actually creating all this mayhem from. And, while you're at it, *please* reveal what method you're using to link everything back to Balance Engineering."

Her fingers flew across the keys. All five monitors flashed and flipped screens, as if an orchestra was playing some kind of cyber-symphony, and Bull was the conductor.

She finished the cigarette, using it to light a fresh one before dropping the filter into the can. Her feet moved as fast as her fingers, doing a kind of hacker's dance, one where she could express her amused excitement without leaving the screen. Her numb, calloused fingers never stopped. Days like this could be painful—cramps, sore back, stinging eyes, a constant, buzzing, mild headache, and swollen, locked-up knuckles—yet hacking was her life, and Killcore was like a god. This was the Super Bowl, World Series, Academy Awards, and Grammys all rolled into one. As good as Bull was, she couldn't even begin to imagine how Killcore was doing some of the things he had done. So far, in a matter of days, he had penetrated the most secure networks in the world, and quietly made a joke of the US intelligence agencies. She wanted to unmask him, to end his reign of terror. But, alone in that room, Bull had to admit to herself that she also wanted to have sex with him.

"Killcore, I hope you turn out to be a guy, because I've got fantasies about you inside me. But, if you're a chick, I'd do some of that, too."

She kept following the trails, only lifting her fingers from the keys long enough to tend her cigarette. Ashes on the keyboard could slow her down.

"What's this?" she muttered, taking her cigarette from her lips. Switching to another screen, she split it into four quadrants, sliding an overlay across each one. "Wow . . . " she said. "How . . . are you doing that?"

Killcore had somehow multiplied, and was now leaving two tracks. She shivered, involuntarily looking over her shoulder, suddenly paranoid that Killcore had seen her following. "Are you trying to trap me?"

Being an experienced hacker, she often used evasive tactics to try to trick and mislead pursuers.

Now she was suddenly looking at *six* different Killcores among the malaise of data.

"Which one are you? Are *any* of you the real Killcore, or are you all just decoys now? Dammit!" She crushed out the cigarette, then dropped the butt into the Red Bull can, muttering, "At least I hadn't told the Astronaut or Chase yet."

She began coding a new tracing program which would merge all the separate tracks and find every common imprint. Eventually she'd get an empty one, and then another. As long as Killcore kept it under forty-eight, she might catch him again.

Seventeen minutes later, she found something beyond her skills, a *scary* piece of code, and knew she had to reach the Astronaut immediately.

Chapter Thirty

Tess had agreed to hold the meeting with her top analysts in Secure. As was protocol, each attendee had surrendered their cell phones, leaving them in a locker inside Mission Control. Initially, it wasn't clear to all those in attendance why the meeting was being held in Secure.

"We have a prepared list of suspects," Tess began. "As you know, Killcore's profile states that he is a forty-one-year-old white male, five-foot eleven, one hundred-ninety pounds, originally from Indianapolis." The large screen at the end of the table filled with the stats she had just announced, plus his employment and educational history, along with social media photos of the man they were pursuing.

"That's his name?" one of the analysts asked. "Fetzer Mills?"

"We don't know yet," Linda responded. "It may just be a name he borrowed. One he wants us to think is his. He also goes by Colin Willis."

"The FBI is in the process of visiting his current and prior addresses, and checking out those former employers."

"Thus far, they have not been able to locate this man," Tess said. "It's a possibility that Killcore is simply pointing us toward this individual, as he has done with Chase Malone."

"That brings us back to the list of suspects," Linda said. "On top of the list remains Chase Malone." Linda looked over at Tess, who wore a disapproving expression. "I know that Tess does not believe this is Chase, however, seemingly all indicators *do* point to him still, and we would be foolish to ignore that, and—"

"And I agree with you," Tess interrupted. "That is why we've kept him on the list, but we all know enough about Chase Malone. We have a comprehensive and detailed profile on him, and have worked with him on numerous occasions. So let's move on."

"Of course," Linda said. "If you look down at number two, you'll understand why this had to be done inside Secure."

"Yes, thank you," someone said.

"Some of the other suspects are also familiar to us. Several of the astronauts possess the intelligence, and perhaps motives, to be pursuing Killcore's agenda. Start with Astronaut Nash Graham, who is known to be affiliated with Chase Malone." She nodded toward Tess, as if to remind her this was another connection. "He is also working with WOLF, the fringe antiestablishment group sometimes referred to as The Cause. Many of you have been on astronaut cases before, and are aware that Nash Graham has extraordinary capabilities and is considered the most dangerous astronaut. However, there is also Astronaut Latif Bolat. He's worked with the Russians and Chinese more than with us. Bolat, like Graham, is a math savant, and was last known to be operating in Hong Kong."

"Graham and Bolat are the two most likely astronauts to be Killcore," an NSA official stated with some authority.

"Yes, among others," Tess agreed. "Bolat is one of the more mysterious astronauts. He has a way with money and markets."

"Bolat has been involved with several Middle Eastern agencies," the NSA man added.

"Correct. Bolat is a Turkish national," Linda said. "We are also looking at Wyatt Tennison, another astronaut who is perhaps even more intelligent and dangerous than Nash Graham. He has worked for British intelligence, the French, and freelanced for several major corporations. Finally, there is Durga Darshan, another savant from India. She takes on any cause that could affect Pakistan or China negatively."

"What is her specialty?" a CIA officer asked.

"No one knows," Linda said. "She seems to excel in numerous areas."

"They call her Durga Darshan after the Hindu goddess Durga, who is the protector of the righteous and destroyer of evil. Durga represents the fiery powers of the gods, and is usually portrayed riding a lion and carrying weapons in her many arms."

"Durga?"

"Yes. Durga Darshan."

"Sounds a little wild," the CIA officer said, shaking her head.

"You have no idea," Tess said.

"Okay, so there are other astronauts that could potentially be involved," Linda said. "However, our analysis points to these four. If an astronaut is Killcore, it's most likely to be one of them."

"We're working on locating them," Tess said. "As you know, this is not an easy task. Seems we're always trying to track down astronauts."

"However, none of those are the reason why we're conducting this meeting inside Secure," Linda said, squelching further speculation about astronauts. "There are two suspects within the US intelligence community. These are highly placed individuals, and were only identified through the most rigorous and arduous screenings."

"I don't need to tell you all why that could be such a serious problem," Tess said.

Two people gasped loudly, and an urgent murmur filled the room as Linda said Dean Johnson's name.

"I know we've all worked with Dean," Tess said. "And it's shocking that he fits the potential profile."

"But Killcore is claiming to be Chase Malone. What if he's also attempting to make us believe he's Dean?" somebody asked.

"It is, of course, possible Dean has done nothing wrong. However, due to specific material that Dean knows, and certain other criteria in the profile, many models point to Dean."

Several people sat visibly stunned.

"It could also be Dr. Valentine."

More collective shock rippled through the room.

"Valentine has long been an analyst inside the CIA, specializing in cybercrime encryption, etcetera. And as with Dean, he has access to a cross-section of information that puts him in the position to be Killcore."

"What criteria?" the NSA man asked.

"We have crossed patterns with all data related to Killcore's attacks," Linda replied. "Only certain people have access to these things."

"And the other suspect?" the woman from the CIA asked.

"Edward Snowden."

"Isn't he already in enough trouble?"

"How could he be doing all this from Russia?"

"Chase Malone *just* met with Snowden."

More murmurs.

"Snowden, obviously, would like to further expose the system and bring down the US intelligence apparatus," Tess began. "Because, let's make no mistake, this may *look* like an attack on the modern world, but we all know that the modern world is run by the six major intelligence communities."

"Then Snowden does make sense," someone said. "He could make fools of us all, expose everything we've done, and he's clearly shown himself to be reckless. I mean, this character gave up his freedom and risked his life in order to expose our surveillance programs."

"And no one really cared," someone else added.

"You talked to Malone. What does he say?" the NSA man asked.

"He said it could be another mysterious group he calls 'the shadow people.'"

"Who are *they*?"

"No one knows," Tess replied a little too quickly.

Chapter Thirty-One

Chase and Wen had only been in Des Moines, Iowa, for half an hour when they suddenly found themselves cut off from their vehicle and surrounded by FBI agents, or shadow people, or somebody else not on their side. After turning down the street where Bull had said Killcore's address was located, the quiet, urban area quickly lit up with guns and dozens of adversaries. They dashed to a rundown strip mall.

"There are too many of them!" Wen yelled as she ducked behind a dry cleaner's van.

"They're everywhere!" Chase barked, getting his gun out. "See them blocking the roads?"

"Obviously expecting us."

"How?"

"We'll figure that out later! Right now, we have about five seconds to get out of here."

Barely concealed behind a Dusty's Dry Cleaners van, Wen could see a group of eight armed personnel rushing toward them. The other side of the parking lot was blocked by more guns, and at least four black SUVs that they could see.

"Looks like we might go out in a blaze of glory," Chase said, checking the magazine of his MP7.

"What glory?" Wen asked, looking for any way out. "If we could get up on the roof . . ."

"If we could fly and had bulletproof vests."

Wen instinctively recalled the first lesson of her MSS training—*Never surrender*—but it was looking bleak, and she didn't want Chase to die. *If only* . . .

As if by magic, a bucket truck pulled into the parking lot and set up to take down an old sign less than twenty feet from them. "High ground!" Wen yelled as she raced them both across the pavement.

A minute later, they were running on the roof, shielded from the danger by the worn, decorative, western façade fronting the long building.

Pinned atop the old strip mall, they had no time to dissect the events which had led them into this death trap—a bad tip, tracking systems gone wrong, and a desperation to find Killcore.

The urban decay in this part of Des Moines seemed ready made for a high-tech ambush. A used record store still struggled to survive next to a space that had once been a toy store, but was now part of a call center. Beyond that, chemical fumes still lingering in the air advertised a hair and nail salon.

"If we can get to the other end," Wen shouted breathlessly, "we might be able to—"

The explosion was loud, rolling and filled with lies.

Chapter Thirty-Two

Wen's gun landed fifteen feet away on the shabby service road. Even if she could've gotten to it, it was tangled beneath a scrap pile of rusted metal rebar and perforated cables.

After the explosion, the jump/fall from the roof had knocked her into a lucky bounce off a soft black composite dumpster lid. She didn't know if Chase had survived. Suddenly, her intuition flashed a warning—the close presence of a man. She knew it wasn't Chase.

The man grabbed her leg before she could shout. Wen reeled around and saw two things in his eyes that told her this might be the end. The first was a jealous kind of killer-anger that showed him to be a casual taker of life. The second came with an eerie recognition that she *knew* him, or at least had encountered him before.

A shadow person, she thought, quickly accessing the encyclopedia of suspects and rogues in her mind. *Where do I know him from . . . where was it? Somewhere in Europe . . . we killed them all, but one got away. It's him.*

She and Chase had been ambushed by the shadow people all over the world, but there was one time in Prague . . . Wen recalled the incident. She could've taken a shot and killed him, but there'd been so much blood that day, and she had hesitated.

Did I let him go on purpose?

"You remember me don't you?" he asked, his gun aimed at her forehead. He seemed to sense her striking distance, and kept just out of reach of it.

"Yes," she said. "I let you live."

He nodded, as if she was confirming something he had only suspected. The surprise that somebody like Wen had intentionally let him live surprised and confused him. "Why?"

"Sometimes killing isn't necessary in our line of work . . ." She motioned very slightly to him, then back to herself, trying to buy as much time as possible, hardly aware of the words she was speaking while she was formulating a plan, looking for an escape, checking angles, recalculating the distance to her gun, the obstacles in the way, the tangle of metal—it was all too much. Her attention and strategic mind moved back to her opponent. He was smart, still keeping a good distance. It would be impossible, even with all her skills, to get to him before the bullets got to her.

But there must be a way.

"In our line of work," she repeated, "we have to kill a lot of people. You know how they haunt us in our sleep."

He nodded thoughtfully, staring at her, as if not caring what she was saying, but wanting to hear it anyway.

"So when a time comes that we don't *have* to kill," she continued, "I prefer not to."

"You let me live because you *could*?" he asked in a bitter tone. "What? Do you think you're some kind of god? That you can just choose who lives or dies? Does that make you feel important, Wen Sung?"

She'd been in hiding and using assumed identities for so long, it startled her to hear him use her real name.

"You should have killed me while you had the chance," he growled, re-steadying his gun. "I won't make that same mistake."

"I don't think I'm a god. That's why I only kill when I have to." Wen watched the shadows, hoping for any distraction. If something or somebody took his attention for even an instant, she would have a chance. "Maybe I did make a mistake in letting you live, but what have you been doing since then? What would you have missed?"

She considered suggesting he repay the favor, saying he was only there because she had saved his life and now maybe he should spare hers. Sizing up the assassin, however, she knew that would infuriate him, and that he would pull the trigger the moment she asked him not to, so instead she posed a different question.

"Before I die, will you tell me who sent you?"

He seemed amused and surprised again, as if he'd been expecting her to plead for her life, but instead she wanted her curiosity satisfied. "Maybe I could tell you. It might be the right thing to do."

But he hesitated, and all Wen's training and experience told her he was about to pull the trigger.

"I let you live," she repeated to him.

"You did," he said. "It was your worst mistake."

As if in slow motion, she could see his finger twitch on the trigger. An instant knowing filled her with searing dread. In less than a tenth of a second, she would die.

Chapter Thirty-Three

The sound of the gun firing echoed through her entire body, as if she'd been split open by a chainsaw. The bullets had not belonged to the shadow man, who, instead, fell dead beside her. The blood on her chest had been his, not hers.

"Wen!" someone called out from above. "Wen! Malachite, malachite!"

"Incredible," Wen breathed. Malachite was an obscure code word only one other person in the world knew.

"Astaria?" Wen said, trying to see the woman yelling at her. *If she's here, the worst situation I've ever been in just got worse,* she thought.

"It's me."

"What are you doing here?"

"You mean other than saving your life?" the woman responded, still above Wen's view. "And, at the moment, I'm about to have to kill your boyfriend."

"*What?*"

"Chase is pointing a gun at me, and you know how that's going to end."

"Chase, she's friendly!" Wen yelled, still unable to see either one of them, but knowing it would only take an instant for Astaria to kill him.

"Are you sure?" he replied. "I thought she was shooting at you."

"No. She saved me. I know her. Lower your gun. You're only still alive because she knows I love you."

Realizing his peril, he quickly complied. A few seconds later, he appeared next to Wen. "I'd found a concealed ladder and headed back to the roof. You taught me always get the high ground. Then I saw this female agent shooting down where I guessed you were . . . Who is she?"

"Take me to the ladder," Wen said. "Astaria is a Mossad agent. We've worked together in the past."

Astaria dropped down the ladder as they reached it. Almost simultaneously, a van pulled up.

"He's with me," Astaria said, motioning to the van as an armed man ran out. Then she embraced Wen, kissing her fully on the lips.

Chase and the man shared a questioning glance, as if to say they felt left out.

After the kiss, Wen smiled at Chase and offered a throwaway line. "Astaria is a little eccentric, and a lot passionate." She turned back to Astaria. "What's going on? Why are you here?"

"Killcore," Astaria replied. "He's CIA."

"How do you know?"

"I can't tell you that."

"How did you find us?"

"I can't tell you that, either."

Wen wondered if Astaria knew who the shadow people

were, or where Killcore was. "I need that information," she said, following Astaria into the van.

"Killcore is CIA?" Chase said as he climbed in. "That's a big problem."

"Actually," Astaria said, flipping her long, black, voluptuous, frizzy ponytail from her shoulder, "you have a much bigger problem. The MSS has identified Wen, and they're coming."

Tess adjourned the meeting as soon as she received a private alert that Chase and Wen had been located in Des Moines. "What the hell are they doing there?" she asked an analyst monitoring the situation in Mission Control.

"Shooting people and getting shot at."

"What leads on Killcore are there in Des Moines?"

"None we know of."

Tess whirled around. "Get on it, people. Chase isn't in Des Moines visiting relatives, something brought him there. Killcore must have a presence in Iowa. Find it! And don't lose Chase!"

Dean Johnson hated O'Hare airport, and didn't particularly like Chicago. The fact that he had to endure both in a single day was beyond annoying. However, there was a computer located in a building in Buffalo Grove, a suburb of the windy city.

This computer didn't act like any ordinary computer, and few could operate it. The access points were called "the gauntlet" due to the seemingly endless biometric and key-test security required to get near it. Nothing could reach it via network connections, and its firewalls and protocols were the most advanced in the world.

Dean hoped it would be his last visit.

It would.

Chapter Thirty-Four

Astaria sat shotgun, aiming an Uzi out the van's passenger window as the driver punched the accelerator. They raced away until six heavily armed men suddenly emerged from behind an abandoned car with flattened tires. A large Suburban screeched in to close the gap.

"We're boxed in!" Chase yelled, looking out the back window to see a garbage truck pulling in to empty the dumpsters.

Astaria leaned out the window and tossed two tech-grenades. Half a second later, their van burst through a smoky mess of bodies, blood, and mangled wreckage.

"Who were they?" Wen asked as Chase marveled at the ease of their escape.

"Oh, my sweet, you know the rules."

"There *are* no rules!"

"Forget about them."

"I *can't*."

"Maybe the MSS will make you forget."

Wen looked at Chase. Their eyes flashed with fear of the

nightmare that had haunted them since Wen had fled China.

"I didn't know the MSS and the Mossad did joint operations," Chase said, suspicious of Astaria, even though Wen seemed to trust her.

"We worked together on a covert matter in Iran," Astaria said. "Another time in Syria, and then that whole misadventure in Nigeria."

"They don't," Wen added, answering Chase's question. "These were not officially sanctioned. I saved her life . . . She saved mine."

"Do you trust her?" Chase asked, not afraid of Astaria hearing.

"With my life," Wen replied. "But that is not to say we are always on the same side. It's possible our objectives occasionally cross."

"True," Astaria said, laughing.

"What does that mean?" Chase asked.

"It is difficult to say," Wen said, as if in deep thought. "If it comes down to saving me or failing to meet her objectives…"

"Which would she choose?"

Wen just shook her head.

"Oh, but Wen, I love you," Astaria said, puckering her lusciously painted lips. "Saving you *always* complies with my objectives."

"Where are we going?" Chase asked, while Wen looked out the back window.

"You wanted Killcore, right?"

"Yes," Chase replied. "We had a lead."

"It was old. Killcore is in Chicago."

"How do you know all this?"

"Simple. I am Astaria."

"Astaria is a legendary operative that some in the intelligence community do not believe even exists," Wen explained. "Her contacts are endless."

"You flatter me."

"Contacts on which sides?" Chase asked.

"*All* sides." Wen replied.

"Of course." Astaria winked. "That reminds me, I haven't heard from Twag."

He had been a top Taiwanese operative from The Cause, and a mutual friend they had both worked with. Wen knew Astaria was very fond of him, so she answered gently. "We lost him in Vancouver."

"Oh no," she said, suddenly sounding less like a swaggering killer and more like a grieving human. "What happened?"

"He died for The Cause."

Chase said nothing. Twag had died saving his life.

Astaria was visibly saddened by the news. Chase marveled at how quickly her hardness and invincibility crumbled. Yet as fast as her vulnerability showed, it vanished again. "Causes make people careless."

"What is your interest in Killcore?" Wen asked Astaria. "Have you been sent to assassinate him, or capture him?"

"Oh, my sweet friend, I can't tell you that, either," she said, turning sideways in her seat so she could face Wen and Chase. "I'm sorry, it's very thin just now."

Wen knew if she had been sent to eliminate Killcore, then their objectives would match. But if her orders were to take him alive, their objectives would clash.

"Those people back there?" Chase began. "We really need to know who they worked for."

"I'm sure you do," she said. "I was only here to warn

you about the MSS, and to *possibly* compare notes on Killcore. Maybe we can help each other."

"Nice coincidence," Chase said sarcastically.

"You're welcome," Astaria replied, staring him down. "Wen is usually more *polite* after I save *her* life."

"Why are you here?" Wen asked. "It's a fair question."

"Once I discovered you were pursuing Killcore, I wanted—"

"How did *you* hear we were hunting Killcore?"

Astaria smiled. "You keep trying, but you know I can't tell you that."

"You could've only found out from somebody inside." Wen was desperate to know. The implications were so significant. Yet Astaria's refusal to answer anything about her sources was not surprising. The world's intelligence communities were more intertwined than the governments would like to admit. An agent with the sophistication and connections of Astaria was especially talented at gathering vital information from multiple agencies with an underworld of sources at crosscurrents in global events.

"Killcore is part of a group that includes a rogue CIA tech genius, and an ex-GlobeTec security chief."

"Not Franco Madden?" Chase blurted out, the realization hitting him like a brick.

"Yes. How did you know?"

Chapter Thirty-Five

Tess paced along the back wall of Mission Control, her preferred vantage point, where she could survey what each technician and analyst had going on while still viewing all the wall monitors. She watched the crisis board and kept a computer tablet in her hand that allowed her control of all the screens at once. However, Tess generally preferred to shout commands and let someone else produce the visual changes she needed.

A representative from the FBI stood nearby, only in attendance because two dozen Bureau antiterrorism agents were along on this mission—another chance to get Killcore. CISS, with five IT-Squads on site, would lead the operation.

As they watched the center monitor, Tess had a sense of déjà vu. "Please don't let this be another Denver," she muttered quietly to herself. Frustration piled on top of frustration as, less than thirty minutes earlier, she'd been informed Chase had slipped away yet again. She turned to another screen, showing a shabby section of Des Moines.

How does Chase do it?

"Here we go," a technician announced, pulling Tess back to Killcore.

The two-story building, situated on the outskirts of Henderson Nevada, sat in the desert, oddly inconspicuous for its enormous size, blending into the terrain with a roof and exterior walls colored the same shade of dusty-sand as the surrounding rocks.

"It must be hundreds of thousands of square-feet," Tess observed absently. "What are they doing with a building that big?"

The native vegetation, growing along a winding, packed-dirt road that led to the facility, reminded Tess of the desertscape around her favorite town—Taos, New Mexico.

"The entire property is surrounded by a double ring of twelve-foot perimeter chain-link fencing topped with razor wire," an analyst said. "Gives it the appearance of a prison yard."

"What is Killcore doing with a facility like this?" the FBI man asked. "It's an odd looking structure, mirrored windows only on the ends and center."

"We're trying to locate plans and blueprints," another analyst said. "However, right now, we're having a difficult time even tracing and confirming the ownership of the property—which also encompasses several thousand acres."

"Team leader, team leader, we are in position. Are we a-go?"

The director of CISS field operations looked at Tess, who nodded. "You are a-go."

The FBI counter-terrorism director walked over to Tess. "Why is this different than Denver?" he asked. "I mean, we have the same signals coming out, and nothing going in."

"As you know, our analysts believe someone has to be inside, generating the hacking commands."

"That was the same scenario in Denver, and yet—"

"I know. He must have been in there, and then found a way out. Not this time. We have everything covered, and we absolutely *have* to get ahold of his servers before they're destroyed."

"How is he *doing* it, though?" he asked with a perplexed expression.

She shook her head. "I've got Dartmouth working on it."

"I kind of feel as if Killcore *wants* us to be here. Think about it. If he's smart enough to carry out all these operations, diversions, break-ins, contrive situations, manipulate and breach all of our networks' and security systems . . . why does he keep letting us find his facilities?"

She wanted to say, *Because we're smart, too. We have the best there is working on tracking this guy, looking for every seam into his world. Even the biggest geniuses make mistakes, and that's how criminals and terrorists get caught—they make mistakes.* But her confidence had been shattered by recent events, and instead, she gave a simple and honest reply.

"I don't know."

The screens filled with interior images of the Henderson building, and it wasn't at all what they'd expected. It turned out to be a hanger-like structure. No second-floor, just a massive void filled with endless rows of servers on three levels of metal grates.

"Clearly those solar panels we saw are providing power for this massive server farm, and for the cooling units that are keeping them from overheating," the FBI man said.

"Careful," Tess said.

Dozens of federal agents treaded lightly as they

streamed into the cavernous space, having been briefed extensively on the need to preserve the data on the servers. Many were veterans of the Denver raid, and had experienced "the meltdown," as it was now being called. The front team donned gas masks and quickly spread out among the cages, locating the entry points and exit points of all com-cables, assessing the grid layout, and determining the master servers.

As each minute ticked by without screens of smoke, Tess grew more tense. *We're getting closer and closer to the prize,* she thought, absently squeezing her computer tablet. She knew it could all be snatched away at any second.

The FBI antiterrorism director asked the question she'd been avoiding. "Where is Killcore?"

She shook her head and held up her hand as the teams scoured the outer perimeters of the walls, which contained locked doors.

"He's there," she said unconvincingly.

The IT-Squads, careful to avoid any traps that might damage the servers or set off a chain reaction, moved around the rooms very cautiously.

"There are only three doors left," the FBI man said. "Killcore has to be behind one of them."

Tess flashed back on the five steel doors in Denver. Her head started to ache.

"Room one, clear!" a Squad member announced.

Tess watched as her teams, the most talented computer forensic technicians in the world, began connecting, downloading, and uploading massive amounts of information from the servers onto skewed satellite links.

"Room two, clear."

The tension inside the Henderson hangar grew as everyone anticipated room three. The exterior and interior walls indicated it to be the largest one, and the farthest from the entry point.

"Logic and experience dictate, this is where Killcore will be," the FBI man said.

Tess quietly agreed, but inwardly, that same logic and experience told her he would not be.

Chapter Thirty-Six

Tess held her breath as analysts inside Mission Control began receiving data from the hangar's servers. The murmur of their conversation rose above the din and hum of the equipment. They zeroed in on the data, looking for the telling points that could indicate high-level threats, and in seconds, could identify any sequences initiated from inside the building that could be about to take out an airliner, or reveal national security secrets, or any number of other dire things.

The door to room three fell in as the IT-Squad rammed. All of CISS command waited to see if the servers would crash and burn. Instead, it felt more anticlimactic than Denver. The room contained a cutout statue of two individuals, Ricardo Montalbán and Hervé Villechaize, two actors dressed in their roles of the mysterious Mr. Rourke and Tattoo from the 1970s hit television show, *Fantasy Island*.

Tess, looking at the two cut-outs standing next to each other in white suits, felt baffled and incredulous.

Audio came through a concealed speaker. "Welcome to Fantasy Island."

"What the hell?" Tess said. "Is this supposed to be funny?"

"I don't share Killcore's sense of humor," the FBI man said.

"More strangeness," an analyst called out. "All the data was legitimate operations for Fortune 500 companies."

Tess shook her head. "Killcore is making fools out of us."

"I found something!" one of the agents in Henderson shouted.

When Mars first arrived to Lompoc, he had been annoyed to learn that all federal prison inmates were required to work unless medically unable. His job at Lompoc Federal Correctional Institute paid twelve cents an hour, but he didn't care about the low wage. He made plenty of money with his "side job."

Being clerk of the prison paint shop allowed him a rare bit of freedom. While the crew of other inmates was painting various buildings and areas around the prison, Mars stayed back at the shop, organizing and ordering supplies—brushes, solvents, drop cloths, gloves, caulk, paint, and a hundred other things. He didn't actually *place* the orders, but he filled out the requisition forms and kept inventories, making sure enough paints and bases were on hand. He also mixed paints, cut the glass for replacement windows, and, at the end of the day, cleaned the brushes and managed returning all the tools and supplies to their appropriate places so they could be counted and secured by the correctional officer who oversaw the shop.

Mars also kept a powerful laptop in a secret compartment of his desk. He used it exclusively to oversee the decoying and confusion process of protecting Chase and Wen.

He pulled out the computer and opened the codes. His desk had been carefully positioned to be safe from surveillance cameras. He'd protected the CO in charge of the paint shop from an OSHA audit by covering up the improper disposal of lead paint and other toxic materials. For that, the man, close to retirement, would have given Mars more freedom. However, Mars had also assisted the guard in obtaining an increasingly sizable portfolio in stocks, which now made for a considerable nest egg in addition to his government pension, and this afforded Mars great privileges.

What greeted him online this time, though, was something both complex and terrifying.

Somebody had gotten into his decoying system.

Franco was tired. Tired of running, tired of Dean, of Killcore, and *especially* of Chase Malone. He didn't understand why Dean was in Chicago, but he'd lied about it, so something was wrong.

I loathe things going wrong, Franco thought, then whispered to the silence of his isolated space, "'It was a wrong number that started it, the telephone ringing three times in the dead of night, and the voice asking for someone he was not.'"

The opening line from *City of Glass* by Douglas Coupland, seemed to fit his mood, as it often did—mystery, trouble, betrayal, and consequences.

"That's my life," he said, adding to the quote and his feeling. "And by God, I will survive it."

Astaria told them about a building belonging to Killcore where a large part of his operations were based. She explained that he'd been trading information to the Mossad and other intelligence agencies for months.

"The CIA, too," Chase said, thinking of the duplicity of Tess Federgreen and wondering what her plan was this time.

"Definitely the CIA. I think they're the ones who gave you up to the MSS," Astaria said.

"No doubt," Wen agreed, wondering how long she could stay alive with the whole of the world's most ruthless agency pursuing her.

"We'll drop you at a car not far from the place," Astaria said.

"Why aren't you coming with us?"

She smiled, then made her lips into a seductive kiss. "Oh, sweet, sweet Wen, you know I can't tell you that. At least not in this lifetime."

Chapter Thirty-Seven

The encrypted machine Mars used for decoying was purposely held separate from another computer, hidden in another location, which contained details of his various business enterprises. He maintained his employees the same way, with convicts on the inside and people on the outside who helped in different aspects of the decoying, as well as in his other projects. Mars kept them all isolated so that none knew the others existed. The structure was meant to protect his operations from collapsing should the authorities discover any associates, his computers, accounts, or in any other way infiltrate his organization. He was making a fortune in prison, but would've gladly given up all his profits in order to keep Chase safe.

Mars stared into the monitor suspiciously, as if searching for intruders who might still be inside his machine. The machine had been compromised, of that he was sure. However, he was certain no one had been able to physically get to it, since the laptop had been concealed in the secret panel of a desk that required a passcode to even get to the regular drawers. Plus, the desk was inside of a building that utilized a biometric sensor for anyone to gain access, within a secure prison compound, which itself was part of a deferral correctional complex. He marveled at the sophistication of the crime.

"The perpetrator would've had to access the machine during shut down, just prior to shut down, or immediately before or right after startup," Mars said to himself.

He knew from Bull and other hackers that there were potential vulnerabilities in running background networking —as he did. The technique allowed for his machine to stay constantly updated through a virtual machine server system located off-site. That meant his computer wouldn't be burdened with long download and upload times, which helped, since he mostly operated within very narrow time windows.

Mars opened a video chat to Bull. "It seems impossible that was his first point of contact."

"That could only be Killcore. He must've gotten in while your machine was ghosting," she said, busily tapping keys as if firing a confetti of data into cyberspace.

"Then he couldn't have gotten much, right?" Mars said hopefully.

"Normally, you would think that," she said absently. "But in this case, it looks like he got everything."

"How?" he asked while opening a chat with one of his outside contacts.

"I've never seen anything like this before. Didn't even think it was possible."

Mars, normally cool and calm in the face of danger, felt suddenly fearful, since this breach could have serious consequences for Chase and Wen. He typed more questions to his outside contact, desperately hoping it wasn't as bad as Bull was suggesting. For the first time, Mars contemplated the possibility that Chase's death could be on his hands.

"Killcore found the server and waited until you started to grab the data."

"He would have only had a few seconds to make the grab. That's a damn powerful computer that can do that, and an unbelievably skilled hacker. Who has those capabilities?"

"No one . . . " she said quietly. She studied multiple screens, thinking there might be another answer out there somewhere, but knowing there was only one possibility. "It could only be Killcore."

"Who the hell is this Killcore?"

"That's what everyone needs to know."

"Then Chase and Wen are exposed."

"Worse than that," she said. "Killcore may know exactly where they are."

In searching for every possible cable or place of concealment in the Henderson facility, the IT-Squads accidentally discovered that one of the server racks moved when an agent tracing conduits came across a loose bolt.

"The paint lines don't match!"

After unbolting the remaining studs, they carefully moved the bulky rack.

"It's a hole. There's a ladder."

Armed with lights and machine guns, the highly trained IT-Squad members descended into another world.

While Tess and the others watched live from Mission Control, several analysts were already working a theory that

Killcore had developed a way to encrypt and manipulate legitimate data and turn it into his criminal codes.

"I'm having difficulty getting my head around the complexities," Tess said, distracted by the images coming in from Henderson.

"Team Leader, are you seeing this?" the lead on-site operative asked as he focused his light and helmet-cam at the underground scene.

"We're looking, but not believing."

A labyrinth of tunnels was lit by the dim glow from a track in the low, arched ceiling, a welcome change from the green night-vision hue of the initial views.

"Tunnels at least fifteen feet across and six high, although up ahead they seem to open to ten feet high at their highest point," the man, whose helmet-cam they were watching, reported. He slowly turned three-hundred-sixty degrees, revealing eight tunnels, leading off in all directions.

The director of field ops ordered a Squad down each tunnel while one remained above with a handful of FBI agents, securing the warehouse.

Tess watched the teams pouring into the elaborate tunnel system. "Let's go find the rat," she said, feeling optimistic they'd finally found his base.

Chapter Thirty-Eight

Mars and Bull both worked independently to patch up the exposure initiated by Killcore into the decoying system. Bull simultaneously increased her efforts to track the super-hacker.

"Damn," Mars said. "I've got to close."

"What is it?" Bull asked over their still-open video chat.

"Just some prison officials heading this way."

"Is it a problem?"

"Everything's a problem in prison, but I'll handle it."

He swiftly shut down the computer, stowed it away, and then looked out the window again. His desk was strategically positioned so he had the best chance of seeing approaching prison personnel. Pulling out inventory requisition forms, Mars pretended to work, and waited for whatever was coming.

On the windowless third floor of the CISS building, a place affectionately known as "Cyber City," dozens of the brightest hot-shot technicians/hackers worked on banks of the most powerful computers and servers available. Tess called the team the CISS "magicians." Inside the vast, dark space, lit only by hundreds of monitors and colored LED indicator lights, which resembled a city skyline at night, they searched, twenty-four hours a day, for Killcore.

Utilizing the darknet and many other covert channels, the NSA-trained techs had also been working on a side mission related to Killcore's exploits: saving the US economy.

"We're losing," one of them said to his superior.

"I know," the woman replied, deciding it was time to notify Tess.

"The stock markets are all over the place," the technician said, as they both looked at the real-time readings coming across one of the monitors. "All the major indices have been plunging hundreds of points at a time and then ricocheting back in the other direction."

She nodded. "It's Killcore."

But they both knew the stock market was the least of their worries. The banks were where the real vulnerability was.

"How far has he gotten?"

"The banks," the technician said.

"Which ones?"

"All of them. Killcore is inside *all* of them."

Tess shattered the silence in Mission Control as everyone watched the footage of the bizarre scene unfolding under the Henderson site. "Find out everything you can about this property, those tunnels. I want to know when they were built, who built them, and why!"

"The whole place gives me the creeps," the FBI man said. "Like our people are walking into a trap."

The giant screens in Mission Control had split into eight feeds, showing what each Squad was seeing as they explored further into the separate tunnels. Tracking fobs showed the deepest teams were already in one hundred thirty feet, while the slowest group was at ninety feet.

"Whoever built these things spent a lot of money, and would've had to hire a big crew," the FBI man said. "There have to be records for all this."

"IT-Squad leader estimates that the tunnels were constructed sometime in the last twenty years."

"We've got infrared detection," the deepest team reported. "Dim red beams crossing the tunnel. No way around without tripping one."

Soon all the teams had reached beams in their tunnels. The FBI man called up for a REOD-V. The remote explosive ordinance disposal vehicle could detonate whatever the beams triggered.

"How many do we have on-site?" Tess asked, trying to calculate how quickly they could proceed.

"Three. It'll take about twenty minutes to get the REOD-Vs into position. The most difficult part will be partially disassembling them to be lowered down the ladder."

Almost half an hour later, the first one was sent into the beams. Immediately, rapid machine-gun fire ripped into the REOD-V. After two full minutes, the ammunition depleted. They repeated the process on the other tunnels, and then moved the vehicles to the next beams, until all eight were cleared.

"I don't like tunnels," Riley, the lead Squad member, said to no one in particular. "Not knowing what's around the next bend, what's lingering beyond the shine of my light . . ."

"At least everything is contained in a manageable space," the agent right behind him said as they advanced deeper. "No threats from above, below, or behind."

"What are you, some kind of an *optimist?*" Riley asked, saying the word *optimist* as if he were Senator Joseph McCarthy saying *communist*.

"It could be worse."

"Really?" Riley asked, as they came to another crossroads with five different tunnels. "It's a maze down here."

He reported back they would have to start splitting into smaller groups to cover the additional openings.

"And splitting up rarely brings good results," Riley mumbled to himself.

Chapter Thirty-Nine

Inside a particularly long section of Killcore's subterranean gauntlet, Riley heard a sound that terrified him.

"Run!" he shouted above the noise of hundreds of thousands of gallons of water heading down the tunnel. "Get out! Get out!"

Tess and the crew in Mission Control watched helplessly as the Squads ran to evacuate the trap-laden catacombs. The rush of water grew louder.

"How close? How deep?" Riley shouted above the roar, but the water still hadn't come around the corner. Judging by how loud it was, he figured the water would fill the tunnels completely. "Keep going! Faster!"

Monitoring the GPS tracking fobs, Mission Control directed the Squads through the agents' earpieces in which way to turn at each intersection, saving them valuable time. Inside the CISS command center, the sound of raging water dominated the room.

"Find more exits!" Tess barked.

"Do we know how soon until the flood reaches our people?" Linda asked.

Analysts, who had been working to map the tunnel system, were using AI programs in an effort to fill out the remaining uncharted areas, and to locate the source of the water. "We haven't determined that yet."

For three tense minutes, they waited and watched as the surviving agents ran at full speed to the hatch, certain the wall of water would engulf them any second.

"Can they get out in time?" the FBI man asked.

"No," a technician said flatly. "Based on the calculations, with this much volume, we've got less than a minute before it buries them. We can only bring them up the ladder one at a time. The swirl and tidal effect of surging water inside that crisscrossing network of tunnels . . . it will suck them down."

Tess had watched people die before, but braced herself for the horror of watching more than seventy of their best people drown in front of her eyes.

The analysts continued their calculations. "The torrent will hit them in nineteen seconds, eighteen, seventeen . . . "

During the frantic evacuation, machine-gun fire tore into several members of one of the Squads, apparently triggered by a hidden photocell or motion detector.

"Amos is dead!" came a shout. "Two injured!"

The water grew louder.

"We see the ladder!" someone yelled as the first Squad found their way through the maze.

"Fifteen seconds."

They'd positioned two ropes at the ladder to pull them up. The method would save a few seconds on each climb, and potentially prevent at least three or four agents from being sucked into the storm.

The first agent was yanked out.

"Ten seconds."

"Five are out. Three more are at the ladder," the field commander announced.

"Seven seconds."

The water was deafening.

"Isn't there another way out?" Tess snapped.

"We haven't found any yet."

"Eight out. Twelve more at the ladder."

"Four seconds."

Chapter Forty

"Three seconds."

"These tunnels must be longer than we think, if it hasn't reached them yet," an analyst speculated.

"I agree," another said. "It would take an awful lot of water to fill that distance. I'm talking a reservoir."

"Two seconds."

"What's going on?" Tess asked.

"Impact!"

"No water," one of the agents, deepest in the tunnels, reported.

"Where's the water?" the FBI man asked.

The sound of the water had grown so loud, they could hardly hear the reports coming in, but the water hadn't arrived yet.

"Minus five."

"What's slowing it down?" the FBI man asked.

"There is no source of water close enough to fill those tunnels," an analyst, who'd been working on locating the origin point of the flood, announced. "There is no way to move water at the velocity to match that sound."

"What are you saying?" Tess asked. But as soon as the words escaped her mouth, she realized what the analyst was suggesting.

"Minus ten."

"There *isn't* any water down there, is there?" Tess asked.

"I believe it's a computer enhanced recording of floodgates being opened at the Three Gorges Dam in China."

"So there's no water?" the FBI man asked. "It's fake?"

"Minus twenty."

"Stop the damned countdown!" Tess shouted.

"Dozens of agents are out, ten more are at the ladder, ready to come up," the field commander reported. "What do you want to do?"

"It's another trick," Tess said. "Killcore fooled us, and has probably escaped out a rabbit hole somewhere. Send them back down. Get me eyes in the air over every *inch* of that desert."

They moved the REOD-vehicles farther ahead. Although the water was still intolerably loud, there was nothing coming. The agents followed and started moving quicker through the tunnels behind the REODs.

Riley's team turned down a previously unexplored section.

"Did you hear that?" Riley asked.

"I can't hear anything above the water," the agent next to him replied.

"Sounded like gunfire."

The water sound stopped as the space ahead filled with men dressed in black trench coats and fedoras, who opened fire with antique Tommy guns. Riley and the others immediately returned fire and hit the ground before they realized they were just seeing black-and-white projections of 1940s and 50s Hollywood gangster movies.

"Killcore has a real sense of humor," Tess said sarcastically, as she watched Riley's team get to their feet and cut through the movie screen.

"Yeah, he's *hilarious*," the FBI man said.

"But you see what this all is?" Tess began. "It's like Denver all over again. He's trying to slow us down from getting to those servers, and these are some major delaying tactics. The servers are underground. He's set this all up to protect them."

"And to give himself time to escape," Linda added.

"Exactly. Show me the aerials. I want to see his escape route to the surface. We need more personnel down there. And we for damn sure need to find those servers, *now!*"

Franco watched the raid on his own screen. *It's the funniest movie I've ever seen*, he texted Killcore. Although Franco couldn't recall the last time he'd actually laughed this hard, he appreciated irony, sarcasm, and poetic justice. *They're running around in the tunnels like lost little children.*

He checked the status of their next step. The plan was good. Nothing would stop the darkness and agony.

Riley noted they were now deeper in the tunnels than they had ever been. "Be alert for new traps."

A few minutes later, intensely bright lights temporarily blinded them.

"It's like staring into the sun!" one of them yelled in agony.

"Get down! Assume shooters! Get down!"

"Where's the team whose supposed to be out there at the solar panels?" Tess barked. "We need to cut the power to the place, now!" Tess, upset it hadn't already been done, shouted, "Power is fueling all those traps and tricks."

Tess watched another monitor, showing a team finally reaching the solar panels, and wondered what traps awaited *them*. Her thoughts were interrupted by more gasps and screams from the normally stoic personnel inside Mission Control as they witnessed five operatives electrocuted in one of the tunnels by surging, blue, lightning-like bolts crisscrossing what were apparently now metal walls and metal grating on the floor and ceilings of that section. Tess did not look away as their bodies convulsed and smoked, watching as they were fried alive.

Danner, the fifth member of the team, who had not entered that section yet, could do nothing to help his friends. He told Tess later that if he had been thinking clearly, he would have shot them all.

Riley's team heard the news when Danner radioed in his report with a breaking voice. Riley knew Danner to be a dog-tough warrior, but was not surprised by his display of raw emotions.

"Get out of there Danner!" the field ops director ordered.

"No, you send me to another team. I want to find this bastard!"

"We'll take you, Danner," Riley offered. There happened to be a cross tunnel near them. Command directed him to the rendezvous. Danner reached Riley's group just as the lights were cut.

"Remember, there can still be traps that don't rely on power," the field ops director warned. "It's likely Killcore has independent generators, or other unknown power sources we have yet to discover."

The groups in the different sections moved deeper, utilizing night vision.

Danner, now up front with Riley, discovered several more trip-points along the way that were now without power, and seemingly deactivated.

Then they heard a horrible, loud buzzing, like a million angry bees.

Chapter Forty-One

Chase and Wen had spent the drive to Chicago pushing and prodding to pry whatever information they could from Astaria.

"Did we really learn *anything*?" Chase asked, after they'd been dropped off.

"Astaria will never give anything she doesn't want you to have."

"So do you believe her?" Chase asked, wondering why the super-agent would save them and give them inside information to help them find Killcore.

"She has an agenda. Right now, it aligns with ours."

"If she's so good, why doesn't she go get Killcore herself, or just come with us?"

"Because she's so good," Wen said thoughtfully. "She's giving us the second look."

"What's that mean?"

"She isn't really sure *where* Killcore is. There may be two, maybe even three locations."

"And she's going to the one with the best chance?"

"Yes. Killcore is not easy to find. She's covering herself. She must be tracking us somehow." Wen pulled out her phone.

"Who are you calling?"

"The Astronaut. We need him to track Astaria."

"What the hell is that noise?" Riley asked, donning his headset again in anticipation of another sonic attack.

Danner, leading with his submachine gun, ready to kill anything that moved, still unable to shake the image of his electrocuted, smoldering buddies grinding through his psyche, shook his head and advanced. The buzzing grew louder.

"Swarm drones!" Danner shouted as hundreds of drones, flying in formation, filled the tunnels, soaring toward them. He began firing, knocking dozens off course or out of the air.

"There's too many!" Riley shouted as the seemingly endless supply tore through the air.

As the drone attack raged inside the Henderson tunnels, Linda Moore handed Tess a phone.

Riveted by the unfolding horror in Nevada, Tess looked at her assistant as if she'd just slapped her. "Nothing is more important right now."

"This is."

"What?" Her exasperation was hardly tempered, yet she

knew her assistant would not interrupt unless the earth was opening up somewhere else.

"The Dow is down five thousand."

"That *can't* be right," Tess said in disbelief, looking at the phone in her hand.

"It's Cyber City."

"Oh God, then it's Killcore?" Tess asked, realizing her nemesis had now breached the financial markets themselves.

"Afraid so."

"The market is off five thousand. Tell me what's happening," Tess said, speaking into the phone to the tech up in Cyber City, while keeping an eye on the action in Henderson.

"The composite has already bounced off those lows and is now showing a two thousand point gain. It's been all over the place. And it's not just the Dow. Nasdaq, bonds, commodities, the dollar itself—way too many crazy, out-of-control moves."

"How is he doing it?"

"We're in there right now," the technician said. "I'll send it to a screen."

An instant later, one of the Mission Control monitors filled with hieroglyphic-like data streams of numbers, intermittent graphs, and all sorts of stock ticker symbols she recognized: Exxon-Mobil, Apple, Xerox, Microsoft, Amazon, 3M, Pfizer . . .

"All those stocks are being bought and sold in massive, instantaneous blocks."

"It's computerized trading."

"Yes, he's put in these huge orders buying and selling in blocks at crazy prices that are causing the market gyrations. He's creating a self-fulfilling prophecy of market collapse."

"Can we stop him?"

"It's not just the markets," the tech said in an ominous tone. "Killcore's tearing apart the banks."

Tess's attention was forced back to Henderson as Riley, Danner, and three others fought the onslaught and shot down as many drones as they could. "It's like they're taking evasive actions!" Riley yelled, confounded that they weren't able to get them all.

"Like they know what we're gonna do, where we're gonna shoot!" Danner yelled.

The scene resembled something out of Alfred Hitchcock's *The Birds*, as the five elite soldiers, scattered in a darkened tunnel, tried to fight off hundreds, possibly thousands, of menacing drones, each seemingly on an attack mission.

"Could they be piloted by somebody watching in that tunnel?" Tess asked.

Two analysts said it was technically possible, but highly unlikely, unless Killcore had a team of a hundred or more pilots. Still, from her vantage point, it was hard to imagine that they were autonomous vehicles.

Suddenly, one of the Squad members dropped to the ground.

"What happened!?"

One of the others ran to check on him. "No pulse. He's dead!"

Tess knew all the IT-Squad members personally, and suffered each time harm came to one of them. The electrocutions would haunt her forever. However, the fallen man had been one of the original agents when CISS was first formed. She knew him especially well.

"How?"

Before he could answer, the man who'd gone to his aid also collapsed, dead.

Chapter Forty-Two

"Back that up, replay," Tess demanded. "I want to know what's happening."

While the live-action battle continued on a different screen, an analyst manipulated and enhanced the video feeds, adding more light, zooming in.

"Damn it! Those are darts," Tess said. The two fallen IT-Squad members had been victims of deadly darts, fired from the drones.

"Get out of there " the field ops commander yelled to Riley. "It's poison darts—the drones are *shooting darts!*"

Danner and Riley both pulled down face shields and moved against the wall, but a third Squad member, a close friend of the first victim, ran down the tunnel, unloading two machine guns as she went, taking out large swaths of the tactical offensive hummingbird drones.

Suddenly, as quickly as it had begun, the drone supply appeared exhausted, the attack done. Riley and Danner caught up with the woman, who had cleared the final swarm.

"I'm betting that was the last defense," Tess said, although she'd learned that the only thing predictable about Killcore was his *un*predictableness.

Linda handed Tess another phone. "Treasury Secretary."

Tess shook her head and resumed her conversation with the Cyber City tech. "Is the money he's using real?"

"Is *any* money real anymore?" the tech replied.

"That's not what I mean," she said impatiently. "Is he moving assets from somewhere to do this?"

The analyst realized her concern. The stock markets could just be the tip of the iceberg. If he was moving these hundreds of billions of dollars around from somewhere, then it could cause panic in the money markets, even an economic collapse. "I don't know," he answered breathlessly. "We're trying to trace it right now."

Two women from the other side of Mission Control stood up. One of them was working a tablet computer, which she used to insert her data onto another large monitor on the wall.

"Switch to display fourteen," Tess said. "Do an overlay and merge the data, now."

"We've just received this from upstairs," the woman said, motioning to the large monitor. "On the source of the funds . . . it appears they are legitimate dollars, and the intent is to cause a complete breakdown in confidence for the banking system." The woman hesitated, looking back at her tablet. "It's already working."

"*What?*" Tess asked, realizing the crisis had just instantly moved beyond what she could handle.

"Runs on banks."

The original tech on the phone from third floor's Cyber City interjected, "There appears to be massive withdrawals being made online. People are moving money to what they believe are safe havens. There are unending lines forming at physical bank locations, with customers withdrawing actual cash."

The images on the screens verified the runs. Tess, Linda, and the other women paused for an instant and looked at one another. "Get me the president," Tess said, handing the phone back to Linda and moving to Secure. She continued to watch Henderson while waiting for the call.

Danner soon came to a heavy, barred door. Riley set up an explosive device. The last three remaining members of their unit jogged back down the tunnel and remotely detonated the charge. The sound of the blast, even through their noise canceling headsets, rocked them. With dust and debris still filling the air, they advanced over chunks of the ceiling that now lay on the floor amongst twists of steel. They passed empty shelves and charging ports.

"That's where the drones were based," Danner said. "See how they must've flown between the bars to make the attack."

They quickly came to a vault-like door. Several dozen additional IT-Squad members arrived at the same time.

"Killcore is on the other side of that door," Danner said to the assembled team. "Let's go destroy the bastard!"

When the president finally came on the line, he was on the warpath.

"Tess, you better have good news for me. I'm here with the secretary of the treasury and the Chairman of the Federal Reserve. Is this Killcore?"

"Yes."

"Tell me you know who this guy is."

"No sir, we're still working on it," she said, looking out the glass wall of Secure, where she could see Henderson up on the Mission Control monitors.

"*Working* on it? Then why the hell are you calling me?"

"I wanted to make sure you were aware of—"

"Of course I'm aware. I'm in the situation room. We're dealing with this mess, attempting to find a way to gain control of the crisis because *you've* been unable to neutralize this threat. The economy, something I've spent *years* making strong, is in shambles. Your guy's managed to unravel all that in a matter of *hours*. Even if you stop him now, this could take a decade to recover from. We're talking trillions of dollars in losses and damages. Killcore's screwing us hard, but you know what scares me even more than all that?"

"No."

"If he can do this to the economy, what else can he do? What is he *really* after? We need to know his end game."

She was about to respond when the president continued.

"Call me back when you've got Killcore in cuffs."

The line went dead.

Tess walked back into Mission Control, a little numb and a little panicked, unaccustomed to the feelings and realizing she'd never felt this powerless.

Chapter Forty-Three

The Astronaut almost never showed his feelings. However, Wen's training in psychological perception allowed her to pick up unspoken emotion in voices, and she could tell he was relieved to hear from her.

"I'd been unable to locate you," he said evenly.

"We had a bit of trouble."

"Killcore?"

"No. Shadow people."

"Details." The Astronaut actually meant every specific detail—number of assailants, types of weapons, tactics, descriptions of anyone involved, dialogue. anything that could contribute to his massive database on the shadow people. Other than keeping Chase and Wen alive, identifying the shadow people was his highest priority. And, really, the two missions were one in the same.

"Later," Wen said, knowing it would bother him. "Right now, I need your help with something more important."

"I can't imagine."

"Are you familiar with Astaria?"

"Of course." The Astronaut had worked with every major intelligence agency in the world, so it was no surprise he knew a top agent like Astaria. "Mossad, expert in languages, manipulation, weapons, martial arts, covert strategic operations—a lot like you, actually. Except she is not to be trusted. I've found her agreeable to collaborate with. Is Astaria working with Killcore? Come to think of it, is *she* Killcore?"

Tess looked up at the Henderson monitors, then back at the technicians. A few glanced at her while the rest continued their desperate quest to track and find Killcore. An assistant met her eyes, then quickly looked away, knowing by Tess's face that it was bad.

"Give me an update on global IT-Squads," she said, mustering determination, acting re-galvanized after the president's blasting. She was going to get this Killcore. She *had* to get him. And if he lived through the arrest, Tess would make sure he had a very small, very uncomfortable prison cell for the rest of his life.

The man sitting nearest to Tess gave her the status on the IT-Squads scattered all over the country, and several more around the globe, ready to pounce, moving on every lead. Up until then, they seemed to have been *just* missing him.

"Somehow, he seems to know when we're coming. Like he's always one step ahead."

"Killcore has a link into us," Tess said quietly, thinking of her internal suspects.

"Do you want me to get on that?" he asked, confused.

"Killcore is one of us."

The analyst looked at her questioningly. "He's CIA?"

"Yes, Killcore is CIA," she repeated calmly.

In Henderson, after blasting through what turned out to be the final door, they discovered a massive subterranean server room.

"It looks like the NSA's Utah facility," Tess said.

"I can't see the end of it," Riley marveled. The darkened room, lit only by the glow of the readout lights on the stacks of servers lined in rows and rows, presented an infinite scene.

"The servers still have power, even though we cut it," Tess said. "Where's it coming from?"

Riley expected to get to the end of the room and find a mirrored wall, which would make the space look like it was bigger than it was. Yet, as he moved cautiously through the room, looking for other doorways or Killcore, all he found were more servers. "How big is this place? He could run the world from here."

Cyber City continued sending updates to Tess via her tablet as the big data rolled across several of the peripheral monitors in Mission Control, but she hardly paid attention to it. The US markets were now closed, but cable news had taken up the crisis. Speculation on bank failures, business bankruptcies, crashing commodities and stocks, was spreading across the globe. And no one knew why. The pundits, so called "experts", and a chorus of talking heads theorized and hypothesized, but everyone was waiting for statements from the White House, the Federal Reserve, or even the Oracle of Omaha, but they didn't appear to be forthcoming. "Surely," one financial show host said, "we'll have a statement soon."

However, the president was waiting until he knew what to say. The last thing he intended to do was inform the world that some madman with the screen name *Killcore* was singlehandedly destroying the world's economy. The administration was contemplating going with one of the wild theories circulating instead—an Enron or Madoff-like scandal, a collapsing currency somewhere in the world, another pandemic, unknown Middle East tensions, an incident in the South China Sea—anything but the truth.

Chapter Forty-Four

Mars knew something bad was about to happen, not because of any psychic ability or other prophetic powers, but because he'd been in prison long enough to understand the field of energy, a kind of vibe, that always held the place. He didn't believe in any new age woo-woo mumbo-jumbo, but he couldn't deny that places like prisons held a certain level of intensity. Perhaps it was the collective desire of hundreds and hundreds of men to regain freedom. He didn't know, and didn't spend much time dwelling on it, yet his business required him to know when any kind of shift was going to occur, if trouble might be coming. Although he had a strong network of both inmates and staff supporting his endeavors, he was not without enemies at Lompoc.

Ever since he'd spoken with Bull earlier and encountered the intrusion into his computer, he'd been puzzled and bothered. He didn't know if his feeling concerned Killcore and Chase, or something more immediate.

It never occurred to him that it could be both.

The person who gave him the most problems inside

Lompoc was an inmate called Rattler. Mars had no idea how Rattler had wound up in a minimum security facility. People with weapons charges and other dangerous histories were not supposed to be sent to places for nonviolent offenders. The rumor was that Rattler had snitched on enough people that he had earned his way out of the higher security facilities. In fact, he had been transferred most recently from the medium security penitentiary that was part of the Lompoc prison complex.

Ever since Rattler had arrived about a year earlier, he had been out to get Mars—would've killed him if he'd had the chance. Mars didn't know exactly *why* Rattler despised him, but suspected the angry con was the kind of guy who liked to be the big man, and at Lompoc, no one would dispute that Mars held that role.

Mars had built his reputation and power not through force, but by doing favors—and knowing that was the gold standard of prison currency, he'd done *a lot* of them. Yet there were people there who didn't like him just because he had something they wanted, whether it was clout, connections, money, power, extra freedoms, whatever. They resented him for it.

Rattler had sought out and found those other discontented inmates who would've liked to have seen unhappy results come to Mars. While they were no match for Mars and his allies, which included a surprisingly large contingent of guards and other staff, Mars knew that one day, Rattler would seize an opportunity and make a move. Mars had been working on a long-term plan to get Rattler transferred, but even with all his friends in prison administration, that was still a bit out of his reach. So he did his best to avoid him, while staying vigilant for any sign of movement by Rattler.

He lay on his metal prison bunk, thinking about Chase, Killcore, and, as usual, Rattler. Something wasn't right. His cellmate, asleep above him, separated only by a few feet of stale air and a three-inch-thick mattress, might have calmed him if they could talk, but in prison, you never woke another inmate. The best way to do time was to sleep—close your eyes, then open them and see how many hours had evaporated.

Mars was edgy. Lompoc was in the middle of the four o'clock count, when all federal inmates in the nation were counted. There would be no way Rattler could get to him during the count, and yet he couldn't shake this nervous feeling.

When the count ended and the inmates were free to move about, he planned to convene a group of his closest confidants in the visitor's room, which convicts were permitted to use on certain evenings to play cards and spend some coin in the vending machines for snacks and sodas. It was the most relaxed time there was in federal prison, and yet it was also wrought with tension, as inmates had more immediate access to one another. During that time, grievances could be addressed, and challenges made and answered. Mars figured this was going to be that kind of evening.

Chapter Forty-Five

Tess called Linda over. "Find Chase, get me in touch with him, and while you're doing that, get me Tom."

"NSA Tom?" Linda asked, referring to the director of the NSA.

"Yes. When you get either of them, patch it back through to Secure."

Linda could tell Tess was stressed, more so than she'd ever seen before. Even if she didn't know all the details, her assistant was bright enough to put it together: Killcore, the president, Chase, NSA Tom—the world might be coming apart at the seams, and Tess was the only one who could hold things together.

But the "Queen of Spies" had, for the first time in her career, lost control of a situation at the worst possible moment.

"Tess, we have **GPR** ready," a tech said, referring to the ground penetrating radar they finally had moved into place. The GPR would effectively allow them to see through the earth into the tunnels. The mapping they had done thus far with their helmet and body cams was quickly combined with the images coming from the GPR. "Screen twelve," the tech added, as one of the larger monitors in Mission Control filled with 3D maps of the facility. "That server room is nearly a thousand feet long, and two hundred feet wide."

There were audible gasps in Mission Control, the seasoned professionals reacting to the sheer scope of Killcore's operation.

"This *has* to be his base," Tess said. "He *must* be down there somewhere."

The map continued to expand from the aerial imaging, filling gaps using artificial intelligence to assemble and extrapolate with the images they had collected over the last hour.

"There are these four rooms," a technician said, highlighting areas connected to the server room by short sections of tunnels. "Any one of these could be housing his command center."

"We've also identified a lower level which housed ventilation, cooling, and power generating facilities," a woman reported.

"Those aren't big enough to keep power going to every server," Tess said.

"We think this chamber here," a woman said, highlighting another large room at the end of the server room that appeared densely packed, "contains batteries, probably enough to hold several days' worth of solar charge from the panels."

"So even though we cut power, there's still plenty of charge?" Tess said.

"Correct, and all other power, such as the tunnel lights and the traps, lost power when we cut. He must have some kind of priority override to protect the servers."

"Same reason the cooling units must have a separate generator," another tech explained.

"Let's get teams in those other rooms," Tess said, knowing they couldn't work on the servers until they'd apprehended Killcore. For the first time in days, she felt the tension ease just a little, believing they might finally have Killcore. "How do we look on the surface?"

Additional monitors switched to the exterior views. Special forces troops had landed, and several square miles of the desert around the facility were under total surveillance. "Killcore's not going to slip out this time without getting apprehended."

Tess watched as their own drones, satellite imaging, and cameras on the troops on the ground swept the area. She looked for any stray speck, any way he could possibly squeeze through.

Linda had been working with the team at the far end of Mission Control, analyzing all the threads of data coming from the tunnel site. "It doesn't look good," she quietly said to Tess.

"What is it?"

"The data we're getting from GPR shows there's nobody there. Those rooms are empty."

"How could that be?"

"He must've already left. Maybe he escaped while we were fighting through all the traps. There was a window of time before we got the surface fully covered."

"How long?"

"Twelve minutes."

He can't slip through again. Tess closed her eyes, unable to believe this was happening. "Get in those rooms!" she shouted. But she knew. Linda was thorough and slow to come to serious conclusions. In fact, Tess couldn't recall a time when Linda had ever made the wrong call. "Show me satellite images. I want to see where he went. How he got out. Killcore is like a damned ghost!"

"That'll take an hour, maybe two, to verify all that. By then—"

"By then, he'll be shutting down the Pentagon," Tess finished, imagining the worst-case scenario.

"These are his servers. This is how he operates. We've at least got that."

"He can operate from anywhere and everywhere," Tess said.

"Look at that." Linda pointed to the screens. "This is an unparalleled operation. Without Henderson, he won't be as strong operating from somewhere else. We need to get these off-line."

"We're going to have to analyze everything there," Tess said. "It'll take too long to disassemble it all and bring it back here. We need to know the forensic fingerprints immediately."

Tess was almost sick with frustration and impatience. She could taste the desperation of it all in her throat. A few minutes later, the IT-Squads confirmed the other rooms were empty.

"He's not unstoppable," she yelled into the room, trying to convince herself as much as her people. "It's just as important to find out how he escaped again, as it is to find out what's on the servers. Only those two answers will show us the way to Killcore."

Chapter Forty-Six

The NSA director was on his way to the White House, and took Tess's call from his car. "Tess, aren't you on your way to the White House?" the director asked.

"No, I'm trying to track this guy. I think he's from the company."

The NSA director knew when Tess said "company," she meant CIA.

"I'm surprised."

"I need you to put someone on it. See if he's using any of the forward systems."

"That's very unlikely," the director said. The forward systems were the NSA's most advanced algorithms, applications, artificial intelligence, and encryption processes. "You know there's only a small number with access."

"That's what I'm counting on," she said. "That we'll be able to narrow it down quickly."

"I have to say *again* that it's highly unlikely Killcore has inside help, and almost impossible that he's one of us. I know every single one of the people who have access, and—"

"Yes, and it's also impossible that someone could hack into the entire US financial system and destroy the economy in a day."

"Of course . . . You're right. I'll go full on this. Let me call my office before I get to White House."

"Thanks, Tom. And please get back to me as soon as you can. If I'm right, then the nightmare has only just begun."

The Boeing seven-forty-seven was at cruising altitude when the pilot suddenly felt his controls were no longer responding. The flight crew went through a series of emergency procedures while radioing air traffic control of their dire situation. Nothing worked.

A sudden drop of five thousand feet ratcheted up the urgency of the situation.

"We're losing altitude!" the co-pilot informed the controller. Screams from the passengers created a surreal backdrop as the jumbo jet plunged twelve thousand feet toward the earth. The pilot, a man with seventeen years' flying, busy trying every technique training and experience had given him, notified the passengers to brace for a crash.

But as they plunged another sixteen thousand feet, they didn't need anyone to tell them they were about to die. Among the three hundred-fourteen passengers, several had already passed out, others had vomited, and still more were injured as they'd panicked and tried to escape their seats.

Air traffic control was helpless and inundated as twenty-eight other large passenger planes were in similar free falls.

Even before the first plane crashed, an urgent relay woke the crisis board, a black monitor normally on a high corner wall of Mission Control. Linda saw that more than one plane had lost control, and immediately put an analyst on it. At the same time, she set up a link-con with the White House, FAA, FBI, NTSB, and several other agencies. There was little doubt that Killcore had found another area to cause mayhem.

Linda buzzed in to Secure as soon as she knew Tess's call had ended. "I still haven't tracked Chase down."

"Keep trying."

"It's gotten worse," Linda said.

"What?" Tess couldn't imagine *how*. "Are planes dropping out of the sky?"

Linda's grim expression removed all sarcastic humor from the scene. "Yes."

Tess stared back at her, speechless.

"Six crashes already. Twenty-three more about to happen."

"Oh, no." Tess went into the cold, detached mode her job often required. There would be time to think about the innocent victims later. Right now, she needed facts, a way to beat back the evil. "When did it start?"

"In the past seventeen minutes."

"Passenger or military?"

"Commercial Flights. More than five thousand total passengers and crews aboard the planes."

As the two women raced back into Mission Control, an analyst announced that all major cellular networks were down.

"The FAA has just grounded all flights," someone shouted.

"Killcore is not in Henderson, and we have no evidence he left there in the past twenty-four hours," another analyst said as Tess passed his station.

She scanned the monitors of the burning plane wreckage, the financial havoc, the bodies being carried out of Henderson, then looked intently at all the CISS personnel working inside Mission Control, wondering if Killcore was among them.

Chapter Forty-Seven

Mars had only been inside the visitor's room for a couple of minutes when the hum of inmates talking fell silent as a siren wailed through the air. A mandatory "return-to-cell" announcement followed. Every inmate understood that failure to comply with the order meant they could be shot by the corrections officers in the towers.

Mars was about to walk briskly back to the cell house when he heard a loud *boom*. Guessing it was an explosion, he ran to the window to try to see the source of the sound. Even before he reached that side of the visitor's room, a second explosion shattered the windows. The force sent him flying back onto the floor, crashing among glass and other debris.

Unsure of what was happening, Mars slid under a table. A dozen other inmates, who hadn't yet evacuated, did the same. A third explosion shook the building. It had been closer than the first two. Mars got back to his feet and jogged to the window again.

Hell if I'm going to stay in here until this building blows.

Looking out the window, framed in jagged glass, he saw billows of smoke pouring out above the fences separating the administrative building from the higher security cellblocks. The razor wire glistened orange in the late afternoon sun, making the barriers seem all the more menacing against the plumes of dark black smoke.

Warning sirens and mandatory return-to-cell announcements were still blaring. A couple of his buddies joined him at the window. "Holy gargoyles, look at that!" one of them said. They watched as the higher security convicts—all violent offenders—scattered through the yards like furious ants. Shots rang out from the towers.

"Damn, those tower guards just took out three guys."

"All the gates are open," Mars said. "How did that happen?"

"Gotta be a big-time planned escape," one of them answered.

"Heard there's a connected mafia guy in there. Maybe it's his day to fly."

Mars believed he knew the one word solution to the puzzle: Killcore.

Some of the inmates behind them were talking loudly. "I ain't going back to my effing cell! They shootin' effin people!"

"I'm just waitin' right here," another said.

"Maybe it's going to full scale riot. Bunch of us be dead."

"While the man's busy with the inside ants, I'm gonna slip out here."

"*Look* out here. *Crazy*, man."

More gunshots. "They gettin' closer."

Mars and his crew huddled around the window, watching and listening to the continuing debate behind them. "You walk out of here, that's five years added to your sentence soon as they catch you."

"Yeah, but they gotta *catch* me. Anyway, my lawyer'll tell them it wasn't safe for me to stay here. Self-preservation ain't no crime."

"Oh *yes* it is. If you escape federal custody, they don't care 'bout the reasons. *Everything* is a crime."

As the inmates argued about whether or not to escape, and Mars's buddies joined the conversation, dozens of dangerous criminals streamed out from the medium security section. Two guard towers were now on fire.

Mars blocked it all out. He was concentrating on Killcore.

He needed to reach Bull.

He had to get to Chase.

Where's my closest phone? Killcore must've done something—hacked into the prison system, opened all the gates . . . this is no accident.

Another explosion rocked the next building.

Killcore isn't doing this to create a headache for the Bureau of Prisons, or the Department of Justice. He's doing it to get to me. He wants me to stop hiding Chase's whereabouts . . .

Killcore's coming for me.

Tess tried unsuccessfully to reach Chase and Wen. She had long ago lost the battle of maintaining his innocence. Law enforcement all over the country and throughout the world were looking for him. As the president had said: "Even if Chase *isn't* Killcore, there's still some connection, and we need to know what it is."

There were now more than forty Killcore investigations

underway, and while they were still coordinating with CISS, Tess was no longer in charge of the overall operation. She had been one of the most powerful women in the world before Killcore set out to do whatever it was he intended. If he succeeded, Tess wouldn't have a career left. But it wouldn't matter, because there wouldn't even be a *country* left.

Not used to being in a subordinate position, Tess had admitted to her deputy that she wanted to personally pull the switch at Killcore's execution. In truth, she'd rather pull the trigger of the gun that killed him, knowing trials were unreliable, and Killcore needed to die.

She checked the crisis board and saw the ninth fully-loaded airliner explode as it slammed into the ground. So far, Killcore had not been able to compromise their satellite coverage, but she suspected he had only allowed it to remain so that they could easily see his destructive power. The country was in full panic mode now, the media frenzied —scared themselves—as mass power and cell phone outages swept the nation, runs on banks increased, and the global stock markets collapsed.

Killcore was personally bringing about Armageddon, and two of the people who had a chance to stop him couldn't be reached, and were erroneously being targeted by law enforcement. At that very moment, they could already have been in custody, while Killcore remained free. She could picture him laughing like a lunatic.

Chapter Forty-Eight

After another tense call with the president, Tess was in her office, gazing at photographs of Taos, New Mexico, the place where she'd rather be; a magical town filled with music and dancing and heartache. She'd taken a moment to calm herself, clear her mind, but it didn't last long. She turned back to the Killcore file. "Who the hell *are* you?"

She was about to head back down to Mission Control when Linda knocked on the door.

"We've got a crisis," Linda said, letting herself in.

Tess was about to respond sarcastically that they were already in the middle of the biggest crisis *ever*, which was why she'd slept in her office last night, when she snapped.

"Calling it a crisis is an *understatement*, seeing how it's the *largest* seismic event of my career. *Dealing* with this madman—"

She saw something in her deputy's eyes, and stopped talking.

"It's gotten much worse."

Tess flashed back, recalling that the president had

hastily ended their call mid-sentence. She'd thought it was because he was tired of her "excuses," but now she feared something even more horrible. "What is it?"

Before Linda could answer, a speaker came to life with a message from Mission Control. "Tess, a helicopter will be here in about three minutes to take you to the White House."

She looked at Linda. "Got it."

"They want you in the situation room," Linda said.

Tess grabbed her laptop and a secure external hard drive, slipping them both into her leather briefcase. "Tell me as we walk."

"Killcore may have some missiles," Linda said breathlessly.

Tess gave her a horrified look.

"We've lost contact with the computer controls of seven nuclear-tipped ICBMs in silos in Wyoming."

"My God," Tess breathed as they got in the elevator. "How long has he had them?"

She checked her smartwatch. "Twenty-three minutes."

"And we're just getting this *now*?"

"Apparently Killcore concealed it with false confirmations or something for the first twelve minutes. And then his cloaking failed, or—"

"We're *sure* it's Killcore?"

"It fits his profile."

"Killcore wants us to know what he's capable of. He wants us scared."

"He's doing a good job," Linda said. "If Killcore launches those missiles, millions dead. And . . . after that . . . it's unimaginable."

"He could send nukes into China or Russia . . . or . . . the United States, start a nuclear war." Tess swallowed hard.

"Or send them to cities inside the United States," she repeated.

The helicopter landed as they exited onto the upper-level parking platform. Tess looked at her deputy as if she might never see her again.

"Find Chase. Tell him this. Give them everything we've got on it."

"Is that wise?" Linda asked. The wind and the roar of the blades caused the two women to yell at each other.

"Of course it's not wise."

"It's classified. Need-to-know only."

"He *needs* to know!" Tess shouted, then turned and jogged to the chopper and climbed in.

Linda stood and watched it lift off, worried the helicopter might explode, wondering why Tess would want someone without clearance to have information that could cause absolute hysteria through the population; a man who, *himself*, was the prime suspect of being the one who was causing so much mayhem.

But she would do what Tess wanted. She had too much respect for her to question her orders or motives.

Ever since Killcore came onto the scene, nothing makes sense anymore.

Linda had been looking for Chase for hours with no luck, but then remembered he had a brother. She quickly tracked down Boone Malone. She told him who she was, and begged him that if he knew of any way he could contact Chase, they needed to talk to him immediately.

"It's an extremely urgent matter."

"It always is with Chase," Boone said, not impressed by her government credentials.

"Life and death," Linda insisted, more than a little frustrated with the response.

"Chase's life?"

"His, and millions of others."

Boone was silent for a moment. "He's a hard guy to reach, but I'll give it a shot."

Boone had been polite, almost charming, a trait he shared with his younger brother, but also noncommittal and brief. She wondered if he'd do anything at all.

However, within twenty minutes, Chase called the number Linda had given Boone. Linda would never know it, but Boone had a way to reach the Astronaut through an encrypted and coded website. The Astronaut had actually been on the phone with Chase when the message came in.

"Chase, thank you for calling. This is Linda Moore. I'm Tess's deputy."

"I'm calling for Tess. I'm only talking *to* Tess," Chase said in a firm, yet polite tone.

"Tess is at the White House, in the situation room, and can't be reached," she began. "Killcore struck again, and this time, he has control of nuclear tipped ICBMs."

Linda could hear a gasp in the background and assumed it must've been Wen hearing the news on speaker phone. Chase remained silent as she continued.

"Tess wanted you to have this information." Linda proceeded to read off the specifics of the missiles, their location range, time estimates of potential destinations—everything. "Chase, I have to inform you that everything I just told you is *highly* classified. Only the people inside the White House situation room, and possibly a dozen others, are privy to this information. I'm sure you can appreciate the catastrophic results not just within the United States, with the population panicking, but around the world, and the heightened dangers that would happen if other countries knew a terrorist might be about to target them with American nuclear-loaded missiles." Linda tried to keep a stable gait to her voice, but a slight tremble in it quickly became obvious.

"I understand," Chase said evenly. "Nothing will come from me, you can be assured of that. However, I have to ask—what does Tess think *I* can do?"

"I don't know," she replied. "I think it was wrong to convey this information to you, given all the circumstances, but it was the last thing she asked as she was boarding a helicopter for the White House, and you know Tess. If she wanted you to have this information, then she must believe you can do some good with it. Can you?" Linda was surprised at her own question, and the slip from professionalism.

"We'll do everything we can," he said.

"Is there a way I can reach you directly?" Linda asked.

"No," Chase said. "But I'll check back."

After the call, Chase turned to Wen. "Killcore just changed the rules. I don't think he wants to take over the world . . . I think he means to destroy it."

Chapter Forty-Nine

The Lompoc Federal Prison Complex had taken on the jagged, smoky look of a war zone. Sirens, explosions, gunfire, and shouting only added to the chaotic scene.

"Mars, are you coming with us?" one of his buddies asked.

Tipping at almost six-foot-four-inches tall, the tan, well-built, soft spoken con hadn't been paying attention to their debate while trying to decide on a course of action for himself. Answering their question with more questions wouldn't help. Instead, Mars told them the truth.

"I'm thinking."

"We should blow this pop stand," another said, encouraging their defacto leader.

Why would Killcore be ravaging the prison around me? What does this get him? Mars wondered. *Obviously I'm not going to be able to get to a computer during a full-scale riot and lockdown.*

One of his closest friends hit his shoulder, as if trying to pull him back into the volatile situation. "Man, you gotta decide quick."

This riot potentially knocks me out of assisting Chase with decoying for several days. Impressive that Killcore would go to this much trouble, and amazing that he could actually pull all this off from some remote location.

"Our cell house is on fire!" an inmate from the other group shouted.

Mars glanced out the window again. Several more buildings were burning. At least seven inmates had been shot.

There'll be no way to help Chase unless I leave Lompoc.

It was a heart-rending decision, because if he stayed in prison, Chase would likely die, but if he left and continued to help him, Mars would either get five more years added to his sentence, or have to spend the rest of his life running.

Chase is spending his life running, but that's different in a lot of ways. Although, at the moment, I can't think of any . . .

"Yeah, I'll go," Mars finally said.

One of the guys looked surprised. "Really?"

The building they were in erupted in flames. The gunshots sounded closer. Nearby, inmates' screams could be heard as correctional officers gunned them down. A smoky haze enveloped the two joined prisons.

"We gotta go!" one of his buddies yelled, as the last of the other inmates bolted out the doors.

I wish I could get to the paint shop. His best computer and phone were there, but that wasn't going to be possible. It was on the other side of the complex. He had another stashed near a laundry room in the cell block building—impossible to reach. One, though, in the back of the chow hall, *might* be attainable.

Mars did a mental calculation. Could they get there? It would be the last place his fellow inmates would want to go.

"We need a plan," Mars said.

"Screw that, let's just boogie."

Mars needed to try to get to the kitchen. No escape was going to be worthwhile if he didn't have a phone. He looked at the rag-tag crew of inmates around him: a forger named Carpenter, a bank robber called Bakersfield, and Tucson, who never would say *what* he'd been convicted of. They were a pretty tight crew he trusted enough in prison, but during an escape, out in the real world, on the loose, was definitely another issue.

"I've got something in the chow hall," he said. All three of them knew what he meant, and nodded, each silently agreeing that escaping with a phone gave them far better chances.

"Okay," Tucson said. Another look out the broken window. Several correctional officers had been caught and were being beaten. The number of dead inmates had multiplied.

"Maybe we shouldn't leave the safety of the visitors' room," Carpenter said.

"Need I remind you that the commissary backs up to the visitor's room?" Tucson said. "I'm assuming a hundred inmates are about to raid and loot the place."

Carpenter nodded. "After you."

The four inmates jogged out the back door and ran low toward the chow hall. Relieved to make it, their mood was shattered as soon as they discovered another group of inmates had already begun to entrench themselves inside, bracing for a standoff with plenty of food. The cons were filling large containers with water, knowing the authorities would eventually cut it off in an effort to regain control.

Mars needed to get through them to a supply room to retrieve his phone. Normally this wouldn't have been a problem. *Normally* the inmates would've been happy to do a favor for Mars. However, nothing was normal about this day. Normal was blown to shreds with the first explosion.

And the man leading the chow hall group was Rattler.

"Hey, look what sludge just slid into the kitchen," Rattler sneered.

Mars groaned inwardly. This was the last thing he needed. Almost any other inmate could be reasoned with, or bought, but Rattler had a screw loose, and wouldn't listen. He had a dozen men, Mars only had three, and already he didn't like the odds.

Then he saw that one of Rattler's men had a gun.

Chapter Fifty

"We have a Launch Facilities Down," the director of national intelligence said as Tess and a dozen other top officials huddled inside the situation room at the White House. "Someone has control of a squadron of nuclear-tipped intercontinental ballistic missiles."

"Where?" Tess asked.

"Wyoming."

"Seven?"

"That was the initial report, we now believe there are twenty-two missiles that have been compromised."

"We're talking about enough firepower to remove more than *forty million* American citizens from the face of the earth. Or, the ability to systematically ignite World War III, should they choose a preemptive launch."

"How did this happen?" someone asked, as the president sat silent, absorbing the data for a second time. His initial brief had taken place only ten minutes earlier.

"The facility lost computer communications between its human controllers fifty-two minutes ago."

"Aren't there additional safeguards to protect against an unauthorized launch?" Tess asked.

He nodded. "Yes, but . . . "

"Everything has been compromised," the president finished. "Those protocols that keep missiles on launch-ready alert have priority, rather than to *prevent* accidental launch."

Tess shook her head, closing her eyes in dismay.

"The underground launch centers that control the ICBMs no longer have the ability to detect and cancel an unauthorized launch attempt," the presenter continued.

"Tess, this must be Killcore," the president said.

She nodded, positive it could be no one else.

"The initial occurrence came during a blackout. Clearly, Killcore, or *whoever*, hacked into the ICBMs' radio receivers."

"How is that even possible?" someone else asked.

"Apparently they tuned into a backup launch-control aircraft, but we're still investigating."

"It's also possible they physically spliced into cabling that connects the missiles to launch control."

"Where?"

"Hard to say. There are thousands of miles of cable. We're trying to find it."

"That's not the most pressing thing at the moment," a general said.

"If we know how he got in, it would help our search, " Tess started. "We need every data point we can get. What about the communications and computer networks used to control the missiles?"

"They are obviously firewalled against computer-attack. We successfully defend against thousands of hostile intrusion attempts every day."

"Then how did he do it?"

"He found a weakness."

"Obviously."

"Aren't the missiles set to land in the middle of the ocean in the event of an accidental launch?" someone asked.

"Yes, but that doesn't apply if they're hard targeted."

"And the terrorist can do that?"

"Targeting is not an obstacle. It only takes a few keystrokes."

"How soon can he launch?" the same man asked.

The presenter looked at the president, who looked at Tess before answering. "Now. Killcore could launch one, ten, or all twenty-two ICBMs at any second."

"The rockets have a wait period of approximately thirty minutes in which crews could cancel an illicit command," the presenter explained. "However, in this case, our personnel are unable to reach the computer, meaning the rockets have already accepted the launch instructions."

"Can't we stop them?"

"These missiles can cross the globe in thirty minutes, traveling at nearly four miles a second."

"But there's a self-destruct mechanism, *right*?"

"No. Once gone, the rockets cannot be recalled or destroyed."

The room fell silent.

"Mr. Mars," Rattler said, a demented smile on his face. "You don't have your guards here to protect you, do you?"

"Seems they're all busy with a riot."

"Yeah, don't you just *hate* when that happens?"

"Not necessarily."

"Neither do I." Rattler looked as if he could have slithered out of some backwoods swamp. His shaggy, greasy hair and spiderweb neck tattoo screamed redneck biker. "Tell me, Mr. Mars, do you get a paycheck from the Department of Justice for your work here at the prison?"

"Listen Rattler, there's enough trouble going down today. Let's not add to it. How about we push our differences to another day?"

"Oh, I guess you're a little nervous without having your guards in here." Several of Rattler's men moved in closer around Mars and his three buddies. "Funny, just before you walked in, I was saying to the boys that it seemed awfully warm in here, and then you turned up, and I knew what made it hotter. Old Mr. Mars. You're so hot you change the temperature in the room."

Mars, annoyed by Rattler's inference, just stared back at him. Being "hot" in prison meant you were cooperating with the warden's administration, federal authorities, or otherwise engaging in something that harmed your fellow inmates. This wasn't a game Mars normally would have bothered playing, but he knew for certain that Rattler was *actually* a snitch, and he couldn't let it go, not even in the current circumstances. There was a code in prison. Even with the echo of gunfire and the smoke drifting through the air outside, the tension inside quickly reached the boiling point.

Mars clenched his jaw, staring hard at Rattler, then stepped toward him. "You want to talk about hot, Rattler? I don't know how *you* look in the mirror without it steaming up, because I've never known a bigger snitch than you."

Rattler's face turned hateful as he took a swing.

Mars, no great fighter, knew the punch was coming and

ducked away. He also knew that in less than a minute, there'd be three or four of them fighting, and if Rattler started to lose, the man with the gun would use it.

Mars came out of the duck and roll close enough to Bakersfield to tell him, under his breath, to move on the gun. He was lucky Bakersfield was one of the men with him, because Bakersfield, who'd done two tours in Afghanistan, understood threats and weapons, but most of all was crazy-brave. In a final bit of irony, it had been a snitch who'd sent Bakersfield to federal lock-up. Still, they were vastly outnumbered, and the prison was in a full-scale riot.

Rattler came at Mars with murder in his eyes.

Chapter Fifty-One

Chase and Wen sat in a car, trying to make sense of the conflicting reports they were receiving.

"Astaria said Killcore was at Westpark Plaza in Chicago," Chase said. "Could she be wrong?"

"With Killcore, anything is possible," Wen said while responding to a text from Bull. "Bull's showing him somewhere on the east coast."

"Where?"

"She's trying to isolate it now."

"Oh good, that narrows it down. The east coast is something like two thousand miles long."

"And the Astronaut says CISS and the FBI both believe they have Killcore in a massive Nevada facility where most of his hacks and other operations have been coming from."

"Plus we've got Wyoming . . . "

"The Astronaut is also working a major lead of Killcore in Texas."

"How could he be in all those places at once?"

"What if he's more than one person?"

"You mean a group? Like The Cause?"

She nodded hesitantly.

"Could Killcore be a branch of WOLF?" she asked, taking up from their earlier conversation on the subject.

"I hope not."

"I know, but what if they are?"

"Why target you?"

"Maybe it was an accident. Maybe because of our affiliation with The Cause, it just looked like I was Killcore."

"Let's go to Westpark Plaza before we speculate anymore," Wen said. "At least we can personally cross that one off the list."

"Sounds fun," Chase said, pulling out into traffic.

"And I would not bet against Astaria."

"Okay, but the next question after 'Where is Killcore?' is where's Astaria?"

The men shuffled around until Mars landed a hard blow on Rattler's temple. The big man stumbled and almost fell before recovering and coming back with a shank. The homemade knives were common in prison, even though getting caught with one would get an inmate a new weapons charge and more time.

"You're gonna die, Mars!" Rattler charged at Mars, waving and jabbing the blade.

"I'm not your enemy," Mars tried.

"You're sure as hell not my friend!"

Mars, not an experienced fighter, and only having a second to anticipate where Rattler would thrust his shank, moved the wrong way. Although he avoided taking the knife in his gut, he caught the worst of it, taking a deep gash across his forearm and bicep.

"Damn you!" Mars yelled, grabbing his bleeding arm as he stumbled away.

A fight had erupted between his guys and three of Rattler's men.

Rattler pursued, waving his knife wildly. With a quick glance, Mars could see that Bakersfield was making a move for the gun. Mars tripped into a stack of cafeteria chairs, grabbed one up with his good arm, and launched it at Rattler. The chair connected, but hardly slowed the raging redneck.

Bakersfield engaged two other men closest to the guy with the gun, attempting to conceal his intent to go for the weapon. With Bakersfield's superior military training, he quickly overpowered an inmate with a sizable beer belly who'd only been in prison a few months. Next up was a young, athletic man who'd clearly had some training somewhere. He took a little more work, but Bakersfield was able to keep him on the defensive while moving their skirmish closer to the man with the gun. His plan was to stay in the fight until he could get the pistol.

Mars got another chair into Rattler's chest, and sent a third flying past his head. One of the windows to the chow hall suddenly shattered as the outside chaos bled into their space. The screams and gunfire from the prison yard invaded the building, and Mars knew guards and other inmates would soon follow.

A long table now separated him from Rattler, but the snake was coming over its top.

I have to get out of here. If Killcore's going to so much trouble to stop me from helping Chase, then Chase is in more danger than he real-

izes. I'd rather spend five more years in prison than five years free in a world without Chase.

Rattler caught Mars, slamming him onto the table. Mars felt Rattler's large hands lock around his neck. He clawed at his hands, trying to force Rattler to release the death grip he had on him.

As he struggled, Mars feared there would be no escape. The big man had him. There was little air left. Mars kicked wildly and tugged at Rattler's angry hands, but had no strength remaining.

Chapter Fifty-Two

"The Astronaut just sent me a link," Wen said as Chase pulled into the tight alley that lead to a parking area behind Killcore's building.

"Of what?"

"I'm looking inside the building," Wen said.

"What building? *This* building?" He pointed outside the car.

"Yes. I don't know how the Astronaut got the cameras on, and how Astaria knew Killcore would be here, but it's always nice to have such talented friends."

Inside the room on Wen's screen, a man hurriedly gathered papers and three laptops, shoving them into a bag.

"That's our man," Chase said, checking the streaming images against the stills on his computer tablet that Tess had sent earlier.

"Looks like I owe Astaria big on this one."

"Juicy kisses?" Chase asked with a smile amidst the world falling apart around them.

"Do I hear a hint of jealousy? Anyway, we don't have

him yet," Wen cautioned. "Looks like he knows we're coming." She motioned to several visible exterior cameras.

"Seems we're not the only ones watching," Chase said. They both observed the man checking a bank of monitors that displayed their arrival, among other scenes.

"The same system the Astronaut tapped into."

The now panicking man rushed out of the office. Chase pulled into an empty parking space. "Did we lose him?"

"Not yet." Wen switched to a hallway camera. "He's heading down the back stairs."

Wen bolted from the car, gun in hand. Chase scanned the cars in the lot, checking for any clues to Killcore's presence, while Wen ran to the back entrance. She waited at the door, counting, anticipating his movements as soon as he entered the stairwell. Chase kept checking the computer, but there were apparently no cameras in the stairs.

Wen looked back at the car, gave Chase a look, and mouthed, "*What's taking so long?*"

He checked the computer again. Nothing. "Could he have gotten off on another floor?" Chase yelled.

Wen shrugged, then pointed to her ear. Chase clicked on the communicators. "Sorry, I forgot."

She continued counting—it had already taken twenty seconds longer than it should have—as Chase's voice came through her in-ear receiver.

"I don't see him on any of the cameras."

"He couldn't just vanish," she said, in spite of knowing that Killcore had a history of doing just that.

Wen pulled out a device from her pack and quickly punched in a code, which provided her with the keycode needed to bypass the entry's security system. As the door opened, she prepared to fire, but didn't expect him to be there. She dropped a prop-mark in the doorjamb, which would allow Chase to get through if necessary, then inched inside. She heard a door shut above her, guessing it was two floors up.

She abandoned caution and burst out of the stairwell on the third floor. "Where is he?" she asked in a quiet voice.

"Still nothing."

"Did he get out the front?"

"Negative."

"Where *is* he?"

She ran back to the stairs and headed up another flight.

"I've got him," Chase said. "Fourth floor. But I can't quite count the doors from the angle of the camera. I think it's going to be the third room on the left."

Wen crept out into the hall.

"He's in some kind of a breakroom—a refrigerator, table cluttered with Styrofoam cups and to-go containers," Chase said into her ear. "Looks like somebody just finished a meal and forgot to clean up."

Wen took one glance behind her, then advanced to the door. "What's he doing in there?" she whispered softly.

"Can't see him. He might be behind the door."

She slammed the door open fast and wide, using all her strength to shove it hard, hoping to trap him between the wall and door.

The man moaned, dropped his bag, and tried to push back. By then she was on the other side and quickly had him pinned against the wall. He wriggled free, ending up on his knees, and pulled at her legs. Wen threw the door shut so he couldn't escape.

He spun around and dove toward the other end of the room, rolled, and pulled a gun. Chase could see them both on camera again. His gun was pointed at Wen, hers pointed at him.

"You're not going to win this fight," she said.

Chase abandoned the computer and his station in the car, no longer worried Killcore could slip out of the building, instead wanting to help Wen. "I'm coming," Chase said to Wen as he took the stairs two at a time.

"You've already lost the fight," the man said to Wen. Chase listened through his earpiece.

"You're wrong about that," Wen replied. "I could kill you now before you even think about pulling that trigger. But I don't want you dead."

"Really? Why not?"

"You need to stop, and then we want to know how you've done everything."

He laughed hard. "Just who do you think I am?"

"Killcore."

He laughed even harder. "You fool. *I'm* not Killcore."

"I don't believe you."

"Like I said, you're a fool."

"If you're not Killcore, who are you?" Chase demanded, bursting into the room, his gun aimed at the man.

"None of your business, Chase," the man said, smirking, but keeping his gun and attention on Wen.

"He's Killcore," Chase said to Wen. "He's trying to trick us."

Chapter Fifty-Three

Wen continued to slowly inch closer to the man.

"Where is Killcore?" Wen asked, sounding as if she believed his denial. "Is he in this building?"

Chase still thought the man was Killcore, but as usual, followed Wen's lead.

"You'll never catch Killcore," the man said, so defiantly it was as if he knew they would never leave the building alive.

"You're wrong again," Wen said, still ready to pull the trigger. "We're going to catch him and stop him."

"We're going to find him, stop him, kill him, *and* yell at him," the man mimicked in a chirpy tone, keeping his gun pointed at her head. He didn't give Chase any more than the slightest attention from his peripheral vision, knowing that Wen was the real threat to his survival. "You'll never stop Killcore. Thinking you will just proves you know nothing about Killcore."

"Chase, check the building, the exits, get back on the cameras."

Most people would never have considered leaving their partner in that situation, with a gun pointed at her head, but Chase knew Wen could kill the man five different ways before he even knew she'd moved.

"On it," he said, running back into the hall, not wanting to give Killcore another second to escape.

"I don't have time right now to argue with you about how great your pal is," Wen said. "I want you to put that gun down."

"I'm not putting the gun down. I'm not going anywhere. I'm kind of amused you think I'm such a light-weight threat that you could send your errand boy away."

"Are you going to make me shoot you?"

"*Are you going to make me shoot you?*" the man mimicked again.

"Don't you see the destruction Killcore has done with *your* help?" Wen asked, ignoring his condescension. "If you help us now—"

"What? You'll make sure I don't go to prison?"

"Maybe. Maybe I'll just let you live."

"Listen tough girl, I don't believe you. But it doesn't matter, because I'm not *going* to prison. You don't seem to understand what Killcore's doing."

"Enlighten me."

"The fun's just getting started. You have no idea what's about to happen. Think the last two days were ugly? Worrying about more dams breaking, plane crashes, getting the phones back on." He scoffed. "That's been a picnic."

"We know about the missiles in Wyoming."

She thought it would shock him, yet he seemed unfazed. "You can't stop that, either. Especially because you think it's only Wyoming."

Chase was now running around the perimeter of the building. "No sign of anything," he said in her ear.

"Put the gun down. Help us," Wen said slowly.

"You'll never stop Killcore. Long live Killcore!"

He turned the gun to his temple.

Wen lunged toward him, but she was too late.

He pulled the trigger. She reached him as his body crumpled to the floor.

"Any sign of Killcore?" Wen asked Chase in his earpiece.

"No. I heard a gunshot . . . "

"He's dead," Wen said. "Killed himself."

"Are we sure he's not Killcore?"

"No ID."

"So he could be?"

"No," Wen said, distracted. "He was telling the truth. I'm sure of it."

"Then where is Killcore?"

"Where," Wen replied. "Who."

"Same thing, isn't it?"

"Yes."

"We should call Margot," Chase said. "She runs WOLF. If anyone would know Killcore's connection to The Cause, it would be her."

"If Killcore is a rogue group inside WOLF, she doesn't know about it."

"How can you be so sure?"

"She would have told us. But call her anyway. I have another call to make."

"The Astronaut?"

"Bull."

"So we search the entire east coast?"

"She'll be much closer by now. It takes a hacker to find a hacker."

"You might be underestimating Killcore."

She shook her head. "Killcore may be a lot of things, and the biggest threat the world has ever faced, but at the end of the day, he's basically just a hacker."

"What about the dead man upstairs?" Chase asked as Wen joined him in the parking lot.

"He's still dead. I took lots of pictures, and a finger." She held up a Ziplock bag. "Call Tess. Let her clean it up."

Chapter Fifty-Four

"Dean Johnson is missing," the director of the CIA told Tess when she answered the call in her office. Normally, she would've seen the incident as part of a written daily briefing, that she might or might not have skimmed. Tess usually relied on her subordinates to glean anything important enough to bother her with, or to find data which might apply to an ongoing situation. However, in this case, nothing was normal, and the director of the CIA personally calling her with this news just amplified that fact.

She knew Dean Johnson from many years of working on different situations, and from attending endless meetings where he was part of the background. She immediately clicked a few buttons on her computer and brought up his personnel files. While perusing the information on the screen, she asked the director what they knew.

"Not much. His sister was the one who first noticed he hadn't shown up for their weekly dinner, and hadn't called. She says he *always* shows up or calls. She checked on him at his house, found it empty and everything in order, but he wasn't there—no phone, no car keys. He did not show up for work this morning, with no check-in, and then the police found his car behind a deserted building on the outskirts of Warrenton, Virginia."

"And you believe this is connected to Killcore?"

"I believe this makes it more likely that he *is* Killcore."

"That's quite a leap," Tess said, still trying to put together the pieces of how Dean and Killcore were connected, and why. "Or it makes him *less* likely to be Killcore."

"How so?"

"Killcore could have been done with him, didn't need the loose end, and . . . killed him."

"A deserted car doesn't mean he's dead."

"Doesn't mean he's alive, either."

"It's possible Dean knows we're onto him. Might want us to *think* he's dead."

"Maybe."

"One of the agency's top cybersecurity experts could be the man bringing the world to its knees, and we didn't bring him in?" the director said.

"Would Dean really take nukes and turn them on us?"

"Apparently he has a gambling problem."

"Really? That's a little cliché, don't you think? Sounds like a Killcore set-up."

"It appears to be true."

"Too convenient," Tess said, clicking through a series of data points provided by her analysts, overlaying Killcore's actions with everything known about Dean. "Back to your theory that Dean and Killcore are one and the same, do you think Killcore's a gambler?"

"One could make the argument that that's exactly what he is. He's gambling with the world."

"That's different than having a problem hanging out at casinos with prostitutes," Tess said, reading from the latest file on her screen. "Now we're well into a Movie-of-the-week plot."

"Tess, we're on the brink."

"I know, but Killcore's making us *think* it's Dean, just like he did to Chase."

"The bigger question is, how did Dean slip through the FBI's surveillance?"

"He's a clever man. I had scheduled a meeting with him for first thing in the morning. I spoke with him a few hours ago about Killcore, and he claimed he was all over it."

"I spoke to him, too."

"Did you tell him we were looking for a mole?"

"Of course not, but he seemed to be downplaying the threat, as if he believed we would catch Killcore soon."

"Why would he think that?"

"He didn't know about the nukes, but said there's too much data, too big a digital trail; that the more Killcore did, the closer he would be to getting caught."

"Interesting. Did he mean *him* getting caught, or Killcore?"

"Not sure, but he's right. We're getting close."

"The scary thing is that Killcore knows that, too."

Chase and Wen arranged with Tess's deputy to drop the finger off at the FBI's Federal building in Chicago. While they waited for the results, they walked to a nearby pizza place for a late dinner.

"Any word from Astaria?" Chase asked.

"She still hasn't responded, but here's something from Bull."

Chase read the text on her phone: *He's in NYC.* "Does she mean Killcore?"

Who? Where in the city? Wen texted back.

Killcore. Not sure where, but I'll send you a radius grid. By the time you get there, I'll know an exact address.

"Looks like we're going to New York," Wen said.

"Great, the pizza's better there. Actually . . . uh . . . all flights are grounded."

Chapter Fifty-Five

A loud shot, that Mars barely heard even as it echoed in his ears, dropped Rattler's body on top of him. Mars coughed and gasped for air. At the same time, he felt Rattler's last breath leave before the snake's body went still.

Bakersfield appeared above him a second later. Mars looked at the gun in his hand, then into his friend's eyes. A quick nod between them said all that needed saying.

Flames were now burning in the front of the chow hall.

Bakersfield pulled Rattler off Mars and helped him to his feet.

Several other members of Rattler's posse were down. A couple had fled, but at least seven remained. Bakersfield waved the gun in their direction.

"I'd prefer not to kill you all, but I will."

"We just want to leave," Mars said.

Another fire broke out near one of the windows.

"Dude killed Rattler," one of the men said.

"Rattler tried to strangle me to death," Mars shot back. "For no damned reason."

"Except he hated you," another said.

Mars nodded. "We're leaving." He went slowly against a side wall until he reached a storeroom. Bakersfield, Carpenter, and Tucson moved in the same direction. Bakersfield kept the gun visible, ready. They knew he'd use it.

One of the men grabbed an extinguisher.

"Put it down," Bakersfield said, thinking the man might use it as a weapon.

"I'm putting out the effin fire, man!"

Bakersfield let him go, but kept an eye on him.

A few seconds later, Mars emerged with his phone, and the four of them headed to the back door. Just before they went through, one of Rattler's men yelled, "Hey! This ain't over. You gonna pay for what you did."

A hundred responses flew through Mars's mind, but he just pulled the door closed behind him and looked around at the apocalyptic world they'd just entered.

Tess looked at the monitor inside Mission Control and called the CIA director. "Is he really dead?"

"We haven't confirmed it, but you can see what's left of his face," the director said. "Looks like him to me. You worked with him. Do *you* think it's him?"

"His wallet and CIA ID card?" she asked, confirming what she'd read on the instant report.

"Correct."

"How long until you can confirm?"

"It'll be the morning."

"Do you still think Dean is Killcore?"

"If he is, we just got very lucky."

"Too lucky," Tess said angrily. "Who killed him?"

"I'm sure he was dealing with some unsavory characters."

Tess thought of the dozen names on her list of Killcore suspects—Dean, the astronauts, WOLF, Chase, Dr. Valentine, Snowden, possibly even the shadow people who'd been haunting Chase and Wen—and wondered if the CIA director should be on the list, too. He also had access to everything Dean did. "Let's assume Killcore and Dean are both still alive and can fire those missiles at any moment."

"That seems prudent."

"I have to take this call," Tess said, getting a note from Linda that Chase was waiting on another line. "In the meantime, let's not make the same mistake twice. Arrest Dr. Valentine immediately."

They'd been watching the long-time CIA analyst, who specialized in cybercrime and encryption, since he was one of the few with access to the critical cross-section of information utilized by Killcore.

"You realize if Valentine *isn't* Killcore, then it's entirely possible that Killcore *wants* us to arrest Valentine."

"If Dr. Valentine *isn't* Killcore, then we'll be lucky to arrest him before his butchered body turns up in a field."

Tess stood in Secure and took a deep breath, catching a brief glimpse of her reflection in one of the darkened glass walls. "I look like death warmed over."

"No," Linda said.

Tess smiled, knowing her assistant kindly lied. She pushed a button to connect to Chase. "Your attempts at evading me are somewhat annoying," Tess said.

"We're not so much trying to avoid *you* as we are all the

people out there trying to arrest us. Not to mention the ones that would just prefer to kill us, and then, of course, there's Killcore, who apparently wants *me* blamed for the destruction of the world."

"I don't give a damn about any of that. Killcore *is* trying to destroy the world, or at least modern Western civilization."

"That's why we're out here trying to find him."

"I know," Tess said. "And Killcore's doing a good job at hampering our efforts to locate him. The FAA just grounded all civilian aircraft, and the Pentagon has done the same for all nonessential military flights."

"Why? The media's only speculating about several crashes."

"Killcore can seemingly take any plane out of the sky at will. There's actually twenty-nine down."

Chase looked at Wen. "We've got to get to New York. Are you telling me that's impossible?"

"Nothing is impossible. What's in New York?"

"Our best lead on finding Killcore."

"Tell me where, and I'll have a team there in thirty minutes or less."

"It's not going to work that way. It has to be us."

"Why?"

"Because Killcore wants me," Chase said.

"Killcore is no fool. He's leading you into a trap."

"He doesn't know we're coming."

"Don't kid yourself. Killcore knows *everything*. If you figured out how to get to him, it's only because he *wanted* you to. He's invited you there."

"Of course he has," Chase said. "But we have to go. It's our only chance."

"You're underestimating him."

"Maybe Killcore's underestimating *us*," Wen said. "Do you have a way to get us to New York?"

"Only if you take a couple of IT-Squads with you."

"No deal."

"Then I guess you're not going to New York."

"We'll get there one way or another," Chase said, clicking off and ending the call.

Chapter Fifty-Six

Tess immediately called Chase back. "That was rude," she said when he answered.

"So is unleashing twenty-two nuclear-tipped ICBMs on America."

"Why don't you just tell us where he is? You go in, we'll cover you. You *can't* fool around with this Chase. There's way too much at stake."

Wen signaled Chase to put the phone on mute. "Don't agree with her. We don't need CISS."

"We have to get to New York."

"We can steal a plane. I can fly it. We can get there."

"Nothing's allowed to be flying. The military would shoot us down."

"Tess won't let them."

"Even if that's true, Killcore could take us out of the sky."

"He won't. He could have killed us by now. He wants to see you. Tess is right; he's invited you." Wen looked at him fiercely. She always believed there was a way, that she could do anything, but Killcore was the biggest threat she'd ever faced.

"Tess is our only option," Chase said. "We can shake CISS when we land."

"That won't be easy," Wen said. "She'll be expecting us to try to vanish."

"We'll find a way." He smiled at her. "Someone taught me that there's *always* a way."

Wen knew he was right, but there were a hundred reasons why she didn't want to do this—didn't want to take help from Tess, didn't want to trust her, didn't want the US authorities to get in her way. There were always other options, but in this case, she had to agree with Chase. The only option she could come up with involved Tess. "Okay." She nodded and immediately started thinking of ways to lose the IT-Squads once they landed in New York.

Chase unmuted the call. "You win," he said. "How are we getting to New York?"

"I'll have a plane on a cleared runway at Midway Airport waiting. I'll call you back with the departure time."

"What if Killcore tries to prevent the flight?" Chase asked, imagining with only a few planes in the sky, Killcore wouldn't have much trouble picking theirs out and taking it down.

"It's a special plane. All self-contained, EMP proof, relies on non-networked protocols—he can't touch it."

"It's like you've been *preparing* for Killcore," Chase said suspiciously, worrying that if Killcore was someone in the intelligence community, this could be a short flight.

"We prepare for everything and everyone," Tess said smugly.

"And how did you know to have the plane in Chicago?"

"You two are good, but not *that* good. I'm always right

behind you," she said. "We knew you were there. IT-Squad on the way."

"Convenient."

"And tell Wen I *am* expecting you to try to vanish. And there usually *is* 'always a way,' but not this time."

Linda heard Tess's cowboy boots clicking on the hard floor even before she found her in the hallway between Mission Control and the elevators.

"We just heard from the FBI. They have an ID on the man Chase and Wen killed in Chicago," Linda reported, trying to keep up with Tess.

"Was it Dean?"

"No," she said, surprised her boss had guessed wrong, which seldom happened. "Aaron Costa."

Tess shook her head. She had been expecting to have at least *heard* of the victim. "Who's that?"

"Aaron Costa founded a company called Code-or-Color LLC, a tech firm focusing on identity-theft protection, facial recognition, and hack-proofing computer networks."

"Sounds like a Killcore kind of person."

"Prior to that, he worked for TruNueral and GlobeTec."

"Really?" Tess stopped walking. She certainly knew those names. GlobeTec was a massive multinational controlled by a powerful and influential man simply known as 'The Chairman.' Its subsidiary, TruNueral, had acquired Chase Malone's RAI invention, making him a billionaire.

"And he was an MIT grad."

"How can Chase not know him?" Tess asked as they reached the elevators. "The plot thickens."

"There's more."

Tess stepped into the elevator. "Of course there is."

"Dean's body in Warrenton," Linda began as she followed Tess in and pressed the button for the top floor. "It wasn't Dean's body after all."

Tess nodded, slowly trying to absorb all the new information and piece it into the fractured jigsaw puzzle. "Whose body was it?"

The elevator doors closed.

Chapter Fifty-Seven

Through the encompassing violence, sirens, and smoke, the four inmates made a desperate dash to the trees.

Along the way, they waded through a nightmare: bloody and fallen guards, gangs storming buildings, others fleeing the grounds. There were countless inmates down, some clearly hit by bullets, others having suffered unknown injuries. Mars saw several men who were on his payroll, and he wanted to stop and help, but there wasn't anything he could do. So, he silently wished them well, and kept moving.

On the other side of a low fence was the narrow road that bordered the prison complex, and the first steps to freedom. The Bureau of Prisons counted on the threat of a guaranteed five years of "new time" added to an inmate's sentence if he walked off the minimum-security campus as a deterrent against potential escapes. That, and the gun tower guards with high powered rifles who oversaw the entire complex.

However, today those guards were otherwise occupied. Thanks to Killcore, hell had arrived at Lompoc.

"Are we really going?" Tucson asked at the point of no return.

"I have to," Mars said, thinking of Chase, searching for assassins sent by Killcore.

"We've got to get to the river," Carpenter said, indicating his agreement. The Santa Diaz River, they all knew, was their best chance of getting out of the area undetected.

"The river? It's gonna be dark soon," Tucson said.

"That's the best time to be on the river," Bakersfield assured him.

"We take Ranchos Lompoc Farm Road across, and then down along the river. From there, we can get to Santa Lucia Canyon Road, where it turns into Florida Dale Avenue," Mars said.

"You been planning this break out for a while," Carpenter remarked with a quick laugh.

"Where we can get a car?" Tucson asked, nervous because he didn't know how to swim.

"Maybe."

"That's a long trek," Bakersfield said. "But it's the least risky route."

"We're escaping federal prison in the middle of a full-scale riot," Carpenter said. "I'm not sure we should be worried so much about risk."

"You know we have a limited time window before the state police, National Guard, and who knows who else shows up here," Bakersfield said. "As in a few more *minutes*."

"All right, so what do you propose?" Mars asked.

"Let's get to the parking lot on the other side of the entrance."

"And steal a car?" Tucson asked, astonished. "From the *prison parking lot*? Talk about risk."

"How are we going to get it started?" Carpenter asked.

"I can start any vehicle," Mars said, thinking about some of the happiest times—working for Chase's mother, Daisy, at her auto repair shop.

"I guess it's the fastest way," Tucson said reluctantly. "Then what?"

"We take the car, get a safe distance from here, figure it out from there," Mars said. "Maybe get another car or hop a bus. By then we'll know what's come down on us. We can go our separate ways."

"Look at that," Tucson said, pointing back to the prison. The grounds were in absolute chaos. "End of the world."

They jogged in short bursts, finding any cover they could. Streams of smoke wafted through the air. Two of the towers were still engulfed in flames.

"Look how they got the concrete towers to burn," Carpenter said, sounding almost impressed. "They built makeshift bonfires at the bases, and somehow sent burning projectiles up to the top."

"The odd thing about prison riots," Carpenter began. "They're almost always spontaneous, and yet often appear well-planned. Something about the orderly existence and institutionalization of the convicts, coupled with the precision layouts of the facilities they know so well, gives them an advantage the moment a single crack in the order appears."

"Watch out," Tucson warned, pointing to a mob of far more dangerous and desperate convicts who had broken loose from the inside penitentiary.

"We're in as much danger from them as we are from the guards or other law enforcement," Bakersfield said.

"More," Mars agreed, pointing ahead. "There's a minivan." It sat among the fifteen or so scattered cars in the lot.

"It's not going to win any races, but it does blend in well," Bakersfield said. "You hear that? Choppers! Could be the cops or National Guard. Every second's working against us now."

Mars had the van started even before they were all inside.

"Damn. If I didn't know better, I'd swear you had a set of keys," Tucson said.

Mars ended up being the driver since there was no time to switch seats. He glanced in the rearview mirror as he backed out of the space, and saw the burning turmoil of the prison where he'd spent the last seven years of his life. In an anti-climatic moment, he pulled out of the parking lot, drove past the abandoned entrance post, and onto . . . a street. An open street.

As they rolled onto the street, Mars could feel the five years being added onto his sentence, and knew there was no turning back. The outside world felt strange as a tense silence filled the van, each man reflecting on the dangerous choice they'd made. Mars felt as if he were wandering through a world where he didn't belong, in a place he knew he couldn't stay.

What have I done? he asked himself. *What have I done?*

Chapter Fifty-Eight

Alone in a darkened room, in front of an eighty-inch screen containing millions of moving characters, the Astronaut marveled at a matrix going by at a dizzying speed. Zeros and ones interspersed with characters from every known alphabet. He'd tracked the basis of Killcore's central commands, and now sat in awe.

"It's genius," the Astronaut whispered to the empty space.

The glow strained his eyes. He rubbed them, the fatigue of staring at the endless stream of numbers and characters whisking across the field taking its toll.

They suddenly teared. He was shaken by the rare flare of emotion, but immediately knew the cause. In what he called a splendid catastrophe, the Astronaut felt like a small child as the data edged just beyond his comprehension, as if some higher being was instructing him in all that was possible. The matrix blew his mind, teaching him things so fast that he couldn't really keep up.

"Who *are* you Killcore?"

Earlier in the day, he had become convinced that Killcore must be another astronaut, and had pulled together a complete dossier on what he knew of each of them. He'd even gone to considerable trouble and risked accessing Heaven, the ultra-secret and complex cloud network connecting all US intelligence agencies. They had little more than he did on the other astronauts. From there, he'd narrowed it down to four prime suspects:

Latif Bolat—a Turkish national, and another math savant, like himself, who had mostly worked with the Russians and Chinese, as well as several Middle Eastern agencies. Hong Kong was believed to be his base, but Nash knew he was most likely in New York. He was addicted to manipulating the financial markets.

Wyatt Tennison—possibly the most intelligent of all the astronauts, he favored British intelligence and the French, but made most of his money freelancing for major corporations. He was last known to be in Monaco.

Durga Darshan—based in India. She was smart enough and crazy enough to be Killcore, but it didn't match her normal slate of only taking on jobs that could affect Pakistan or China negatively. Still, Killcore's ultimate objectives remained in question. Durga's mystery and potential involvement fascinated Nash.

Taz Killmer—the irony of his name amused and worried Nash. Taz had recent residences in Mexico, Thailand, Chile, South Africa, and various places in Australia.

The Astronaut urgently needed to find them. He was good at tracking other astronauts, but they were also good at not being found. It would take time to locate Taz and the others, but there was no time. Yet, as he studied the numbers and letters blinding his intelligence, and extracted another quick pattern from the orchestra, he doubted his earlier theory that it could be *an* Astronaut.

"Maybe it is several of you." He squinted at a specific line of numbers. "Perhaps it is someone who is employing one, or many, of you to do this diabolical work."

The complexities of the matrix playing out before him continually stunning his rapid mind.

"Somebody with greater capacity than I did this, but who? Who is Killcore?"

He continued tapping the keyboard every time he isolated a pattern, freezing the frame for a split second to capture a screenshot and send it to a database he'd built earlier. "There is always a pattern of patterns."

He'd told Bull: "You have to go through the data to get there. Just choosing a suspect from a list of astronauts, or other tech geniuses and mathematicians who might be out there, would take too long." There were, frankly, too many possibilities.

Thinking about his last conversation with Bull, he realized there was something in her data. She'd been closing in on Killcore using trajectories of his attack back through the digital abyss. The Astronaut pulled up everything she'd uploaded into their cloud vault.

"There it is!"

He created a grid, extrapolating from the patterns Bull had been able to loop. He relayed across the screen, deep into the data, and overlaid cross grids to produce multilayers.

"A key . . . All this time, a *key!*"

His hunch had been right. The Astronaut was generally driven by the zones and colors of numbers, the silent sounds equations made when they worked. In this case, it was the sounds as numbers clicked into place like tumblers in a lock.

Killcore's complex puzzle made the sphere of numbers contained in our solar system seem inadequate. Solving it had required colors and possibilities from the entire galaxy. The ramifications excited him beyond anything he'd ever known.

Killcore *could* have been Chase Malone. The drip of clues, digital trails, and server originations from Balance Engineering were only part of it. But because it appeared that Killcore had invented something—and not just a singular program, but a considerable *collection* of systems, including a new key number, one that wasn't used for a key equation, but for codes . . .

"A new alphanumeric set of symbols that can unlock anything," the Astronaut said, hardly believing his eyes. "Killcore has changed equations and the security of computers forever. This is how he's getting in. If we can reverse engineer the key, we can stop the nukes, and, maybe just as important, we can find Killcore himself and stop *him*."

His elation was quickly tempered by the realization that with all this, Killcore could easily find and target him, or Bull, or whoever he told about his discovery.

"I must share this information before Killcore discovers me, but who should I put that death sentence on?"

Chapter Fifty-Nine

Chase looked at his phone, frustrated. "I haven't heard from Mars, Tess still hasn't given us a departure time, and we have no idea where Astaria is."

"Take a deep breath. You can't just *will* the phone to ring. We have to wait."

Chase looked at the screen one more time and decided she was right. It rang as he was putting it into his pocket.

"See?" Wen said. "You let go, and it happened."

"Are you kidding? It rang because I *willed* it to ring."

Wen rolled her eyes. "Who is it?"

"Tess."

"The man you killed was probably not Killcore," she said as soon as he tapped to accept her call.

"Anyone I know?"

"He should be. Aaron Costa. Used to work for TruNueral."

"That's the company who bought RAI."

"I know."

"He also went to MIT, but you didn't recognize him?"

"Just because we were in the same circles doesn't mean I *knew* him."

"But he knew you."

"Apparently."

"Does the name Dean Johnson mean anything to you?"

"No, should it?"

"What about Ron Walker?"

"Nope. Who are these people?"

"Dean Johnson may be Killcore. He's Deputy Director of Cyber Security."

"Inside job. CIA?"

"*Technically* no."

"But technically yes?"

"Right."

"And the other guy?"

"He's CIA. Turned up dead. Mutilated body made it hard to ID, but he was carrying Dean's wallet, ID, and CIA credentials."

"Nice."

"Yeah, well."

"So where's Dean Johnson now?"

"We don't know, but we've just learned he had contact with your friend, Costa."

"Not my friend."

"You killed him—or was it Wen?"

"I'm pleading the fifth."

"Save it for the Senate hearings."

"That'll never happen."

"No, it won't," Tess said, putting her feet up on the conference table in Secure, ignoring, for a moment, all the buzz of Mission Control. Her exhaustion was taking a toll. She checked the time, realizing it was well past dark in both

DC and Chicago, wishing she could sleep. "Dean could be in Chicago."

"Really?" Chase looked at Wen.

"Costa was there to meet someone."

"What about New York?"

"He could be there, too."

"Doesn't the *I* in CIA stand for intelligence?"

"Hey, save your judgement for your own life. Want to tell me why you were meeting with Astaria?"

Chase might have been surprised that Tess knew Astaria, but Wen wasn't. Astaria was a legend.

"Why does it matter?" Wen asked.

"*Everything* matters right now!" Tess snapped. "Killcore has twenty-two nuclear missiles under his control, he's taken control of the airspace over the entire country, obliterated the financial markets and banks, *and* he's taking cell phones up and down just for fun. Wen, you should know better. Astaria isn't here by accident. Could she be working for Killcore, or someone else, trying to cover up Dean or other moles? Did she and Dean set you and Chase up to kill Costa or help him escape?"

"I don't know," Wen replied irritably. "Do *you* know?"

"I need to know everything."

"Shadow people ambushed us," Chase said. "Astaria showed up out of nowhere and saved us."

"And gave you the lead to Costa?"

"Yeah," Chase said. "But she told us it was where Killcore might be."

A flash came across Tess's screen in Secure. "We just received intelligence confirming that Killcore might be in New York."

"Great, when do we leave?" Chase asked, worried that Tess would no longer need to send them.

"Killcore's fooled us before. In fact, we've been positive we had him on five separate occasions, and our intelligence was wrong. Every. Single. Time."

"They could be right this time."

"Are you willing to bet forty million lives on that?"

"We have to."

"Why?"

"Because that's all we've got."

"I'll have a plane at Midway at three AM, Central time."

"That might be too late," Wen said.

"It's as soon as we can be there."

"What do we do in the meantime?" Chase asked.

"Killcore wants you in New York, which means he might still be in Chicago. Find him, or Dean Johnson."

"And if they're one and the same?"

"Then you'll probably never make it to New York."

Chapter Sixty

Bull appreciated why Chase had sent her to a remote cabin in the woods alone, and although she was definitely a loner, she still preferred to work from densely populated urban areas where she could get lost in a sea of humanity and there were plenty of choices for take-out. She constantly felt out-of-place, lost, alone, but with a keyboard under her hands and a monitor glowing in front of her, she was invincible.

The Astronaut and Bull had been communicating on and off for several hours via voice-activated screen chat.

Bull smiled as the Astronaut's words came across one of her monitors. *"I'm tracking Killcore right now."*

"I know," Bull said, her words typing themselves into his message box. "Have you broken through the layers?"

"Yes, I'm into the subterranean." Their words in hacking lingo might have confused those not accustomed to the way data stacked on the web.

"I've been on him for almost ninety minutes."

"Why didn't you report it?"

"I'm chasing a ghost," she said. "He split."

"He split? How many?"

"First four, then six, now fourteen."

"Do you see me?"

"No."

"Wait, I'll send you a marker."

"Nothing."

"Coordinates."

She read him a long series of more than eighty numbers.

"I'm not there."

"Then which one is following the real Killcore?"

"Check the cloaking."

She gave him the results of her review.

"We both may have him. He must be using some kind of delay, record, magnification set-up."

"But is that possible?" she asked. "So many?"

"I've done it myself."

"You did? That's incredible, how did you do it?"

"I'm the Astronaut."

"No, really. How?"

"It's complicated."

"I sure hope so."

"I mean I'll tell you later when we have more time. Right now, I've got to keep after this before the seam closes."

"How close are you?"

"I don't know yet. You know how these things are. I could be at the final veil, or just going down another rabbit hole."

"I'm still in the layers."

"Yes, but you can see him, which means you are able to triangulate the other side."

"Okay, I get it. See what you think of this." Bull typed on two keyboards simultaneously, putting in commands, copying and pasting long scripts of code from pre-positioned commands custom created long ago in her arsenal of nuanced seek-and-destroy alphanumeric weapons.

The Astronaut shot back an occasional eighty-eight. Each one made her smile, as she knew it was shorthand for him being impressed with her work.

For the next twenty minutes, the two of them concentrated with little exchange as they played a silent and dangerous cyber game of cat and mouse, hoping that the mouse was not aware of their presence. However, they both feared Killcore was aware of everything.

Soon their false and fragile hope completely fell apart.

"I think we've got him," Bull said, wishing the keyed letters on the screen could convey the excitement in her voice. Yet, at the same time, something told her it'd been too easy. She'd spent too much time chasing treasure, thieves, and secrets across the internet to believe somebody as powerful and talented as Killcore could fall so easily. Just as that realization came to her, and even before it sank in, the Astronaut's words, racing across the screen, confirmed her fear. In the letters of the Astronaut's message, she could almost hear Killcore laughing.

"It's a trap! It's a trap! He's coming after you!"

"I can handle it," she fired back, not really believing her own words, but safe in the knowledge that she was a million miles from anywhere, isolated in a secret location, protected by layers of servers and routers and reroutes and criss-crossing circuits he could never physically penetrate. "I've got him. I'll have his true IP address and actual location any second!"

"Bull, you're one of the best hackers I've ever seen, but Killcore is a monster. A god compared to what you can do. Shut down now and get out of there!"

Chapter Sixty-One

Franco looked into his screen and read the update from Killcore.

"It has begun," he whispered.

After reading the last line, he smiled.

"So, Chase Malone is in Chicago? I wonder if he knows how close he has come? No matter, he'll soon understand."

After trying unsuccessfully to reach Costa, who was also in Chicago, he had grown increasingly worried, but hearing from Killcore put his mind at ease.

"'Nights dark beyond darkness and the days more gray each one than what had gone before. Like the onset of some cold glaucoma dimming away the world,'" he said out loud, in a foreboding tone, quoting from the opening paragraph of *The Road* by Cormac McCarthy. He wanted so badly to reply to Killcore with those words, but he knew it wouldn't be appreciated.

Wen checked her ammo and kept her pack close. The entire city of Chicago and, as far as they knew, the world, had gone completely dark minutes after their call with Tess. That was more than three hours ago. The city had quickly descended into a dystopian hell.

They both had the lights on their cell phones, which was about all they were good for, with cell service now completely out. Wen also had a high-powered LED headband, but she kept it off. They weren't looking to attract any attention. All they really wanted to do was get to the airport, but there was a lot of trouble between here and there.

"It seems quieter," Chase said in a hushed tone as they walked softly down what had once been a street of small businesses—a deli, electronics shop, clothing store, a discount shoe store, bakery, and other assorted establishments. Now all that remained were smashed windows, doors, and remnants of strewn inventory. "The evidence of a looting block party," Chase said, shining his light down as he moved, careful to avoid clanking over the security grates laying in the streets.

Wen knew that quiet didn't always mean safety. There were many threats to consider. The shadow people were clearly not going to let a massive power failure and civil unrest slow their pursuit of them. However, the more urgent concern was the marauding gangs, looking for easy robbery targets, or just the thrill of attacking. Plus, the greatest threat, Killcore, who had seemingly sent Chicago into ruin in still another attempt to get at Chase. They'd already lost their rental vehicle as all the streets were blocked by various obstructions.

"I just can't let this go," Chase whispered, staying in the middle of the street so they couldn't be surprised by somebody leaping out of a doorway, "but what if shadow people really do work for Killcore? I mean, we've been treating Killcore and the shadow people as two different enemies, but maybe this is just the final battle."

"You think Killcore was the one looking for us all along, and he got tired of not catching us?" Wen asked, tired of revisiting this idea. "So maybe he did all this, the nukes and everything, to get to us?"

"It's possible."

"I don't think so," Wen said.

"Why not?"

"At the MSS, we study our opponents in the light of every great strategist in history; Sun Tzu, Genghis Khan, Hannibal, Attila the Hun, Rommel, Napoleon, and many others. People are who they are. It's like a fingerprint. They act how they do, and that doesn't change. Even if they try to change, it's within the scope of who they are. Whoever has been sending and directing the shadow people has always acted a certain way."

Chase accidentally kicked a glass bottle, causing it to smash against a curb.

Wen stood still, listening for a moment in an attempt to detect any movement toward them in response to the sound. After a few seconds, she began walking again, continuing her answer. "Killcore acts entirely different."

"What if the shadow people hired Killcore?"

"If that were the case—" Wen began when a Molotov cocktail exploded at their feet. Flames raced up Chase's leg, but he was able to smother them as they ran for cover into a ransacked and ruined corner shop.

Wen glanced out of the shop's mangled door. "There's a gang of at least two dozen coming toward us from across the street."

Chapter Sixty-Two

Everything Bull did was immediately covered and countered by Killcore. "It's like he's reading my mind," she typed in panicked frustration.

As the words appeared across the screen they changed to: *"I like him reading my mind."*

"Oh my God, how did he do that?" she blurted.

"But he could be a woman," Killcore responded.

Wen's words echoed in Bull's head, as if Killcore had heard them, heard that conversation. *How much does he know?* she wondered, and at that same moment, similar words raced across the screen.

"How much does he know? How much does he know? But remember, he could be a she."

"Stop it!"

"How is Killcore doing it?" Killcore wrote. *"He's reading my mind."*

Bull shivered, unsure if any of her words were getting to the Astronaut or if he was seeing any of the stuff coming from Killcore. "Can you see this?" she attempted to ask the Astronaut.

Killcore filled the screen with thousands of number eights, a code only the Astronaut knew.

She desperately tried to figure out a way around him, needing help from the Astronaut. The dual had unnerved her, yet Bull knew that Killcore was likely thousands of miles away and couldn't *physically* hurt her.

The screen lit up. *"Do you feel the danger? Because I can reach you whenever I want."*

Once again, his apparent mindreading freaked her out. *How is Killcore calculating my thoughts so accurately?* Bull absently moved a hand across her head, as if searching for an implant she knew wasn't there. *Could Killcore have gotten to me? Could he have some sort of neural technology?*

"I know everything," Killcore said. *"Even that."*

She'd read a psychology book that belonged to a boyfriend who was taking psych 101 at Penn State. She knew Killcore was playing a game with her. *He couldn't possibly know what I'm thinking. Someone could say that to anyone to induce fear of a hidden secret, the skeleton in the closet nobody should know about.*

"Do you remember the smoke?"

She shivered again and considered powering down the computer. Maybe he didn't know, maybe he did.

"The fire? You do recall the fire, don't you, Bull?"

She thought back in a terrifying flash. The fire . . . it hadn't really been her fault, but if she had been there, it wouldn't have happened. Bull thought of all that smoke, as if it were choking her even now.

She and a fellow hacker had gotten into an oil company's network, linked into the safety system of a major refinery. They'd wanted to shut it down, thinking they were environmental terrorists, but instead had done something that caused a fire.

It had really been Green-led's fault, the guy who had taught her the earliest lessons about hacking. He'd been the aggressive one, showing off, wanting to prove that they could change the world. His words had seemed so important and powerful at the time: *"God gave us all this technology, all these computers, so we could liberate the planet and humanity from the greedy scum that has polluted everything good in the world, and the planet itself."*

Bull had believed him. She'd been absolutely amazed at what they could do with computers, how they could reach around the globe, change things, control things, unhinge things. But the day they'd tried to shut down the refinery, everything had changed in her world instead. The fire had sent her farther away from the normal world, the living world. After, she'd never felt safe again unless she was inside a digital cave, in the dark recesses, the colored blinks of zeros and ones. She needed to hear the hum of servers, the digital connections.

"Are you there, Bull? Or are you back at the refinery, counting bodies?"

"Leave me alone!" she screamed.

"How many died that day?"

She stared at the screen, terrified now.

"More are going to die today. So many more are going to die."

Chapter Sixty-Three

Tess's assistant, Linda Moore, like her boss, worked long hours. She had barely gotten six hours of sleep, and was already heading back into the office. She had thought about driving, but preferred the subway, especially since it was so early; hardly anyone would be riding. Opening in 1976, the Washington DC Metroline was one of the newer and more modern systems in America, and it made Linda's daily commute much easier, instead of fighting Beltway traffic.

She was reviewing files on her tablet when the lights went out and the train slammed to a halt. Linda, like the few other passengers, at first assumed it was some kind of maintenance issue. There was no cell coverage, and no announcements, so all they could do was wait. Several passengers used the lights on their phones to make sure everyone was okay. Someone helped an older man who'd fallen into the aisle.

After a minute or so, Linda began to get nervous. She couldn't help but think of what she knew from working at

CISS. Linda wondered if Killcore had shut down all the subways.

She moved forward. The cars were nearly empty since she was commuting against traffic—heading out to the suburbs where CISS headquarters was the last stop on the orange line. She peered out between the cars to see if anything was blocking the train.

A man grabbed her roughly, pushing her into the metal end of the car. She felt a gun pressing hard into her ribs.

"If you scream, Linda Moore, I will kill you."

The panic of being attacked gave way to the sheer terror that he knew her name, that he'd been waiting for her.

"Then I will kill your boss, Tess Federgreen."

Wen wasted no time firing her MP7 above their heads. But instead of scaring them off, the move seemed to embolden them.

"A hundred dollars to whoever gets me that gun!" the apparent leader shouted to his scattering crew as they sought cover behind burnt-out vehicles. "A thousand if you bring me the person who fired it at me!"

The members yelled and hollered. There was almost no light on the street other than what came from the remnants of a distant fire.

"I can just make out seven or eight males—athletic builds, probably late teens, early twenties. The rest of them seem younger," Wen said. "I don't really want to kill a bunch of kids."

"I don't think they want to be friends," Chase said.

Some of the group came out from behind their cover and started moving toward them.

"What do we want to do?" Chase asked.

"I'm not sure. I'm not used to being in the position of being attacked by strange kids who I'd prefer *not* to kill."

"Yeah, kinda takes the fun out of it." Chase wasn't used to Wen not having a plan, but there wasn't much time, particularly after a second Molotov cocktail landed in the shop where they'd taken cover.

They moved to the side without flames. "The three in front have guns," Wen said, pulling out her Glock and shooting one in the leg, then a second one.

"We're in Chicago," Chase said. "They probably *all* have guns!"

Her impressive display of marksmanship stopped them. As her two victims moaned and limped back to the mob, the leader yelled out again. "Dim light, moving targets, in quick succession, without using your fancy machine gun—nice shooting."

"We just want to be left alone!" Wen replied.

"I can't allow that, especially with you shooting up my friends!" he yelled. "Get them!"

The entire gang surged toward them.

"There's more than we thought!" Chase yelled. "There's got to be at least forty!"

Chapter Sixty-Four

"Wh-what, what do you want?" Linda stuttered.

"I want you to tell Tess to stop looking for me. If she doesn't, then, next time, I *will* kill you. And if she doesn't believe me, tell her what you see in the next car."

"What is it?"

"You'll see for yourself. Tell her next time, it will be you. Tell her the time after that, it will be her."

"Who *are* you?"

"You know who I am, Linda. You've been looking for me. *Everybody's* been looking for me." He slammed her head against the cold steel wall. "But I don't want to be found."

Linda felt woozy from the blow. "I'll tell her . . . please . . . don't hurt me."

He pushed her to the ground and kicked her. "Don't forget to look in the next car. You tell her what you saw."

Linda stuttered something again, not knowing what she'd even said. He didn't answer. She realized her eyes had been closed as she lay curled up between the cars. Opening them, she looked tentatively around. He was gone.

She started to cry, but then remembered the next car. Crawling to her feet, ignoring the pain in her head and side, she stumbled to the door. Just then, the lights came on, and the train began moving again.

The door slid open and she screamed. Four people lay on the ground, twisted in a pool of blood. Their throats had been cut.

Her loud, terror-filled screams drew passengers from her car. As they took in the scene, she scanned in every direction, looking for the man she knew was Killcore, but he was nowhere to be seen. When she caught her own reflection in the window, it startled her. She didn't recognize herself, but it wasn't because of the tear-stained, agonized face she saw looking back at her.

It was because he had cut all her hair off.

"Oh God," she breathed, reaching a shaky hand up to her head. It seemed impossible, but somehow, while he'd been talking to her, while he'd slammed her head around, while he'd kicked her on the floor, he had cut her hair. "Why?" she cried out loud, sobbing again, unsure how a monster could kill those other people, and only cut her hair off.

He wanted me to be the messenger. He wanted Tess to understand he would come for her. But he'd already hacked into CISS, and if he knew how to find me, surely he must know Tess isn't going to stop. Even if he had killed me, Tess would not stop.

Linda turned away and somehow made it back to her car, collapsing into a seat. Her fear and bewilderment turned to anger.

Tess will work even harder after this. She'll find him. Tess won't rest until she finds him. He must know that. So why did he do this? Why did he waste those lives, and risk getting captured, just to send her a message she would never heed?

The questions rumbled through Linda's pounding head. The burning need for an answer made her forget the ache in her ribs, made her numb to everything that had just happened. He'd made a mistake not killing her. She wasn't going to leave Mission Control again until Killcore was in custody, or dead, and she knew Tess would do the same.

Does he really think he can get into Mission Control? A subway is one thing, CISS headquarters is something entirely different.

But then she started making herself crazy.

Maybe that's what he wants. Maybe he wants us all to stay in Mission Control so he can blow the whole building up.

She didn't know what to think, but she knew Tess would. Linda checked her phone. It was working again.

Bull heard it. It wasn't very loud, and she was no secret agent, but it was out of place. She had grown accustomed to the surrounding sounds—or rather, to its silence. This was neither silence, nor anything she'd heard before. In the instant that the sonic awareness traveled from her ear to her brain, it was processed for fight or flight.

She wondered if paranoia had gotten the best of her. If somehow the Killcore sightings on the net and her cloak and dagger conversations with the Astronaut had scared her. But the one thing she could always count on—her intuition and street smarts—were the instincts that had kept her alive. Just barely, but alive nonetheless. Now, that caffeine riddled, nicotine addicted little voice inside her screamed one word:

Run!

Bull's computers and monitors shut down an instant before everything else in the cabin went dark. Knowing this was no coincidence, she dropped to the floor with only a fleeting thought to protect her work, but there wouldn't be time. All she could do was grab what she called "the jigger," a flash drive containing an app that constantly backed up critical data as she went. But whoever might be out there would be able to trace her work and see where she'd been, know what she knew.

The front door erupted in a violent crash of splinters and smoke. Bull rolled twice before slithering into the kitchen. Heavy boot steps storming into the house filled her swirling mind, as if thunder from the heavens had just swallowed the small cabin.

Chapter Sixty-Five

Wen and Chase, crouched behind the store's large metal shelving unit—that might, or might not, stop a bullet—tried to think of another option that didn't involve a crowd of teenagers dying. Chase shined his phone light behind them, looking for a way out as the mob dared to move closer.

"I'm going to have to shoot!" Wen yelled to Chase.

The thugs were close enough to hear her. "You can't kill us all!" the leader shouted to cheers from his gang.

"They must be on drugs or something," Chase said to her, before yelling, "Who in their right minds *willingly* walks into machinegun fire?"

"That's *my* machine gun!" the leader responded. "And what kind of idiot thinks they can win with odds of fifty-to-two?"

"I can shoot at their legs," Wen said, just loud enough for Chase to hear. "Maybe once a dozen of them drop, the rest will scatter."

"We've got no choice," Chase replied. "But those in front with the guns aren't kids. They're adults who are about to kill us, *over a gun*, in the middle of America's third largest city."

Wen aimed for the leader. "I'll shoot him first, and then sweep to their legs."

Chase aimed his pistol at the man next to the leader, who appeared to be wielding a shotgun. "On the count of three. "One, two . . . "

The jigger clutched in her hand, Bull slid the device into the pocket of her tight jeans. She caught a glimpse of the red laser-sights from their weapons crisscrossing the room as she crawled into the bathroom. In all her time spent with Chase and Wen, not much secret agent stuff had rubbed off.

No regrets, she thought, trying to calm her breathing. She asked herself, *What would Wen do?* No answer came.

She crawled into the cabinet under the sink. The light from her smartwatch allowed her to find two catches that let a concealed panel open. Bull had only accidentally noticed the panel while looking for bubble bath—something she indulged in whenever she could, the only pampering she gave herself. But this time there'd been none, and she didn't like to sit in the tub with only water, so, instead, she'd taken a shower. But the trapdoor had intrigued her curious nature, so, after the shower, she'd lifted it up and seen beyond the crude, itchy insulation that it went into the crawlspace beneath the cabin. She hadn't explored it then because it hadn't mattered after she knew where it went, but now it might be the only thing that could save her.

She quickly maneuvered her lithe frame and dropped down beneath the cabin. Replacing the panel would take precious seconds, and she almost decided to skip it, but knew she'd be dead if they found the passage too soon.

Inside the cramped space, with only about two feet of clearance, she suddenly feared she'd made a mistake.

I'm trapped in this tomb.

The uneven dirt floor was filled with pipes wrapped in more insulation, and too much clutter. Bull frantically searched for an exit she wasn't sure existed.

I wish I'd come down here earlier, when it was light.

The dark space was bitter cold.

I wish I'd grabbed my jacket.

The pounding feet above her made it impossible to think straight.

It sounds like an army.

She fought through the maze of pipes, footings, forgotten buckets, and random tools, trying to get to the exterior wall.

I wish Wen was here.

She bumped her head as the space narrowed in the middle to no more than eighteen inches. The thundering footsteps above her told her they were almost done searching the house.

I have to get out!

Trying to estimate, it sounded to Bull as if at least ten people were on top of her, but it could have been fifteen.

It doesn't matter how many, it's a hell of a lot.

She finally reached the edge and quickly found a foundation vent big enough to squeeze through. Looking out, she was horrified to already see flashlight beams cutting through the darkness. There were enough lights outside that she could see the surrounding forest.

How long will it take them to find me out there?

Even if I make it to the trees, how far will I get? Where will I go?

Chapter Sixty-Six

Tess took one look at Linda and said, "You should not be here."

In spite of the cold greeting, Linda fell into her boss's arms. Tess hugged her deputy. In the forty minutes since Linda had called her from the subway, Tess had gone from being truly shaken by the attack, to raging anger. The FBI, National Guard, and every elite special ops unit she could enlist had initiated a massive manhunt for Killcore, fanning out from the site of his subway strike, but she couldn't be sure it had actually been him. They still had strong intelligence showing he was in Chicago or New York.

Holding her sobbing assistant outside of Mission Control, Tess had the awful reoccurring thought that Killcore was more than one person.

Even if we catch him, even if we kill him, he'll keep coming.

The mob of youths was dangerously close to Chase and Wen, but before Chase got to count to three, the dark street lit up as if the sun itself had crashed to earth in that very spot.

"What happened?" Chase yelled, turning away from the blinding light.

"Flash bombs!" Wen replied.

"I happened!" Astaria said, appearing about twelve feet away from them. "You're welcome."

"How did you find us?" Chase asked.

"She can't tell us that," Wen said.

"I never lost you, actually," Astaria said, holding a massive gun that, to Chase, appeared to be a combination of a rocket launcher and a machinegun. "We should go, don't you think?"

"Where?" Chase asked.

"Don't you two have a plane to catch?"

Chase was about to ask how she knew that, but realized what her answer would be.

The man she'd been with earlier slipped out of the darkness and fired into the light. "We don't have much time," he said.

"This way," Astaria said, exiting the way they'd come. "We have a vehicle not far from here."

"Aren't most of the roads blocked?" Chase asked as he followed her. Wen took up the rear, keeping her MP7 trained toward the dwindling light.

"I didn't say it was that kind of vehicle," Astaria said, launching another flash bomb back toward the mob.

"That should hold them," Chase said.

"Oh, they're nothing," Astaria said. "The real enemy is just ahead."

Bull peered out. *It's definitely an army.* She could hear their shouting from above. The element of surprise had evaporated. *Killcore sent them. His power knows no limits.*

Still staring at the trees, searching for an opening, Bull could feel the clock ticking.

I wish I had a gun, or something. Killcore had gotten close, too close. *Could he be here, with them?*

Her panic paralyzed her for a moment. All Bull wanted was to smoke a cigarette and curl up in a corner and pretend none of it was happening. The Astronaut had been right—she'd pushed too far, had gotten overconfident. She'd been in sticky situations before. The one Chase and Wen had extracted her from had been the worst, up until now.

"She's hiding somewhere! Find her!"

The muffled yells through the floor ripped her back into action-mode. Bull pulled up the contact list on her phone, found the name Lisa, which was really Wen's number, and pushed.

"Damn . . ."

No cell service.

She pulled the vent grate off.

"There's a panel under the sink!" she heard a man shout.

Bull slithered out of the narrow opening, crouching for an instant to try to get her bearings as her heart threatened to beat out of her chest. "Here goes nothing!" she muttered under her breath, and bolted toward the trees.

The lights hit her two seconds later. "Freeze!" someone shouted.

She kept running.

"Stop or we'll shoot!"
It's only thirty more feet.
The thick forest, her best chance of escape, came closer with each pounding, breathless step.

Gunshots ripped apart the cold night air like a car crash on a foggy Sunday morning.

She didn't even slow.

An impossibly bright light hit her from behind, actually helping her to see the trees ahead more clearly.

Twenty more feet. She could hear them coming after her. It sounded like hoofbeats. *They can't have horses!*

"Stop!"

The shout was louder, closer.

I have a good head start. Somehow she managed to harness the adrenaline and push her skinny legs faster.

More shots. They missed.

Ten more feet!

They'd lit the area up so much, Bull easily picked the route she would take into the forest.

Just five more feet. I can lose them in those trees.

"Stop!"

More shots.

I'm going to make it!

Two feet!

By the time Bull heard the shots that hit her, she was already reeling in agony on the ground. It felt as if ten bullets had gone through her flesh, and she couldn't understand why she'd only heard two. In her floating-faintness, she tried to understand.

Why didn't I hear . . . how could I have felt the bullets even before I heard them? Why did they do this? Why?

Suddenly it was very bright.

Am I dead?

The lights and soldiers, black shadows, and trees, merged all around her. Bull's mind slipped from awareness. She forgot who she was, where she was, even what life was.

Then everything merged into total blackness.

Chapter Sixty-Seven

Finally, a block and a half away from the gang, the light from the flash bombs was no more.

"Where's the vehicle?" Chase asked.

"On the other side of a National Guard checkpoint," Astaria replied easily, as if it were no big deal.

"We're stealing a helicopter?" Chase said.

"Know another way to get to your flight on time?"

"They'll be armed."

Astaria laughed. "So are we."

Wen, who'd been mostly quiet since Astaria had shown up, pulled her old friend into an alley. "Why did you send us to kill Costa? You knew he wasn't Killcore."

"He was in on it," she said, shaking Wen's grip.

"Why didn't *you* just kill him?"

"I had to do something else."

"What?"

"I can't tell you."

"You were taking out Dean Johnson at the same time, weren't you?"

She smiled, as if pleased Wen had figured it out. "Maybe."

"Were you working with him?"

"I can't answer that."

"Wait, what?" Chase asked. "Back up."

"How deep are you in with Killcore?" Wen asked.

"Don't get ahead of yourself, Wen. You're too smart for that."

Wen pointed her gun at Astaria. "Tell me the truth."

The other man pointed his gun at Wen.

"Whoa!" Chase said.

"Is this what you want to do?" Astaria asked, icy calm.

"I want the truth."

"Which truth?"

Chase wasn't sure if he should do something, and if so, what?

"Who is Killcore?"

Astaria laughed. "If I knew that, do you think I'd be running around the dark streets of Chicago with you?"

"You do know."

Chase decided to trust that Wen had it under control.

"I know a lot, Wen, but I don't know who Killcore is. You're so good at reading people, but not me. You know you can't read me, so stop trying. You're embarrassing yourself."

"Why did you want Costa and Dean dead?"

"I told you, they were part of Killcore's operation."

"Are you really trying to stop Killcore?" Wen asked, knowing that Astaria knew the questions she was asking weren't necessarily the ones she was *really* asking, and that Astaria might answer a different question altogether.

"We don't have time for this!" Astaria snapped.

"This is not a Mossad operation. Who are you working for?"

Astaria grabbed Wen's gun, and in a blur, the two super-agents were on the ground, fighting.

The other man turned his gun on Chase before he could jump in to help Wen. Chase thought about pointing his gun at the man, but figured he might shoot him, so instead, kept the pistol slack at his side.

After almost two exhausting minutes of a hand-to-hand combat death match, the man shouted, "Star, alto!"

"How is this helping?" Astaria asked Wen, as the two women remained locked together.

"I don't know whose side you're on!"

"There *are* no sides!"

"Not true," Wen said, struggling against Astaria's grip.

"Yes, that's the difference between you and I, but do you *really* want to kill me? Do you really think you can?"

"You *know* I can."

"Maybe," Astaria said breathlessly. "But I don't wanna kill you."

Wen broke loose and backed away.

An instant later, both agents had their guns pointed at each other.

The man said something else to Astaria in Spanish that Chase didn't understand.

"Do you want to get on that plane to New York?" Astaria asked.

Wen nodded slowly.

"We'll keep them busy while you steal the bird."

The man lowered his gun. Chase took a deep breath.

Wen lowered her gun as well. "Where is it?"

"Just on the other side of those buildings."

The truce held.

The weekend warriors were no match for the ultra-skilled foursome. Wen piloted the helicopter while Chase fired cover shots to help suppress the guardsmen. Astaria and her partner slipped back into the shadows. Less than twelve minutes had elapsed since Wen and Astaria had ended their skirmish.

They flew low and landed at Midway airport after a very short flight. As promised, a plane was waiting with two IT-Squads aboard.

Another benefit of the special spy plane was they had a network connection. Just after takeoff, Tess briefed them from Mission Control. She told them of the latest Killcore sighting outside Washington, without going into detail, and Chase told her they believed that Dean Johnson was dead.

"Then who the hell is Killcore?"

Chapter Sixty-Eight

Halfway to New York, after the call with Tess, Wen received a very distressing message from the Astronaut.

"Killcore went after Bull," Wen told Chase.

"Is she okay?"

"She's alive, but in the hospital . . . paralyzed from the waist down."

"Oh . . . oh no . . . "

"The Astronaut is patching us through."

Chase looked across the small hospital room at Bull and flashed back to when his partner, Dez, had lost his leg. In this case, Bull would keep her legs, but would never walk again.

Dez had been doing a lot of research with exoskeletons, nerve implants, and other cutting-edge methods to assist paraplegics, quadriplegics, and amputees, in finding a way to walk again. Chase would get a message to Dez, and knew he would visit her.

"We didn't mean to wake you," Chase said.

"You shouldn't be here," Bull told him groggily. "They could be using me as bait."

He assumed she meant Killcore, but took it as the collective threat that had arrayed against him. The attackers at the cabin had turned out to be SWAT. Killcore had infiltrated their systems and told them a killer was in the cabin. After the mistake had been discovered, they'd rushed her to the hospital.

"We're not there," Chase said. The nurse holding the large computer tablet he spoke from smiled. "The Astronaut hastily arranged this call so we could check on you."

"We wish we could be there," Wen said, crowding into the camera. "How are you feeling?"

"Bad choice of words," Bull said. "I'm *not* feeling my legs."

"I'm sorry," Wen said, embarrassed she had committed such an insensitive faux pas.

"It doesn't matter," Bull said. "I sit at a computer all day anyway. But I guess I'll never dance again . . . I really wasn't much of a dancer."

"This isn't going to be permanent," Chase said. "I don't care what the doctors say, we'll spend whatever it takes. Dez is already pushing the boundaries of research."

"I don't want to be wearing metal-erector-set pants, looking like some sort of Terminator or something."

"It doesn't have to be like that. Just don't lose hope. You'll be dancing yet."

Bull glared at them. "You don't have to feel guilty. It's not your fault. If it wasn't for you two, I would have been dead long before those men came to the cabin."

She was a tough woman, yet Chase could see that even the mention of the cabin had caused a bit of her hard ass façade to crumble. "I'm not saying it because I feel guilty, I'm saying it because it's true. It's about technology."

"I'm a technology babe," Bull said, smiling, then turning serious. "I know the world's changing, but he's still out there. And until Killcore is dead, the future . . . none of us are safe, not even the future."

"Forget him."

"Bring me a computer," Bull said to the nurse.

"No." Chase shook his head. "You need to rest."

"I'm in bed. You can see me resting."

"You've got six bullet holes in your body. You've only just survived emergency surgery. You don't need to be working."

"I found him. Before they came, I found him."

Wen and Chase looked at her. "Killcore?"

"Yeah. That's why he sent the gunmen." Her voice shook. The little remaining color in her face left for a moment, and she paused hesitantly.

"Where?" Chase asked, unable to resist. "Is it different than what we already have?"

"It's definitely still New York. I can't tell if it's the same physical address yet. I was chasing him across the internet, the dark web. He keeps moving. But I know how to find him."

"It's too risky," Chase said.

"Bring me a friggin' computer!" she demanded, the frustration evident in her voice that she couldn't just walk down the hall and commandeer one from the nurse's station.

"No," Chase repeated, even though he wanted nothing more than to get her one.

"I'll get you one," the nurse holding the tablet suddenly blurted. "If a computer can help find the people that did this to you, then by God, I'll get you a computer, honey."

"Thank you," Bull said firmly. "After she gets me the computer, you two need to cut off. And don't try to come here."

The nurse propped the tablet up on the bedside table and went to get a laptop.

"Don't worry about our safety," Chase said.

"I *do* worry about it, but I know that I'm also in more danger when you're connected to me than when you're not. And I'd rather not add another bullet hole to my collection."

Two officers, from the private security company Chase had hired, arrived at Bull's door.

"If it's not a legitimate doctor or nurse, you stop them from going in that room, understood?" Chase said.

"Yes, sir."

Chase wanted police officers on duty, but there was too much chaos out there, and they could not be spared.

"We need to go," Wen said to Chase and Bull. "We're landing soon."

"Be careful," Bull said.

"You, too," Chase said. "You've done enough. We know where he is because of you. We're going to finish it."

Bull nodded, her mind already somewhere else.

"I think she would've been safer without a computer," Chase said after the video chat ended. "That's how he found her last time. If he finds out where she is . . . "

"Bull knows how to cover her tracks," Wen assured him as they prepared to land.

"Then why is she in the hospital?"

"She's learned how to—"

"Yeah, tell that to Tess. Underestimating Killcore has cost how many lives so far?"

Finally alone in her guarded hospital room, Bull rebooted the nurse's laptop, shoved the jigger into it, and quickly accessed the dark web, back on the trail of Killcore.

"I'm coming for you, Killcore," she whispered into the ethers of the dimly lit space. "This time, *you're* the one who's gonna suffer."

Chapter Sixty-Nine

Mars and his crew disembarked from one of the few planes flying, an air national guard KC-135 Stratotanker. Using prison connections and Bakersfield's many contacts, they'd hopscotched their way across the country on military flights in an effort to get to Chase. Mars was spending most of the favors and money he'd accumulated during his time behind bars. He'd convinced Bakersfield and Carpenter to stay with him by assuring them Chase would help them relocate to an obscure part of the world—preferably one without extradition treaties. However, Tucson had immediately headed to Las Vegas, where he had a girlfriend.

While in the air, or waiting for flights, Mars continued working computers to keep the decoying system operable to prevent Killcore, the shadow people, or anyone else from finding and doing harm to Chase and Wen.

"Are you sure your man is coming?" Mars asked Carpenter, nervous that their final ride might not show.

"He'll be here," Carpenter said. "The guy is stand up."

"And he really has a helicopter?" Bakersfield asked skeptically.

"Yes, guy's got a helicopter. I told you, he's cool to get us up to the top of the building. He's got a payload of dozens of fifty-five gallon drums full of foam."

"Right, but you're sure the construction site, where he's delivering them, is near the building?"

"That's what he said."

"Call him again," Mars said, looking at the time. "We're cutting this too close."

From her hospital bed, Bull resumed the Killcore hunt. In a split window, she sent a message to the Astronaut. His response came swiftly.

"You must rest. I am shutting you down."

"No! I need to find him."

"You found him. We know exactly where Killcore is, but no one can protect you if he finds you."

"He won't!"

"Not if you're not online. I'm sorry, Bull. Goodbye."

Her connection gone, Bull begged the nurse to help her leave the hospital. "I can go to a café, get back to where I was."

"You're in no condition—"

"I'm *fine*."

"No, you're not. And it's against the rules."

That made Bull laugh. "Is a cigarette also against the rules?"

"Absolutely."

The nurse finally agreed to help, but not in the way Bull

wanted. They'd sedated her not long before Chase called, checking to make sure the guards were extra alert.

During an encrypted call with the Astronaut, while in flight, he told them that Killcore's building was a modern fortress. "There is no way in."

"How does *he* get in?" Wen asked.

"Hard to say, but it's his building. There is no way to land, or even fly a helicopter close to the building because it employs EMP defenses."

"He's got Electro Magnetic Pulse protection?" Wen sighed, knowing the high tech security would make their job even more daunting. "There still must be a way in."

"Given enough time, we could get in, but if you can't get onto that roof, those missiles are going to be launched."

"Then I'll *climb* the building," Wen said, frustrated.

"They've thought of that. Not only is it a smooth glass skin, there are pulse shocks that would knock you right off."

JFK Airport was a ghost town, at least out on the runways. The terminals were insanity, after virtually all flights had been cancelled. Stranded travelers were camping out, trying to get out on various ground transportation options, and just plain frustrated and angry.

Four helicopters were waiting to take the IT-Squads, along with Chase and Wen, to wherever they said, but they could not land near the runway.

"It's just a quick shuttle ride," the Team Leader said as

the plane taxied to a mid-field area where shuttles would take them to the helicopters.

Wen didn't make eye contact with Chase, but knew what he was thinking: *We're in business.*

As soon as they were on the tarmac, walking to the shuttles, the explosions started. The IT-Squads, believing it was a Killcore attack, immediately took cover while Chase and Wen fled to the shuttles.

"Reminds me of Chicago," Chase said as flash bombs similar to the ones Astaria had used on the gangs lit the predawn sky.

A dark blue panel van squealed up behind the shuttles with its sliding door open. Chase and Wen jumped in as it slowed.

"Astronaut sent me," the driver said as he sped away, across the open concrete field, with his lights off. Out the back window, Wen watched the full-scale assault on the IT-Squads continue. "He sent that surprise welcoming committee, too."

"Amazing," Chase said. "I didn't know he had it in him." Wen had tried to get their friends in the revolutionary group, WOLF, to help, but they didn't have the firepower available.

"Oh, yeah," the driver said. "He's worked with the best mercenaries—ex-black ops, and former spooks. He's got a lot of friends."

"Friends?" Chase echoed, thinking of the anti-social Astronaut. They took a sharp turn and he slid across the bench seat into Wen.

"Well, relatively speaking," the driver continued. "By friends, I really mean fans who owe him favors, owe him their lives."

Wen smiled, happy that the Astronaut wasn't Killcore.

Chapter Seventy

The driver of the panel van slowed as he entered a congested area. "Your stop's coming up," he said. A minute later, he pulled under a covered passenger exchange area. "Time it right."

Wen looked out the windshield and saw a young couple waiting in the crowd. "Is that them?"

"Yep," the driver said, slowing down. "I'll even stop this time."

As Chase and Wen jumped out, the couple climbed in. "Good luck!" the woman shouted.

A couple of minutes later, they were on the air train, headed for the subway.

"I can't believe we're taking the subway into the city."

"Fastest way," Wen said. "Well, assuming you don't want to go on the CISS helicopters."

"Tess is going to kill us," Chase said, unable to suppress a smile.

"Unless Killcore beats her to it."

As they rode the elevator to the roof, Chase tried not to think about what they were about to do.

"I must say, Moscow's subway stations are far nicer than New York's, but I enjoyed our time in these much more."

"Just because no one was shooting at us?" Wen asked.

"Yeah, that probably had a lot to do with it."

They had to use an access code to get onto the roof. "The Astronaut came through again," Wen said as the door buzzed open.

Hidden behind a giant air handler was, what appeared to be a large water tank, and other unidentifiable equipment, they were relieved to find two hang gliders.

Wen shook her head. "I can't imagine what he had to do to get these up here."

"You do realize that the last time we were in a mess involving Franco Madden, and we went to the roof of a skyscraper . . ."

"This time it's different."

"Yeah, it's worse," Chase said as they each harnessed into one of the hang gliders.

Wen gave him some brief instructions, and then they ran to the edge. Stepping off, holding onto the aluminum frame, felt like the craziest thing he'd ever done.

The wind caught them immediately, the stainless steel cables went taut, and the entire airframe creaked as if it were about to fall apart.

"Don't look down," he told himself. "Focus on the building."

The building, which was coming up way too fast.

Tess had just spoken to the president, and assured him that they were closing in on Killcore. The commander in chief was onboard Air Force One, which had been designed to withstand EMP attacks and nuclear blasts. He'd gone "aloft" to maintain the government for the first time since the terrorist attacks of September 11, 2001. She hadn't dared tell him they were working with Chase and Wen on a final attempt to stop Killcore. A minute later, her decision to withhold that detail was vindicated when the Team Leader of one of the IT-Squads accompanying them, called in and informed her that they'd lost the pair.

Tess, seething inside, maintained her calm and began directing satellites and screens. "Get me a back track!" she said, calling for a look at the incident, which had occurred only minutes before. "That blue van, where is it? Follow it."

"We've got a continuous view of the van," an analyst said as they all watched the van merge into traffic outside the airport.

"No sign of the attackers. It appears to have just been a big diversion," one of the IT-Squad members reported.

"Should we take it?" Team Leader asked from one of the helicopters, just taking off.

"No, just follow them," Tess said. "Let them think they got away, and they'll lead us straight to Killcore."

An unexpected updraft blew from the open plaza between the two buildings and tossed the hang gliders. The wide jolt of air pushed Chase sideways. "Damned oversized kite!" Chase cursed while fighting to correct his craft. In his peripheral vision, he saw Wen had somehow navigated her way through.

Seeing the slick, mirrored edifice up close, Chase could see why it would have been virtually impossible to climb, even without its high-tech protections. Its architectural design was something out of the year 2525, with nothing extending, no places to grip.

"Damnit, I'm going to miss the building!" Chase yelled, his words lost to the city noise and flapping polyester sail.

He shifted his weight and turned, moving back on course, but now he was too low.

"I'm going to smash into the building!"

Moving the harness, he pushed down on the control bar and arched his back, but it wasn't going to be enough.

Chapter Seventy-One

The nuclear threat overview appeared on the highest monitor in Mission Control. Tess stared at it as if it might suddenly erupt.

"I have him," Linda said, interrupting her thoughts.

Tess thanked her and decided to take the call in Mission Control rather than Secure. She didn't want to be off the floor for even a second.

"Hello, Tess," Nash Graham said. One of the astronauts working for CISS had been able to get a message to him.

"Thank you for calling. Where is Chase?"

"Isn't he in a blue panel van on West 57th in Manhattan?"

"You know full well he is *not*," Tess said bitterly. A CISS analyst had found a camera inside the passenger exchange area at JFK where Chase and Wen got out. They still hadn't figured out where they'd gone, but they did know they weren't in the van.

"You'd have to ask Chase, then."

"Listen to me. The United States is officially at DEFCON Two for only the *third* time in its history."

"Yes, Defense Readiness Condition. The two highest alert states were during the Cuban Missile Crisis in October 1962, and the Persian Gulf War in January 1991, when the Joint Chiefs of Staff declared DEFCON Two."

"I'm pleased you know your history. Then you should *also* realize that this means the Armed forces are ready to deploy and engage—the next step to *nuclear war*."

"I understand, and that is what Chase and Wen are trying to prevent."

"They can't do it alone."

"Apparently, they aim to try. I know exactly what will happen. Killcore will launch one—or *all*—of his nuclear tipped intercontinental ballistic missiles, anywhere within their range of three to four thousand miles. Upon detonation, an uncontrolled chain reaction will split atomic nuclei. This will produce an incredibly intense wave of heat, with corresponding disruptions to light, air pressure, and radiation. The nuclear explosion will generate and release radioactive particles."

"You make it sound so clinical. It's not—"

"No, it isn't. It will enrage the atmosphere as the radioactive burden is strewn and drawn up into a mushroom cloud. More will die from the deadly dust and debris than from the initial blast—depending on his target and the prevailing winds—as the fallout spreads far and wide to expose great swaths of the population to radiation."

"*Tell me where they are*. I'm trying to *help* them."

"It's too late."

Chase struggled, lifting his body, then bringing it down like a snake. He tried to look up, searching for Wen, but the sail blocked his view. With nothing left to do, he looked down, wondering how he could land on the busy city street.

Then, from out of nowhere, perhaps from a subway grate far below or some other atmospheric condition he'd never understand, a pocket of warm air suddenly jostled him up, sending him soaring toward the building with just enough altitude to make it.

As soon as Chase had the roof in view, he realized landing was going to be the least of his problems.

Wen had sailed right into the hands of a group of armed men. One of them spun, shooting at Chase. Wen kicked the man in the head at the last moment, causing his shots to go just above the glider. Chase soared into the building, his legs kicking desperately, trying to get a few more inches of elevation gain needed. He slid across the roof on his knees, putting the airframe's tip into the gut of one of the men, who staggered backwards. Chase went from his knees to his feet and used the momentum to run over the man's face, adding a hard kick into his jaw.

With the high probability that his victim was not getting up again, Chase released his harness, shoved the hang glider into an approaching man, and kept going. The entire roof was covered with killers.

Wen engaged several men at once from behind a massive piece of equipment concealed in a mirrored dome. Now up close, Chase realized the roof was very different from the photos they'd received from the Astroanut—it was actually a three-story open atrium packed full of catwalks, cooling units, and generators. The machinery broadcast extremely loud, high frequency noise. There was no way for him to communicate with Wen over it.

His only option seemed to be to retreat into the maze of catwalks. Chase couldn't shake the feeling that these men had been waiting for them, that Killcore had arranged every aspect of their showdown, that even winding up among the metal grates submerged in the shiny roof had been choreographed in advance.

That thought made him hesitate, not entering the maze. Instead, he ran back onto the open roof, hoping to join the battle with Wen.

The explosion hit with such force they were thrown backwards in a burst of debris and fire. Chase managed to regain some footing on the edge of the building and spotted Wen a few feet in front of him, flattened on the glassy surface next to a burning dead man. Just as she got to her feet, another explosion came out of nowhere. The shockwave sent her sailing into Chase. Their bodies collided on the edge of the roof, sixty-two stories above the busy streets.

For one slow-motion instant, they teetered. Their eyes locked in a flash of knowing panic.

They were going over.

The glance conveyed, in a nanosecond, apologies, regret, absolute love, and fear—not for their own lives, but that they couldn't save the other's.

Then time sped up again, and they went over together in a screaming tangle.

Chapter Seventy-Two

In the dizzying final moments, fire, bits of metal shrapnel, and melting plastic washed over them in a hellish flood. As the last decisions of his life spun past in a blur, Chase managed two extraordinary feats: the hand of his weaker arm found something to grab onto, and, as he clutched the edge of the building, his right hand caught Wen. Her grip was tight and sure as they dangled above the brutal, unyielding pavement that might as well have been sixty-two miles straight down.

"Hold on!" Wen shouted.

For that second, they had once more cheated death. Yet the sweat on their palms told another story as Wen's fingers began to slip.

"We're still here!" Chase yelled in amazement. "We're still here," he repeated, as if to convince himself, but his celebration was cut short.

"I'm slipping!" Wen screamed.

Chase felt the weight of her struggle pulling him down.

The strength in his fingers on both hands began to loosen. "Don't let go!" he yelled, but he knew what she was thinking. "I. Can. Pull. Us. Up."

"No you can't!"

"Yes!"

"I'm falling."

"No!"

"Let. Me. Go."

"*No!*" He repositioned his body, trying to increase his leverage, instill more strength in his arms, but there was nothing left to draw on. If she didn't let go, they would both go down. He knew this, but was not willing to make the choice.

Wen groaned.

"Pull. Climb up my arm."

Before she even answered, Chase heard more men shouting on the roof. They were coming to the edge. All they would have to do was step on his fingers . . .

"Pull! Climb up!" he yelled again. Still echoing in his thoughts was the realization that they weren't going to survive this. The only chance was to let her go.

I can't, he thought, trying again to pull her up. The fear of losing her was sapping his dwindling energy.

Her nails suddenly dug sharply into his hand, forcing him to involuntarily open his grip and let go.

"*Nooo!*" he screamed as he felt suddenly weightless, and knew she was gone.

In the split second it took him to scream that one long syllable, his mind weighed a hundred options, the biggest of which was deciding whether to let go of the ledge and plummet to his death with his beloved Wen.

But the rage of what had happened took hold, propelling him back up onto the roof and sending him rushing into the waiting men, who could not have underestimated his fury more. As he broke one of their necks, just like Wen had taught him, all he wanted to do was get back to the edge and look over to see the unthinkable.

However, it would have to wait. Another man was shooting at him.

Chase dove at the man, the bullets somehow missing him through the flames. As Chase reached the shooter, he jammed his elbow into the side of the man's head, grabbed the gun, and came out in a spin, as if channeling Wen. After killing the man, he then turned, looking for more. Another came at him from below the catwalks. Chase knew if he was going to get inside the building, he'd have to fight his way through the maze.

Bullets sparked and ricocheted all around him as he dropped into a twisted section of roof damaged by the earlier explosion. Ahead, he found a catwalk with stairs heading up, giving him a back way across the dark shadows. He could hear the other men hunting him and see their powerful beams of lights in the shadowed darkness of the sub-roof. A thatched grid of shadows and lines came across like a kaleidoscope, creating false levels of catwalks. The shafts of alternating light seemed to distract his enemies, because they shot into the deep shadows, not knowing how he could not be where he should have been.

Chase came screaming up behind them, opening fire in an uncontrolled rage. A spray of bullets cut them both down in his gory rampage. He stepped over their torn bodies without a hint of remorse, blaming each of them for Wen's death.

Suddenly, there was silence.

Up on the roof, nothing.

Down in the maze, nothing.

He wanted to die . . . could he and Wen have really only been five men away from victory?

"She died because we didn't get those last five." He spat the words bitterly. "How many times have we survived so much more?"

He looked around again, still pulled to the edge, wanting to see, yet not wanting to know.

Was there any way she could have survived? Wen would want him to go on. To find Killcore. Stop him. Kill him. Pause the nukes.

But he couldn't. Chase *had* to know.

He climbed back to the roof and fought the wind and grief to get back to the spot where he'd lost her. Dropping to his knees, then falling flat, he looked over. It was too far down to see any detail on the ground, but there was nowhere she could have safely landed—no miracle, no chance.

With renewed determination that bordered on madness, Chase launched himself back into the damaged section of the roof.

I have to get inside!

Chase followed the maze of catwalks until, two levels below, he spotted a door. "How do I get there?" he asked the wind.

After a frantic twenty second search, he found part of the grid on the floor could be lifted. He was then able to drop down, and found a concealed metal ladder that took him straight down to the door. It had been left unlocked—apparently by the people who had come through for them. He positioned his gun, stood close and quiet, then pulled open the door, expecting another instant battle.

He found something entirely different.

Chapter Seventy-Three

Mars and his fellow escapees were nervous as the chopper flew in between the tall buildings of Manhattan.

"Keep it low," Mars reminded the pilot through the headset. "We can't get too close to the building." The Astronaut had warned him about the EMP capabilities, and Mars looked up at the building's roof, wondering how they could get inside to help Chase.

"Oh my God, someone's falling!"

"It's a woman!" Bakersfield yelled into his mic.

"It's Wen," Mars said, stunned. "We've got to help her!"

"Impossible," Carpenter said.

The pilot flew to her, careful to keep underneath her. "I don't want her to hit the propellers!"

Wen, spotting the chopper hauling a load, but having no idea who was inside, knew this was her only chance. She positioned her body and skydived toward it.

Got to get to that cargo net.

Her dive to the helicopter meant she was also plummeting to the pavement faster.

The pilot must have spotted me—he's flying this way.

Wen, a trained skydiver, got close enough to see the chopper was hauling fifty-five gallon poly-drums.

Come on, she silently implored the pilot. *A little closer.*

Wen calculated the distance, tried to take into account the wind and updraft, the spinning rotors, her angle of descent . . . and she wasn't sure she'd make it.

I'm going to be within a couple of feet . . .

Mars, barely breathing, pressed against the helicopter's window. "Closer!" he yelled.

"She's too near the building," the pilot countered while fighting the controls. "I don't know where the Electromagnetic border is."

"We've almost got her!" Mars yelled. "She's *so* close!" He could actually *see* the determined expression on her face. "You've got to get closer!"

"The only way is to go lower." The pilot suddenly took it down forty feet and spun the tail around, trying to sweep up against the side of the glass tower. "This is as close as we dare."

The helicopter's rapid drop startled Wen's concentration, sending a surge of momentary panic jolting through her. Then she realized landing a bullseye on the cargo net might be possible now.

If those barrels stop swinging . . . she thought, now factoring in the pendulum-movement of the load.

She did a flip to gain herself another burst of momentum. A second later, she hit dead on, bouncing around on the poly-barrels. Wen slid and rolled, desperately trying to keep hold of the heavy netting. However, the speed of her impact, coupled with the swinging cargo and vibrating, made it almost impossible.

She slipped and nearly went careening off before, at the last instant, she got hold of a cable that ripped into her hand with agonizing pain. The sear helped her hold on.

Mars looked below, but didn't see her falling. "I think we got her!"

Carpenter and Bakersfield cheered.

The pilot moaned a desperate "*No!*" as the rotors stalled, the humming and whirring of the propeller winding down. "We got too close to the building! Too close!" the pilot shouted, pulling off his headset.

Mars braced, knowing Killcore's EMP had taken out the helicopter's instruments. They started plummeting, the four-thousand pound craft going into an eerie, muted, creaking, droning shut down.

"We're low enough that the drums might cushion our landing!" the pilot yelled, knowing the poly-barrels were filled with commercial grade insulation foam. "There's a chance, but brace for the crash!"

Mars worried that Wen, holding on below, would get crushed, but he might be too dead to ever know.

Wen looked up as the crippled helicopter turned into dead weight, catching up to its own load.

I'm going to get sandwiched, she thought, trying to gauge how to get off once they were near enough to the street.

While figuring the impossible odds, gravity won.

The cargo hit first. All the drums smashed, exploding foam into the street. Wen jumped off just as the helicopter crashed on top, rolling clear.

Chapter Seventy-Four

Chase pushed through the wretched grief and agony of Wen's death, knowing he had to complete the mission. They had done so much together—solved problems, thwarted villains, helped the good guys, and did their part to actually save the world a few times. But from the beginning, both he and Wen had known they'd chosen a dangerous road.

Killcore had been different—and the most dangerous thing they'd ever faced—from his first strike. Taking down technology to bring the modern world to its knees, ready to launch nuclear weapons, it all seemed a little too much like a cheap airport thriller—except for the fact that the world really did *need* to be saved.

He stood there, inside some kind of upper level lobby, wondering where to go inside the vast building, when the elevator floor indicator lights began moving. As it swiftly moved up—*twenty-nine, thirty, thirty-one, thirty-two*—Chase searched for a place to hide.

Forty-one, forty-two, forty-three.

Finally, as it zipped up to sixty, sixty-one, he decided to press himself against the wall just beside the elevator doors.

Sixty-two.

The polished silver doors opened. Chase, unsure whether to expect another batch of mercenaries, a CISS IT-Squad, or Killcore himself, desperately clung to the ridiculous hope that Wen would step out of the elevator.

It was not to be. Instead, a weaselly, dangerous, evil little man emerged from the stark box.

"Franco Madden, you worthless piece of trash!" Chase snarled, aiming a machine gun only a couple of feet from an obviously startled Franco. "Tell me one good reason why I shouldn't kill you where you stand!"

"Chase! How nice of you to drop by. I've been expecting you. Where's your trusty sidekick?"

"On her way," Chase lied. He quickly took a pistol and large hunting knife off Franco. "Now I'll ask *again*—"

"Oh, don't be ridiculous. If you kill me, you'll never stop Killcore."

"*You're* Killcore. Once you're dead, problem solved."

Franco laughed. "You idiot, you'll *never* stop Killcore!"

"What are you talking about?" Chase asked, not in the mood for Franco's games. "Is he in this building now?"

"'Behind every man now alive stand thirty ghosts, for that is the ratio by which the dead outnumber the living.' *2001, A Space Odyssey.* Have you read the book, by Arthur C. Clarke? *So much* better than the movie."

"Take me to Killcore!" Chase barked, knowing the nukes could go airborne at any second.

"Oh Chase, you are such a fool."

"Let's go. Twenty-ninth floor," Chase said impatiently, pushing the down arrow button. The elevator doors opened again. "*Move!*"

Franco complied, a sly smile on his face.

"Push twenty-nine, and tell me everything you know about Killcore, or you're of no use to me. And I'm definitely looking for an excuse to shoot you."

"You've seen his whole life, I assume," Franco said as the elevator doors opened on the twenty-ninth floor. "His postings, his correspondence, photographs—he invented *all* of that. The images are all completely composite."

"Why did he target me?" Chase asked, motioning with his machine gun for Franco to exit the elevator.

"Killcore targeted you because you created RAI."

"Why?" Chase asked, standing outside the elevator, so stunned he could hardly move.

"For some tech wizard, you're a little slow on the draw here."

Chase wanted to shoot Franco that instant. "When are the missiles going to launch?"

"I don't know. I told you, that's Killcore's game."

"Game? You think this is a *game*?"

"*Life* is but a game."

"Take me to the master servers, *now!*"

"Fine. Open door number three." Franco pointed down the hall.

"*You* open it," Chase said, not wanting to fall into a trap.

The server room was massive. Chase found a container of zip ties at a tech station and quickly secured Franco's hands and feet. That done, Chase moved back to the tech station and began typing furiously, trying to find access, and wondered if at any moment Killcore and a team of men would burst in, but there was no other choice. He had to find a way to stop the missiles.

Franco chuckled. "I like it on the floor."

"Shut up."

"Do you want to know the secret?"

"If it will help."

"'No one would have believed, in the last years of the nineteenth century, that this world was being watched keenly and closely by intelligences greater than man's, and yet as mortal as his own. That as men busied themselves about their various concerns, they were being scrutinized and studied, perhaps almost as narrowly as a man with a microscope might scrutinize the transient creatures that swarm and multiply in a drop of water.'"

"You're quoting H.G. Wells to me. For the last time, *where is Killcore?*" Chase demanded.

"Right there," Franco said, laughing.

Chase glanced up from the keyboard, and looked at the scariest thing he'd seen in all his life.

"Oh my God!"

Chapter Seventy-Five

Chase stared into the endless servers, their lights and dark presence seeming overwhelmingly sinister.

"Killcore isn't a person?"

"Not even a little," Franco sang.

"Killcore is a damned *program*!?"

"Feel foolish, Mr. Computer Genius?"

Chase turned, stepped hard on Franco's stomach, and pushed the machine gun into his mouth. "Tell me the whole story, or I'll blow your head all over this wall."

"I guess you *do* feel foolish," Franco wheezed. "But I'll tell you, since you're going to die soon anyway. Let's see . . . I guess I'll skip the boring parts."

"Do that," Chase barked, worried about the nukes.

"Dean Johnson and Aaron Costa created Killcore using your invention, Rapid Artificial Intelligence. Yes, that's right," Franco said, smiling at seeing Chase's obvious distress that RAI had been used to facilitate Killcore's reign of terror.

"Dean Johnson, the CIA cyber guy? *That's* how Killcore was able to infiltrate everything?"

"It started that way, but Killcore has taken on a life of his own. I use the term 'his' loosely, but he's already in control of almost everything. You can't stop him. It's impossible."

Chase pushed his foot harder into Franco's gut. "*You'll* do it."

"I can't either," Franco said, gasping.

Chase knew how artificial intelligence could move past its initial programming and develop itself with machine learning to become artificial general intelligence acquiring the ability to understand and learn intellectual tasks. Clearly, Killcore had gone beyond AGI and was in the realm of artificial super intelligence, the point where machines surpass humans. And Chase's own RAI had been the breakthrough to amplify that capability by unimaginable speed and sophistication.

"I . . . can't . . . answer . . . questions," Franco said in a horse whisper.

Chase moved his foot, which had slid onto Franco's throat.

Franco took in a gulp of air.

Chase's mind was racing. "If it's a machine, we can stop it." But even as the words escaped his mouth, he realized the flaw in his argument.

Franco laughed as he saw the realization hit Chase. "Yeah, you can turn off one machine, then you can turn off another, but he's always moving. He's on the network. He's infiltrated servers you will *never* find."

No, there's always a way, Chase thought, remembering Wen's maxim. "I'll shut off the power."

"Sure, shut off the power to the whole world? You amuse me, Chase."

"You *want* him to launch the missiles?"

"Whatever . . ."

"You think that's *okay*?"

"This is the greatest form of intelligence the world has ever known. Killcore already knows everything you could be thinking—hasn't he proven that? You can't come up with anything he hasn't played out to a million moves. Killcore has all the knowledge of human existence, and that's only one-one hundredth of one percent of his capabilities. And every minute, his intelligence grows."

"Killcore wanted me dead, because *I* created RAI . . ." Chase repeated it to himself four or five times, ignoring Franco's rant, until it hit him. "I can get in. Killcore knows I can use my knowledge of RAI to get in and change the programming. *I'm* the unique threat . . . the only threat to Killcore. *That's* why he went after me."

"Wasting your time," Franco said.

There has to be a way. I can write more code, another command to replace what formed Killcore's initial programming . . .

Chase knew that with artificial intelligence, there was always the primary command: its mission. After that, the safeguard was power. For stationary machines, you could always deny power, but with a force like Killcore—spreading around the globe via networks, and already *so* far ahead—the last wall of defense was a command that countered the mission.

"What was the primary command?"

"Yes," Franco said. "Your arrogance is expected. Don't you see, Wonderboy? It doesn't matter what you do. Killcore will deflect anything you put in."

"Tell me!" Chase pulled Franco to his feet and shoved

him against the wall, his hands and legs bound so that after he crashed into the metal slotted partition, he fell back onto the floor, laughing.

"Do you like my maniacal laugh?" he asked. "I've practiced it for hours." He cackled again.

Chase put the gun to his head. "You don't know how badly I want to shoot you, and I will if you don't tell me the primary command."

"'The telephone was ringing wildly, but without result, since there was no one in the room but the corpse.' Have you read *War in Heaven* by Charles Williams?"

Chase shot him in the leg. "Next time I pull this trigger, you won't live long enough to feel the bullets that kill you."

Franco gritted his teeth, somehow enduring the pain without screaming. He slowly gave Chase the primary command.

"I'm only telling you because I want to watch you fail."

The primary command's main purpose is to take away humanity's dependence on technology, Chase thought, playing the idea over in his mind. *Killcore has been assuming control of all technology, thereby removing humanity's role. If I can take control of Killcore, and show Killcore that he is the ultimate technology, he would have to shut himself down to stop us from being dependent on him.*

"How can I do that?" he muttered to himself, knowing there were potentially millions of steps—then remembered why Killcore had come after him.

Through the RAI interface, an access point that only Chase knew existed, he keyed in a command that told Killcore humans were dependent on Killcore—the ultimate technology. The logic held up because humanity's survival truly *was* now dependent on Killcore.

Killcore's main servers instantly began to process the ramifications, sorting and playing out millions and millions of scenarios. Chase held his breath, not knowing if Killcore would find a workaround, or what final solution it might accept.

It took a while, but Chase detected a change in the hum of the room.

Then the first servers went dark.

Chase closed his eyes in relief.

It didn't have to be hard. I just needed to find Killcore. It was right to be afraid of me. Everything it did were just diversions.

"What did you type?" Franco asked urgently. "What have you *done*?"

Chase didn't answer. Only after the last server shut down did he say anything at all.

"It's over."

Chapter Seventy-Six

Chase secured Franco to an anchored server rack. He didn't even look at Franco as he left the room and headed to the elevator. A few floors down, no longer worried that anyone was going to show up with a gun, Chase made a call to the one person who could verify that Killcore was done.

"Where the hell *are* you?" Tess asked angrily.

"You should have control of the missiles back."

Tess snapped her fingers and pointed. Technicians inside Mission Control, having heard his words on speaker, immediately went to work.

"Pentagon confirms—missiles are back online!" an analyst shouted.

"Nice work," Tess said. "I owe you and Wen both a drink."

"Wen didn't make it this time," Chase told her.

Tess, stunned, was silent for a moment. "Sorry, Chase," she finally whispered.

"So am I."

"Killcore's footprint is out of the banks and financial markets," another technician reported.

"We've got people there, but they've only gotten as far as the lobby. They say it's a building inside a building. Can you help them get in?"

"I don't know. I'll see," he said, suddenly feeling old and very tired.

"They'll take you anywhere you want to go."

"I'll bet they will," Chase said.

"Seriously, whatever you need," Tess said.

"FAA is showing no more Killcore interference," Linda reported.

"Franco Madden is on the twenty-ninth floor," Chase told her. "I left him tied to a server rack."

"Good, we've been looking for him."

Chase got to the ground floor and found that he was, in fact, inside some kind of core building within an outer glass shell. "A fortress," he murmured to himself. But without Killcore holding the elaborate security measures together, it was a simple matter of overriding the last protocols, and the vault-like doors released and opened. A moment later, his friends from CISS, the IT-Squad members he'd flown out from Chicago with, poured in around him and secured the building. Even before he reached the street, dozens more CIA, FBI, NSA, and other government intelligence personnel appeared.

There was a crowd outside. Apparently the rooftop explosions had drawn hundreds of onlookers. NYPD was keeping them at a safe distance. Chase barely glanced their way. He wasn't sure where he was going, just knew it wasn't going to be anywhere with the IT-Squads.

Maybe a hotel room under an alias, a long, hot shower, and sleep . . . for a week, or more.

He looked up to find the easiest route through the crowd, and nearly collapsed.

Wen!

She was looking back at him, smiling. Chase ran to her, wrapping his arms around her, smothering her in a hug.

"You're alive! I don't believe it . . . How . . . I'm so sorry I dropped you."

She shook her head. "You didn't. I let go."

"But how did you survive the fall?"

Wen laughed. "I couldn't die without knowing who Killcore is."

"*Was*," Chase corrected. "Killcore is no more."

Epilogue

Chase and Wen walked away from the crowd and the building. "So who was Killcore?" Wen asked.

"A machine," Chase replied. "But first, tell me how you lived."

"Mars."

Chase looked confused.

She explained how Killcore had attacked the prison. Since Mars could no longer do the decoying from there, he escaped and came to find them. Then Wen told him the incredible way she'd made it to the ground.

"Amazing," Chase said, truly stunned by the story. "So Mars is okay?"

"I sure am," Mars said, walking toward them.

Chase ran to meet him, hugging his old friend tightly.

"Of course, now I'm an escaped convict," Mars said when their embrace ended.

Chase nodded. "We'll figure that out."

Mars introduced Carpenter and Bakersfield, explaining

that they'd helped him get out of Lompoc and across the country.

"I owe you all everything," Chase said, looking at Wen, and then to them. "Tess might be able to help us out."

"Let's not call her until we're safely out of the area," Wen suggested. "We deserve some peace."

A few hours later, in a hotel outside Philadelphia, Chase called Tess on his still scrambled phone. He asked to cash in his favor with pardons for Mars, Carpenter, Bakersfield, and even Tucson.

"I'm sure we can do something," she told him. "Tell them to stay out of sight, and don't let them get into any trouble. I'll get back to you as quickly as possible, but a lot is going on right now. Cleaning up after all Killcore's damage is going to take time."

Chase thanked her.

"By the way," Tess said, reading from a report just handed to her, "it turns out Killcore sent SWAT to get Bull. Tapped into their communications and reported that she was a wanted, desperate, and armed killer."

"She's lucky to have lived through that. I guess he did something similar at Lompoc Prison."

"Most likely. It will take us months, maybe years, to learn everything Killcore did."

"Yeah . . . and there's something that's been bothering me since I discovered Killcore wasn't a person," Chase said. "Why did Dean and Costa create Killcore? What was their ultimate objective?"

"I think it was a money-making scheme that got out of control. You know how AI and machine learning can go."

"Yeah, but I think there was more to it. CIA . . . Mossad . . . a cyber war . . . I'm sure Franco can shed some light on it. Have you started questioning him yet?"

"Franco's dead."

"What? He was alive and well when I left him, aside from the gunshot wound to his leg."

"Turns out he killed some people on the Washington Metro line in Virginia on his way to New York," Tess said, looking over at Linda's closely cropped hair.

"So?" Chase asked indignantly, thinking about how tragically coincidental it was that the only three people with direct knowledge of the Killcore program had been killed in the past eighteen hours.

"Virginia is a death penalty state. I guess he didn't want to go that route."

Chase remembered how he'd left Franco tied to the rack, and knew Tess had had him executed.

"I see. So some things we'll never know . . . "

"Isn't that always the way?"

Chase thought of the shadow people and Astaria. "Yeah, but if you live long enough, eventually you learn everything."

Next in the Chase Malone Thriller series

vinci-books.com/chasing-risk

**They know your thoughts, your fears, your every move.
But what if you were the real threat?**

Fugitive billionaire Chase Malone and former spy Wen Zhou uncover a chilling program that's not just about selling products—it's about selling control.

Turn the page for a free preview…

Chasing Risk: Chapter One

"In the daydreams of our imaginations and the whimsical glow of childhood, we forget that a darkness is waiting to snatch our innocence and shatter the illusion."

Chase Malone thought about the cynical words. They had troubled him ever since a friend, called The Astronaut, had uttered them upon learning about the boy.

The Astronaut and the boy were just two of the odd collection of people Chase had accumulated since his flight from "the real world" began.

The billionaire's chiseled face softened in bewilderment and affection at seeing Tu, the little eight-year-old Chinese boy he had come to love. Searching his eyes for wonderment, joy, or any sense of whimsy, it saddened him to not see any sense of childhood excitement. Instead, the "Buddha" child often seemed like an adult, always analyzing and studying.

The product of a Chinese experiment, Tu was a special boy. While still an embryo, his genes had been edited, manipulated for increased intelligence. The results were fantastic, although disturbing. He easily worked incredibly complex math equations in his head, and could quickly reason through intricate problems with machine-like precision.

Chase, a brilliant billionaire with many patents and inventions to his credit, just wanted Tu to have a normal childhood. He looked over at Wen, the woman he shared everything with. The two of them had rescued Tu from a Chinese facility where the boy had been held since birth. Her eyes told him she was thinking the same thing.

Chase and Wen had been living as fugitives, pursued across the globe by numerous enemies. Their dangerous lifestyle grew more complicated after suddenly finding themselves as parents once they'd snatched Tu from his communist captors. Wen, a former Chinese spy, had escaped the same corrupt and brutal government that had "created" Tu. For a while, she had successfully disappeared, having secretly erased her existence, and was free—or was at least some form of that undervalued and overused word.

Now the MSS was hunting all three of them.

They'd safely hidden Tu in America with Wen's grandmother. US officials had no idea the boy was there, but the Chinese knew, and they would not stop looking for Tu. Ever.

"I've lost track of how many people are after us," Chase told Wen that morning, each knowing he hadn't. Yet, it wasn't the MSS who worried him most. The ones who kept them both up at night, the ones they could not seem to evade, was a cabal known only as "the shadow people." The clandestine group had been pursuing them for years, and somehow always seemed to be able to locate them. During all that time, Chase and Wen hadn't been able to discover who was chasing them, or why they wanted them dead.

"Chase," Wen said, pulling him out of his worrying. She pointed at Tu, and gave him a look as if to say, *"Make our little boy smile."* Suddenly, nothing seemed as important. They'd brought Tu to a carnival to celebrate his eighth birthday, hoping to help him find a piece of lost childhood magic. Chase looked around, deciding which ride to suggest while remaining always vigilant, looking for threats. Wen never took her eyes off "the field," as she called it, seeing the world as one infinite battlefield.

They were practiced at moving without detection, with a long protocol of precautions when traveling—non-traceable burner phones, decoys, and elaborate cyber tactics, as well as vIDs, a spray-on application Chase and The Astronaut had invented, used to defeat facial recognition systems. However, when Tu was with them, they also employed Sepio, an elite, private security force whose exorbitant fees matched their skill level, their clientele exclusively billionaires.

The three of them were anonymous, lost in the big carnival outside San Diego. Chase was determined to pack a chunk of childhood, which had been mostly denied to Tu up until that point, into the evening. With that in mind, the colorful lights, happy music and joyous shrieks, the constant hum of loud conversations, and the practiced pitches from the midway's hucksters all came into focus, and Chase welcomed it.

"What's that?" Tu asked, pointing to the Wave Swinger, a massive pillar of lights and murals supporting a tilting disc which resembled the garish ceiling of some futuristic cathedral. Suspended from the kaleidoscope of blinking colors were long chains, each ending in a seat carrying a single passenger who was being swung sixty feet above the ground at a dizzying angle and speed.

"I believe those are called the 'evil swings,'" Chase said, grimacing. He recalled making the mistake of getting on the ride as a twelve-year-old. "It's a vomit-inducing torture device."

Tu looked at him with the same expression he did whenever Chase was being sarcastic. "Why would they have something so horrible here?" he asked innocently. "I thought you said this was fun time."

Wen shot Chase a dirty look. "It is not called the evil swings. That is the Wave Swinger, and it's actually great fun."

Chase shook his head at Tu and pulled a finger across his throat as if to indicate it was a life-threatening proposition to get on. "Not this one," he insisted.

Wen scowled at Chase, quickly switching to a bright smile for Tu. "Which one do you like?" she asked Tu, while making eye contact with one of their security detail. The man indicated an all clear.

Wen tried to relax as she searched for any sign of trouble. She didn't *expect* any, as no one could have any idea where they were, yet she never trusted whatever illusion of safety they found themselves in, even as she attempted to have fun.

None of them knew that less than ninety feet from their precious boy, a clown with a gun was pushing toward them through the happy, excited crowd.

Chasing Risk: Chapter Two

Tu's face lit up as he gazed at the Ferris wheel, mesmerized by its colored lights and magical appearance which seemingly offered excitement and thrills. "That one looks beautiful!"

Chase thought the Ferris wheel was a good choice, but suggested they start with the merry-go-round. However, as soon as the vintage calliope music began and Chase saw Tu sitting on a lion, he realized that even though the boy had only just turned eight years old, his genetically modified adult mind wasn't going to enjoy such a boring ride.

"Why do people like to just go in circles?" Tu asked as they were getting off. "It does not seem a very good use of time."

"You'll like the Ferris wheel better," Wen said.

Chase was about to say something about it being the same thing except turned on its side, when Tu looked up with bright eyes and said, "I do like to go high."

Looking at the other children around them, Chase

suggested getting some cotton candy, which Tu had never had.

"It's sweet," he said, smiling. "Feels funny in my mouth."

The line to the Ferris wheel moved quickly, and soon they were secured in their seat, three across. For a moment, the look on Tu's face was like that of a normal boy. They slowly climbed, taking in the view as the carnival sprawled out below them with its crowds and varied noises.

Tu pointed to the sky ride. "Can we do that next? I'd like to float over the whole park."

"Sure," Chase said, enjoying Tu's excitement.

"Look, you can see the ocean from here," Tu said, as they reached the top. "I like this ride very much."

But Wen wasn't looking out toward the Pacific. She had seen something down below that concerned her, two men that seemed out of place. Although dressed casually—to most people the pair would've appeared as two guys out to enjoy the carnival—Wen could tell by the way they walked they were not interested in the rides, the Midway games, or the junk food. They were looking for someone.

As the Ferris wheel came around lower, she got a better look. They were definitely carrying concealed guns. One had a slip holster inside his pants, the other a shoulder holster hidden under his light parka. As their gondola passed the entry gate, completing their first rotation, the suspect closest made eye contact with her, and moved toward the Ferris wheel.

Wen tapped Chase on the shoulder and motioned with her eyes back to the ground. "Blue parka," she said casually, as if it were nothing, but he never would've picked the man from the crowd without her description.

"Blue parka?" Tu asked.

"I asked Chase if he brought his blue parka."

Tu was normally excellent at detecting lies. However, Wen had been trained to not only beat polygraph machines, but also the world's best interrogators. Tu let the comment go.

A second later, their gondola reached the top of the wheel's arc, and the ride abruptly ground to a halt. Wen tried to look down to see if blue parka had stopped it, or if the operator was giving them the obligatory thrill moment of letting them take in the view. Taking advantage to scour the area, Wen spotted two more figures approaching the Ferris wheel with an out of place determination.

Tu, unknowing, kept shifting in the seat, smiling, trying to take in as much of the whirling lights, streams of laughing people, and saturated rainbows of the carnival. It amused Chase, listening as Tu tried to hum the mix of multiple musical medleys which blended into a cartoonish chorus high above the flashy scene.

"I'm getting out," Wen said, slipping under the safety bar.

"What?" Tu asked, alarmed. "We're at the top!" He looked down, studied the wheel, and said to Chase, "We're approximately twenty meters above the ground. Since you're metrically challenged, that means around sixty feet. If she falls, gravity will pull down on her mass, and there isn't enough air resistance to push back in twenty meters, but enough to kill her. Terminal velocity . . . Wen is small and light . . . yet gravity accelerates all objects at the same rate, regardless of mass . . . I do not want her to fall."

"She'll be okay," Chase assured him.

Tu looked down nervously. "Is someone after us again?"

Chase glanced down at Wen, then back to the innocent face of a scared little boy, a boy who had almost been killed during their escape from China, a boy who had learned fast that the world was nothing like the sheltered existence of the protected "lab" he'd grown up in prior to meeting Chase and Wen. Chase wanted to pretend nothing bad was happening, that they were safe no matter what, but Tu deserved more than that.

"Yes. The killers have returned."

Grab your copy...
vinci-books.com/chasing-risk

About the Author

USA TODAY Bestselling Author Brandt Legg uses his unusual real life experiences to create page-turning novels. He's traveled with CIA agents, dined with senators and congressmen, mingled with astronauts, chatted with governors and presidential candidates, had a private conversation with a Secretary of Defense he still doesn't like to talk about, hung out with Oscar and Grammy winners, had drinks at the State Department, been pursued by tabloid reporters, and spent a birthday at the White House by invitation from the President of the United States.

At age eight, Legg's father died suddenly, plunging his family into poverty. Two years later, while suffering from crippling migraines, he started in business, and turned a hobby into a multi-million-dollar empire. National media dubbed him the "Teen Tycoon," and by the mid-eighties, Legg was one of the top young entrepreneurs in America, appearing as high as number twenty-four on the list (when Steve Jobs was #1, Bill Gates #4, and Michael Dell #6). Legg still jokes that he should have gone into computers.

By his twenties, after years of buying and selling businesses, leveraging, and risk-taking, the high-flying Legg became ensnarled in the financial whirlwind of the junk bond eighties. The stock market crashed and a firestorm of trouble came down. The Teen Tycoon racked up more than a million dollars in legal fees, was betrayed by those closest to him, lost his entire fortune, and ended up serving time for financial improprieties.

After a year, Legg emerged from federal prison, chastened and wiser, and began anew. More than twenty-five years later, he's now using all that hard-earned firsthand knowledge of conspiracies, corruption and high finance to weave his tales. Legg's books pulse with authenticity.

His series have excited nearly a million readers around the world. Although he refused an offer to make a television movie about his life as a teenage millionaire, his autobiography is in the works. There has also been interest from Hollywood to turn his thrillers into films. With any luck, one day you'll see your favorite characters on screen.

He lives in the Pacific Northwest, with his wife and son, writing full time, in several genres, containing the common themes of adventure, conspiracy, and thrillers. Of all his pursuits, being an author and crafting plots for novels is his favorite.

Acknowledgments

Writing some books is harder than others. *Chasing Kill* was a bit of a challenge. I think a big part of that was due to having to wrap it up during the Covid-19 lockdown. Everything seemed to take more time, more effort, and a different kind of energy. Still, it was fun, and the crazy events of the real world did nothing to slow down the characters—who are constantly running in this one—in which might be the most action-packed Chase & Wen Thriller yet.

As always, my wife, Ro, helped so much during the process of creating this story. Not just in reading outside of her preferred genres, but in talking about it . . . a *lot*. Our son, Teakki, also had countless ideas, many of which made it onto these pages. He's definitely an action/adventure kind of guy. I love having them both to share the journey with.

My mother, Barbara Blair, fought her way through the tunnels and never missed a comma, until I made her stop. She also kept the characters honest (the ones that *are* honest, anyway). It's always wonderful having her as part of the process.

I'm always grateful to the keen mind and sharp eyes of Melanie C. Hansen, who can find typos that a hundred others missed. This time, Gil Forbes also volunteered to lend a hand. It's like having the Chase and Wen of proofreaders!

Once again, my great appreciation to Jack Llartin, my copy editor, for getting the manuscript tight and ready for the world.

And, finally, to Teakki, who patiently waited to trade Legos and show me his latest drawings until I finished writing each day (and for handling all the lockdown restrictions like a pro).

Most of all, I can never express enough gratitude to my readers. To all the ones that have read everything I've published, to the ones who have just finished their first Booker thriller or Chasing adventure, it means the world to me that you've decided to spend your money and time on my stories. Please drop me an email anytime – responding to reader emails is one of my favorite times of the day.

A special thanks goes out to the following readers for either their support, kindness, suggestions, and/or encouragement:

Rob Zorger, Robyn Shanti, Bob Browder, Chis Bond, Melanie C. Hansen, Chet Keough, Sue Steel, Jacky Dallaire, Adam Tanner, Frank Murphy, Gil Forbes, Blake Dowling, Sam Rhoades, Karen Markovitz, Kyle Dahlem, Christine Moritz, Tom Strauss, Irene Witoski, Martha Heckel, Sandie Parrish, LA Dumas, Bob Dumas, John Nicholson, Peggy Gulli, Randy Howerter, Ingo Michehl, John McDonald, Kathy Creecy, Susan Norlund, Liz Miller, Cheryl Olson, Jan Dallas, Chuck Gonzalez, Justin Lear, Rick Ferris, Janice Gildea, Vivienne Du Bourdieu, Elaine Dill, Sharon Moffatt, Jean Sink, Julie Price, Judith Anderson, Terry Myers, Carl Howard, Chris Tomlinson, Judy Hammer, Satish Bhatti, Christopher Bowling, Michael Ferrel, Susan McGuyer, Bill Borchert, Samantha Jackson, Debra Harper, Dennis Lowe, Cathie Harrison, Marcel Roy, Terri, Heather, Mary, Hank, Jennifer, and Dave.